THE REVELATION
OF EMMA GRACE

RICHARD REZENDES

Visit our website at **www.StillwaterPress.com** for more information.

First Stillwater River Publications Edition
Library of Congress Control Number: 2019920943

ISBN: 978-1-950339-76-1

1 2 3 4 5 6 7 8 9 10
Written by Richard Rezendes
Published by Stillwater River Publications, Pawtucket, RI, USA.

THE REVELATION OF EMMA GRACE

CONTENTS

1   *THE ISLAND*

In 1985, the United States discovered an island in the middle of the Atlantic, a volcanic dead zone, and wanted to use this island for a nuclear storage facility. They had to get permission from other countries that also put claims on this island, so the U.S. made deals with them to buy their way with agreements.

The island has separate parts and it looks like a naked woman lying in the ocean with her body being covered up. The first part of the island looks like a hairy head covered with trees and a face in a sand dune leading down to a small beach. The second part of the island has two bare rocks with red pointy tops on them like a woman's breasts; both rocks are perfectly round side by side. The third part of this island is where the volcano is; this looks like the in and outside of a woman's vagina. The middle part has burned out area of trees where an eruption may have occurred; its middle is where the crater is that looks like it's caved in and a slit going right down the middle makes it look like the inside of a woman's vagina. The third part is also nice and round and has beaches around it. Finally, the fourth part of the island looks like a pair of legs, the knees pointing on the pair of bare rocks and even feet appear out of the water when flying over in a helicopter.

Due to the threat of a Middle East war, the United States wanted to use this island to practice bombing with nuclear materials; other countries in the Caribbean wanted to make a resort out of it. The U.S. got the OK to start bombing after an underground bunker was built to protect against nuclear fallout. The United States got all rights to start bombing using nuclear smart bombs dropping them on the island on the mountain and in the water setting off nuclear explosions. Some were dropped in the crater to erupt the volcano for testing but no eruption. All the trees and grass and plants died bare completely around the island leaving a burnt black pile of ashes. Rainwater washed the black ash into the ocean leaving the island a dead zone with nothing but a path for more bombing! Nuclear blasts lit the sky up for miles.

Military ships came with supplies of weapons, food, and equipment for military use. Strong bunkers were built under the island's body, arms, legs, etc. Food and equipment were stored in these bunkers through a lighthouse out in the ocean to get into them. A stairway and an elevator go down to a large steel door to get in. A five-number combination and a username and password are used to get in the bunkers located deep under sea embedded in solid rock for protection. The bunkers have living facilities, bedrooms, washrooms, kitchens, tunnels, computers, and TV monitors everywhere!

People on the island had to wear a spacesuit form of clothing to protect them from nuclear poison when exposed to outside when ships come in and planes and helicopters were landing. B-52 planes were used to drop the bombs. People in the bunkers had to go into private rooms and put on jackets with belts on them to buckle up when nuclear testing was done because everything was shaking like a violent earthquake! The bunk beds have seat belts to buckle up, even on chairs and couches. There are even seatbelts in the shower rooms, along walls in the tunnels and straps on floors to buckle up in. The bunkers are a safe haven and hold more than 100,000 people. Lighting, cooking, and bathing was run by giant generators!

The bombings went on for ten years preparing for WWIII starting in 1985, until 1995 when nuclear testing stopped. President George Bush ordered to stop the bombing after the Gulf War in Iraq. In 1998, India and Pakistan started testing nuclear bombs putting this island on alert and ready again! Battleships destroyers and aircraft carriers started docking on this island with nuclear warheads! On September 11th, 2001, the World Trade Center, the Pentagon and a plane crashing in a field heading for the White House got U.S. warships ready for war! The nuclear warheads were stored on these ships ready for action. Then the second war in Iraq, Syria and Afghanistan, U.S. military had military training on this island, some bombs were launched; it's been an ongoing thing for 20 years!

In 2005 the military started building a base here. More bunkers were built, and heavy equipment and bulldozers were digging holes in the mountain to store nuclear bombs guns tanks military vehicles war weapons etc. A steel vault was built to get into storage areas and an entrance to the bunkers. During the last ten years clean-up was done to make a base here. The nuclear fallout was removed, and the island was clean enough to train on. Grass and trees were growing on the mountain and military workers raked down the mountain from the summit down to the beaches and planted trees. Grass and vegetables treated by rain and sunshine started growing all over the mountain to be picked to eat and there were plenty of fish here. The military-built piers and docks for ships to come here and the island is starting to look like a resort building here. The ships imported food and weapons for protection; loading up the bunkers with food and living facilities.

Weapons were stored in private storerooms in the mountain. More bunkers were built with steel vault doors to enter.

Arms, legs, hands, feet, even fingernails and toes were carved and a body with the two rocks on each side, and nipples were painted to make it look like a naked lady in the water, with big tits! The face in the sand was carved out and eyes were carved out and a nose was made and ears and a smile with teeth. Trees and plants planted to look like the hair leading down to a beach. *What else is there to do in ten years for artists to make the island look nice for people to visit?* A heliport was built for military helicopters to land and take off. Prop planes and fighter jets landed on aircraft carriers.

In 2007 a cruise ship arrived for a visit and a group of people came to visit the new base in the middle of the Atlantic Ocean. The cruise ship pulled up along a battleship and docked there and National Guard troops greeted them as they vacated the cruise ship for a tour of the island. Tents were set up on the island's body where food and drinks were served.

"Greetings, welcome cruise ship Delta to the lady in the water island. My name is Sergeant Adam Santini this island is a mid-Atlantic military port for the United States Operation Stand Down. We are located here to intercept international terror and are a protected area in case of nuclear war! You would never believe it in the middle of the ocean, but we have underground bunkers that hold about 100,000 people to live in case a war breaks out. We have a volcano here that last erupted in 1969 and this island was used for a bombing pad for more than ten years, but we have had no more problems with any eruptions. This mountain has been dormant since then. With bomb after bomb with violent explosions and no problems! The bombing stopped in 1995 and the island was built up to start bringing visitors. We plan on building military housing and a port alongside the mountain, docking military ships emergency vessels and cruise ships. We have earthquakes once in a while and we can get some serious weather such as thunderstorms there's one coming right now! We get these storms almost every day around 4 p.m. Heavy rain strong winds, and sometimes we get waterspouts."

"What's a waterspout Sgt. Santini?" asked a lady.

"A waterspout is a tornado over water! Look to the right there's one right there!" The lightning was flashing like a strobe light and the rain came down in buckets and waterspouts were sliding across the water. The wind was whipping like a hurricane and the tied down tents were blowing in the wind. The tourist and National Guardsmen-women had to hold food and drinks in place to avoid them getting blown away! The storm came and went in five minutes then the sun came out! While everyone was eating and having a few drinks and watching the sunset a rich man introduced himself.

"Mr. Sgt. Adam Santini, my name is David L. Sanberg the owner of Dave and Lories, Limited. I would like to make an offer to buy this island and turn it into a resort. I would like to make a millionaires' paradise out of this island by building a hotel and better piers and loading docks and bring cruise ships and open this island to the public. I will need a military presence to help me build my dream. I believe I can make a lot of money and bring in a good crowd and make this happen."

"David let's make a deal! I will show you around, take a helicopter tour and show you the bunkers. Then we'll see what we can do. The only thing; we have to be here to protect the United States and Caribbean islands. I agree to have a resort here so if you want to go halves, let's do it!" Sgt. Adam Santini shook hands with David L. Sanberg and took him on a tour of the island on a golf cart around the mountain during a mild earthquake showing him the mountain and beaches before going up in the helicopter.

"Sergeant, what is all that shaking!?" asked David.

"That was an earthquake we have them once in a while, they're mild! We also get some big rainstorms here!" Later, Sgt. Adam Santini and David L. Sanberg went for a boat ride to a lighthouse to get to the bunkers and a tour through the great maze under the sea!

"It's amazing down here!" said David. Then they went on a helicopter tour of the island.

"Mr. David L. Sanberg this is Richard Dennis who's going to take you on a helicopter tour," said Sgt. Adam Santini.

"Nice to meet you Mr. Sanberg, let's go for a ride." The rotors went *wop* and the little propeller in the back went *ginnyginny* and they were off! Flying over the volcano crater it looked like a woman's vagina.

David said, "It looks like the inside of a woman!"

"That's right Mr. Sanberg. This is Mount Flow it has a split inside the crater and the rest of the mountain looks like a black hairy curly bush!" said the pilot.

"I have an idea; I would like to name this island Clitoris!" said David L. Sanberg. The helicopter flew over the rest of the island and they got a good laugh!

A few days later, Dave and Lories Ltd. made agreements to start building a resort with the help of the National Guard. First the beaches were cleaned up and palm trees were planted, and the arms legs and the women features were built up then the foundation was laid to start building the hotel. Military barracks and homes were built along the mountain and soon later a resort.

2 THE RESORT

Eleven years later in February 2018 it was a different look to this island with how it was built up. Ten years later the island was ready for tourists. First the hotel was built with seven floors, 700 rooms and a swimming pool a food court, a casino and night club, show rooms, conference rooms a huge comfort lobby with French doors with gold knobs and handles at the entrance, wall to wall red and white carpeting, beige colored walls with big lamps and chandeliers hanging above everywhere! The hotel is a solid white wood building with red shutters on each window outside every room. The rooms have mahogany furniture and the room doors are made of mahogany wood with gold room numbers, wall to wall carpeting in every room. A breakfast is served in the comfort lobby every day. Finally, a big event hall or convention room to hold big meetings and special events. There is a huge solid mahogany table with about 300 chairs around it. The hotel is well built and it's beautiful!

The hotel sits in front of the volcano, the pool views the hotel and volcano. The pool has hot tubs at each end, tents and Tiki bars where food and drinks are served and palm trees surrounding the pool deck and the hotel. A walking path goes around the mountain and a fire house a police sub-station a tourist support center, a weather station a village camp area, military homes and barracks and a mess hall and living facilities for the natives and Indians. A church and an all grade school, from k to 12. A gymnasium and a whorehouse.

All the walking or riding paths had palm trees on both sides of the paths, trees, plants and vegetables grew on the mountain from the beaches all the way up to the summit. The rest of the island had little shops and food vendors. It took more than 10 years to build this island into a resort. Tiki bars everywhere! The beaches also had umbrellas, Tiki bars, dressing rooms, restrooms, and lounge chairs, beach chairs, folding beds and cabanas. Military ships were docked on one side and cruise ships and fishing boats and other vessels were docked on other side.

The resort was private and opened to the public in 2020. From February 2018 until August 2020 only private world leaders were invited. In the spring of 2018 was the international food market for visitors from Dave and Lories, ltd. All kinds of food were brought in from different countries all over the world. Fishing boats brought in swordfish, marlin, tuna and all kinds of fresh fish from the ocean and potatoes, peppers and vegetables were served from the natives in salads. Food vendors were set up with all kinds of world culture food and a fish fry. The Indians were doing a dance during the fish fry!

Meanwhile hundreds of seagulls came out of nowhere and started attacking the fish and the natives got wooden clubs to bash the seagulls and gunfire to get rid of them! The dead seagulls were scooped up in wheelbarrows and laid on a beach to be burned! Leftover food was given to the natives. The natives and Indians took care of the mountain side where they lived. The leftovers went to more seagulls and sea birds and the hotel workers hosed down the remains and cleaned up the island.

The name of the hotel and properties around it was kept quiet until the island opened to the public. Summer 2018 world leaders' meetings were held in the event conference room in the hotel. Fall and winter and through 2019 private events were held by the U.S. National Guard and island management until the grand opening.

August 20th, 2020: "The grand opening!" Cruise ship Irene arrives, and Admiral Quonset Point is the tour guide from that ship. The tour departed the ship and was greeted by the new owner of the island.

"Welcome to the island of Q'klitores. My name is David L. Sanberg the new owner of this island and hotel where you will meet your tour guide after checking in. His name is Admiral Quonset Point, he will show you the hotel first and take you around the island. After checking in you will meet him in the comfort lobby. Welcome to the David L. Sanberg Inn." The guests from cruise ship Irene were checking into their rooms and went back to the lobby to wait. A couple checked into room 413 and an angry looking woman appeared in a mirror and faded away; it was a faint apparition then it went away!

The women said to her husband, "Did you see what I saw in the mirror?"

"No what!" he said.

"I thought I saw a ghost in the bedroom mirror, but I'm not sure!" The husband looked out of the window and he saw a group of women gathering outside.

He said, "It could be a shadow from people outside standing around Linda." The couple were taking clothes out of their suitcases and the spirit in the room was roaming around in black shadows but the couple paid no mind and went back down to the lobby to meet the gang and a complimentary breakfast was served before the island tour. The tour had ham, eggs, bacon, muffins, bagels, croissants, bread, fruit, orange juice, and coffee.

"Good morning my name is Admiral Quonset Point, your tour guide. After breakfast we will take a tour through the hotel and then we will board golf cart trolleys and will ride around the mountain and around the island."

"Sir, my name is Willy Bird and I'm from North Attleboro, Massachusetts and my dad is in the National Guard and his plane is located at Quonset Point Naval Air Station in Rhode Island. And I'm a diehard Patriots fan!"

"I never knew I had a twin in Rhode Island, but my name is Admiral Quonset Point."

"Are you from there sir?" said Willy.

"No sir, where's Quonset Point, Rhode Island-Massachusetts!?"

"It's part of the New England states in the United States!" said Willy.

"Oh wow! That's interesting, I would like to see this place sometime; I will Google it later. Who are the Patriots?" asked Admiral Quonset Point.

"They're a football team that wins super bowls!" said Willy.

"Congratulations that's a nice story Willy. OK ladies and gentlemen let's take a tour through the hotel. Here is the hotel comfort lobby with luxury couches and mahogany furniture big lamps and chandeliers and pictures of famous leaders of the world from wall to wall and carpeting with red gold and white coloring. Over here is the check in desk where we checked in this morning.

"Let's walk through the halls where the rooms are located on both sides and we will see what our rooms look like. Here is room 111 overlooking the island's body, if you look out the windows you can see what looks like a naked woman with her body showing her boobs hands and her head features, her fingers and her bellybutton where the helicopters land for the island tours. This room is the model room to be shown to visitors. All the rooms are similar to this one. All the doors, frames and furniture are made out of solid mahogany wood with gold handles and knobs. Some rooms have two queen beds like this one, or a king bed all made out of mahogany wood. A large mirror is placed over the middle of the bedroom and dressers and a 50-inch flat screen TV in each room. The bathroom has a tub and shower. A sink with gold faucets, red white and gold tile floor. All rooms have wall to wall carpeting. All the rooms are all the same on floors one through 6. The seventh floor has a few suites that can sleep up to eight people; same material but those rooms are different.

"Let's go back to the lobby, the entrance has French doors with single pane glass the same windows in each room with a screen. This hotel is air-conditioned run by generators. Over here are the elevators that go to all the floors with gold doors and gold interiors. Let's take these elevators down to the basement.

"Down here are no bedrooms. Here is the laundry room with 12 washers and 12 dryers and soap dispensers and a dry cleaner and press tailor. The next room is the exercise and weight room with stationary bikes and tread mills. The next room is a snack bar with candy machines, a microwave and a refrigerator. The next room is the corporate management office. The next four rooms: two on each side are conference rooms.

"The next room is the event convention center located in the middle of the hotel on the ground floor and rises up to the fourth floor with seating all around the room up above. The ceiling is 52 feet high from the ground with four chandeliers hanging from one end to another, the table is 150 feet long; a solid mahogany wood with 300 surrounding chairs from one end to another, all mahogany wood and eight feet wide. We have six large lamps on each side and couches surrounding this room. Wall to wall red, white, and gold colored rugs. Conventions meetings and special events are held in this room and there are four double doors on each side to enter. This is quite a room.

"Let's exit to the other side of the ground floor. Here is the pool entrance going up stairs to the pool deck through those French doors. The rooms on the left are male and female dressing rooms. The rooms on the right are maintenance rooms and restrooms. Let's go upstairs to the pool. Out here we have an Olympic size swimming pool for people who don't like saltwater or beaches. The pool deck has Tiki bars to order drinks and food, beach umbrellas chairs and lounge chairs and a hot tub on both ends of the pool and outdoor dressing rooms and restrooms. Palm trees everywhere!

"Let's all walk to the next set of doors enters the casino. We are in the volcano casino and we have slot machines and table games; it's not a big casino but it's a pretty good size. We have the night club called Nathan's Rock House and the Lories High Limit Room and the volcano room for simulcasting and rest area. Also, Benjamin's Steakhouse here in the casino. Finally, the food court. We have quite a food court here! We have McDonald's, Dunkin' Donuts, Long Wang Chinese Rice and Bean factory, Popeye's Fried Chicken, devil's fried ghost peppers grill, Charley's Philly steaks, parrot fish market, Dave and Lori's Charter House, and finally Dave and Buster's Game Restaurant. We have ten classic restaurants here in our food court.

"I forgot to show you a couple more rooms located in the casino. Here we have Fado Irish Restaurant and Dave's Palace Show Room that seats 1500 people and Las Vegas style shows are held in this room; it looks like Radio City Music Hall in New York City. We have upper and lower decks and we also hold concerts here.

"Now, let's go back to the elevators and go to the seventh floor and show you the suites. After we will go back to the comfort lobby and meet the hotel and island leaders. The suites are big rooms like the regular rooms, but these rooms are like apartments. Let's go inside. Here we have four bedrooms all queen beds and four pull out couch beds. All the suites sleep eight to sixteen people. This suite is one of the biggest ones: room 764. Overlooking the volcano. All the furniture is made out of mahogany wood and double mahogany doors to enter. There are two full bathrooms, in each bathroom is a jacuzzi a separate shower, two sinks, a toilet, urinal and a wash basin. Women like to use the wash basin to clean between their legs. Crocodile Dundee always says to clean your backside," said Admiral Quonset Point! Everyone laughed!

Then the admiral continued his tour. "Out here we have two kitchen areas and two lounges. Four windows overlooking the mountain. The kitchens have a full refrigerator a cooking stove, microwave oven and a table with 6 chairs; both kitchens are the same. Out here is the hallway and another on the other side of this suite. We have big lamps in each room eight of them and chandeliers in the lounges. These suites are very nice! Let's go back to the comfort lobby and meet the hotel management and hosts," said Admiral Quonset Point.

During the tour there was an earthquake, the ground shook and swayed back and forth rattling as everyone screamed; it was a pretty good jolt!

"Don't worry ladies and gentlemen, we get earthquakes here all the time, most of them are very weak and some we feel; but this one was unusually strong! We have some people to meet, David L. Sanberg you met earlier the owner of this hotel. Dick Dickey is the casino host and pool manager. Next is Helen Kladova the show and fashion manager. Next is Randy Austin the island's grounds manager. Richard Dennis, he's the National Guard air manager. He will take you on a helicopter tour for those who would like. Donald Perderka is the bunkers and hotel manager and the casino pit boss. Chi Chung from Ding Dong Tours, he's the convention and events manager. Doctor Raymound W. Hallowmostraphoniagalleriabarringtoncommonwealth, he's the islands' doctor; he likes to be called Dr. It! Sergeant Adam Santini. The National Guard and heavy arms manager, he's the one who runs the vaults leading to the bunkers and he is also the island's bank manager. Randy Austin also is the military manager who organizes all the ships that come and go; he's also a casino host! You met Randy earlier. Lori Stack is the beach and lounge manager and she's the room and maintenance manager, as well, and a hotel host.

"I think we met them all, let's meet and greet until lunch is served and then we'll go outside and continue our tour. Thanks again my name is Admiral Quonset Point manager of cruise ship Irene and island tour guide. Have fun and see you in a couple of hours to finish our tour. Lunch will be served in the food court by Dave and Lori's Catering Service."

The cruise ship Irene tour met all the managers and they were on their own until lunch. August 20th, 2020 at noontime lunch was served in the food court all the tours were invited. Salad, chicken noodle soup and ham, tuna fish and chicken salad sandwiches were served with potato salad and chips and Oreo cookies for dessert and coffee. After lunch the tour met outside the hotel where the tour continued with Admiral Quonset Point.

"OK let's all group together. This hotel is made out of wood shingles white with red close shutters around each window and a slate red roof with solar panels to keep the hotel cool. The attic is the eighth floor and the hotel's storage space. There is no admittance up there except for hotel staff. Now let's board these golf cart trolleys and ride around the island and visit other places."

"Are there any golf courses here, Admiral?" said Willy Bird.

"No sir; just a naked lady in the water with a volcano between her legs!" Everyone laughed!

"Before we tour the rest of the island, we need to know what island where on! This resort was known as the lady in the water for 50 years or more it was always here! Today is the grand opening of resort island Q'klitores. It's spelled q-k-l-i-t-o-r-e-s! The management renamed this island because the crater on top of this mountain looks like a woman's vagina! The spelling was changed to suit an exotic resort, but with the name visitors will still get a good laugh!" said Admiral Quonset Point. Everyone had a good laugh!

Then the admiral continued! "By the way, this mountain is a volcano, it last erupted in 1969 on July 20th, the day Apollo 11 landed on the moon. This is Mount Flow! The Indians and natives live on this mountain that keeps us fed. They live in huts, tents and housing they own this mountain and they plant vegetables, potatoes and all kinds of greens. They plant trees and keep the mountain clean and nice, for the people here.

"The first building facing the mountain is a police and fire substation. The trail and beach below belong to them, it's building number one. The next building is the weather station and they have their beach, building number two. The third building is the Indian-natives village. They have a private beach. The next set of buildings called level four: the military living barracks. These areas are off limits for tourists, the beaches below are also private. The next building number five is the E.R. When people are sick, they come here! For severe cases they get transferred to a hospital boat.

"Look straight ahead you will see a leg with feet and toes and boats tied around them and a beach below also off limits. Outside the right leg are emergency vessels such as the hospital ship, fire-police boats and military ships. The inside of both legs are fishing boats, luxury boats sail boats etc. The beach between the legs is named Nudeass Beach! It's a private military beach. The left leg is where the tugboats are docked and around the feet. Cargo ships also dock along the left leg! Now we come to the left side of the island of Q'klitores.

"Building number six is the military mess hall and private living facilities and Indians and natives private village all fenced off with black gates. The beaches below are private. Most of Mount Flow is off limits to tourist only the military, Indians and island natives has the rights on this mountain. This area is called level seven. The next building is the international house of worship assembly church, building number eight. This building is open to the public. Let's go in and meet Pastor In," said Admiral Quonset Point.

"Good afternoon cruise Irene tour! My name is Pastor In. Welcome to the international house of worship: we have a church for everyone to go on the island. We hold services on Sunday and this church seats 1500 people, and the service is about an hour in a half and the Indians and natives takes care of this church. We have colorful stained windows and mahogany wood seating and the floor is smooth volcanic lava rock and it gets buffed out twice a week to give it a good shine. The only bad thing it gets slippery when it gets wet on rainy days. It's raining now! So, you better get out! Just kidding!

"We have a rectory living facility for the church. The next building is the reading academy a private k through 12 school, gym and ball field. The school is building number nine and the ball field and gym is level ten. The school and ball fields and the gym is private. Over here is building number eight B is the church learning center prayer service is held on Wednesdays and Fridays. Building number eight A is the rectory. Take a walk through our complex and buildings, you may take pictures and our tour is over with me then the admiral will take you to the last two buildings and you use your own judgment!"

said Pastor In.

"Ladies and gentlemen, we have two more sites to see. The next building number eleven is a whorehouse, that's right you heard right! Tongue Kiss Cafe house of sex! It's open to the public and you can get laid here for 100 U.S. dollars! Prostitution is legal on the island of Q'klitores. Tours are not allowed to enter the whorehouse; you're on your own!

"The last building is a support center, building number twelve. 'Culture united national translations', c-u-n-t! It's not under a very nice name, but it is what it is: we will meet Dr. It, here! Let's go inside," said Admiral Quonset Point. The tour laughed hysterically!!!!!!!!!!!! Over the last two buildings!

The tour is not over yet!

"Good afternoon welcome to the C.U.N.T. building! My name is Dr. It. We met earlier and we have a variety of things here! This building is a culture center for all nationalities for tourist information and language changers. All foreign languages are spoken here! We have counseling, home schooling, religious studies, island tours, boat rides, a place for the homeless, for handicapped people. Entertainment organizations, child's day care, we have a hospice center and believe it or not, we have a six lane ten pin bowling alley connecting to the volcano casino and the hotel. We have access to the hotel and casino but not here. We have only the main entrance to the C.U.N.T. building. Take a look around and take pictures and feel free!" said Dr. It.

After the mountain tour the golf cart trolley made its way by the hotel pool area and stopped on the island's stomach. "Ladies and gentlemen, over here is the island's bellybutton! It's a red circle with a hot tub in the middle; a natural hot spring from the volcano. The water temperature is 120 degrees. Look straight ahead you see two round rocks with red pointy tops that looks like woman's breast! Yes!

It's the island's titties!

"On the right hand is where all the cruise ships and luxury boats dock and around the hand to the other side. Tugboats dock behind the right hand. The right pinky finger is a tattoo shop. The fourth finger is a hair salon, the middle finger is a candy store and it sticks straight up as if to tell other vessels where to go! The second finger is an ice cream parlor and the first finger is the cruise line ticket office. The beaches below both hands and behind the head are open to the public. The right-hand beaches halfway around the mountain are open to anyone.

"Our next stop is the islands head with a face and ears and nose carved out with eyes painted on the rock and a smile with teeth and a tongue sticking out of the mouth and trees, bushes and straw to make it look like a lady laying in the middle of the ocean. We'll let you off here to take pictures when our tour is over.

"The left hand is where all the military ships dock. We have battleships, destroyers and aircraft carriers on both sides of the hand and tugboats dock behind the hand. The circle between the island's titties and bellybutton is the heliport where you go on helicopter tours. The middle finger is the immigration office you go to before you leave the island and for tours checking in. The finger tells the left side where to go and tells you where to go if you don't show your passport! The left hand is private, but the beaches below are open to the public. On the right side of the left hand are battleships and destroyers; aircraft carriers dock on the left side and other military boats, and cargo ships. The pinky finger on the left hand is a military gift shop. The fourth finger is a military command center. Don't forget to show your passport here before you leave, or you're fucked!!!!!!!!!!" said Admiral Quonset Point. Everybody laughed! Then the admiral continued.

"The second finger is a military clothes store. Finally, the first finger is a military visiting center; you can buy day passes here to tour all the ships. If you want to go on a helicopter tour, you buy the tickets here. The five to ten-minute tour over Mount Flow crater is $111.00 U.S. dollars. And you can change international money here as well; finger number one is the island's bank.

"Let's go over to the island's head where our tour ends. You get out here to take pictures and you are on your own. Dinner will be served tonight at 7 p.m. at Benjamin's Steakhouse located in the volcano casino. Thank you very much and enjoy your stay on the island of Q'klitores!" said Admiral Quonset Point.

"Good afternoon ladies and gentlemen from Irene tours, my name is Peter Peckershaw the island picture entertainer! Welcome to the head of the lady. Right here is the mouth painted in a smile with her teeth and tongue hanging out like she's waiting to get laid! Her nose and ears carved out of rocks and sexy eyes painted on the rocks with her sexy eyebrows and trees, grass, rhubarb straws to make her look like a sexy lady to take home, the beach below has hors d'oeuvres and Jell-O shots, my tour ends here enjoy, have a good day!"

The tour was invited to a tiki bar party on the beach with topless girls dancing around on the beach. Two couples decided to go on a helicopter tour, and they went to the left-hand finger one to get tickets and the chopper landed waiting for the next tour.

"Hi, my name is Willy Bird and my friend Nicole Nickelson, Patty McGroin and Dick Hurts. We're from Bangor, Maine, U.S.A. and we would like to go for a flight over the lit volcano!"

"Sure, hop aboard, my name is Richard Dennis the pilot and Chet Nugget the co-pilot! Welcome to the island of Q'klitores and we are going to tour the volcano crater, Mount Flow, and fly over the island; fasten your seat belts and we'll be on our way!"

The pilot started the helicopter the rotor started turning, *wop-wop-wop-wop-wop-wop-wop-wop-wop*! And the propeller in the back went, *ginny-ginny-ginny-ginny-ginny-ginny-ginny-ginny-ginny*! And the copter lifted off and flew over the volcano crater.

"Look at that juicy cunt below, she's squirting like a hose!!!!!!" said the co-pilot.

"Chet! What the hell is the matter with you! You're disgusting! Have class! We have women aboard!" said Richard Dennis the pilot.

The crater looked like a vagina waiting to get fucked! It looked pink inside with rain washing mud out of the crater and down the mountain. The top of the crater was a red rock that looks like the clit and a light-colored mud was washing from this clit-rock washing through the pink colored slit crater and down the sides of the mountain!

Everyone got a good laugh in the helicopter then it flew over the island over the ships and beaches, the hotel then it landed, and the tour was over in ten minutes. The four visitors went to the hotel to meet the rest of the Irene tour for dinner at Benjamin's Steakhouse. The tour will be staying for a couple of nights and now they're on their own.

3   THE TOURISTS

The Irene tour eats at Benjamin's Steakhouse, a very classy place. After dinner everyone is free to do their thing. The restaurant is beautiful! It has leather seating and mahogany and glass tables and woodwork, chandeliers and big lamps and cathedral ceilings. It's a five-star restaurant and the cruise ship Irene tour was eating dinner. The meal is $30.00 each and a soup of choice then a chef salad then the meal; an eight-inch filet mignon, broccoli and cheese, and loaded mashed or baked potato. The meal is served in a wine sauce, it's delicious! A marble cake with chocolate frosting or ice cream with coffee for dessert.

Someone came to all the tables where the tour was eating and serenaded them with music playing a violin and a flute, some had a guitar and a cello, and a piano was playing, and dancers were doing the tango. It was a fun night for everyone at Benjamin's Steakhouse!

Then about 10 p.m. the tour broke up and everyone went their separate ways; some went to the night club and others went to the casino. Willy Bird, Nicole Nickelson, Patty McGroin and Dick Hurts were in the casino gambling and Willy Bird hit big on a dollar machine, he won $300.00; his friends were playing the tables, blackjack, poker, roulette and craps. Willy left his friends and he went to the pool area to have a couple of drinks and he went to the whorehouse to get laid!

A woman met him at the door and she said, "Can I help you?"

"Yes ma'am! I want to get laid!"

"It's $100.00 U.S. dollars. Go upstairs first door on the left and see Hurricane Matha!" said the lady at the door. Willy pulled a hundred dollar bill out of his pants pocket and he put it in the madame's hand and he raced upstairs to the girl!

"Are you Hurricane Matha?"

"Yes, get your clothes off and lay down on the bed!"

The hurricane started blowing wind on Willy, he said, "What are you doing?"

"That's the warm wind from the hurricane!" Then she ripped her shirt and she started slapping Willy in the face with her tits and forcing them in Willy's mouth.

Willy laughed and he said, "Wow! What are you doing now!?"

"It's the coconuts from the palm trees from the hurricane!" Then she stood up over Willy's body and she started pissing all over him!

"Hey, what the hell are you doing!?"

"That's the warm rain from the hurricane!" Willy quickly got up and he started getting dressed!

"Get undressed and get back on the bed I am not through with you yet!"

"I'm sorry I can't fuck in this kind of weather!" said Willy and he ran out of the Hurricane's room and he went back downstairs, and he said to the madam:

"Get me someone else, she's a freak! I can't fuck her!"

"You have me!" said the madam and she took Willy in another room and she stripped down!

Willy said, "What can you do!?"

"I may have winter in my hair, but I have summer in my heart!"

Willy said, "If you don't get some spring in your ass we'll be here until fall!"

"My name is Linda, and you are a very fresh man!" Willy picked her up and threw her down on the bed and he fucked her brains out! Willy Bird was an animal!!!!!!!!!!!!

He left Linda's naked body there and he left the whorehouse and he went back to the hotel pool. He stripped down to his underwear and he jumped in the pool for a swim for a while then he got dressed and he went to the casino and his friends were not there and he went to the night club looking for them and they were not there then he went to his room and he went to bed.

It was 2:30 in the morning and all the action was quiet. A thunderstorm rolled through and the rain came down in buckets! Willy was staying in room 413 where Olivia's ghost visits! The ghost was appearing in the mirror, she's a woman with big tits! But Willy was sound to sleep he never noticed! ! *He's got a big surprise tomorrow night!'*

The next day August 21st, 2020. Willy woke up and he went downstairs for continental breakfast and he met his friends there.

"Willy where did you go last night, we were looking for you!?" asked Nicole Nickelson.

"I was at the casino and I went to the whorehouse and got laid last night!"

"Willy, you dog!" said Nicole. Later the four of them went to the beach for the day to ride a few waves, they had a few drinks and some lunch at the tiki bars on the beach.

Around 2 p.m. there was an earthquake and sirens were going off and the lifeguards told everyone, "Get off the beach and get to higher ground!" Everyone went running up the rocks and mountainside fearing a threat of a tsunami coming. The waves were twice the size just minutes after the earthquake struck and it was a pretty good one! The island rocked, rolled and shook strong enough to knock people down! Everyone ran to the hotel from the beaches and were directed to the pool area and met with Dick Dickey, and he said:

"Ladies and gentlemen don't panic we get these earthquakes all the time, some of them can be strong! The National Guard will direct you where to go when these earthquakes happen. The protocol is the same as a thunderstorm, wait 30 minutes and it will be over! You may feel aftershocks for a while several times during the day. These earthquakes are triggered from this volcano, the volcano is monitored every day. It's not dangerous! We will be fine you're going to feel a little shaking the ground is shaking a little right now can you feel it! We're on a volcanic island we get these almost every day. Stay here in the pool area don't go in any building until the sirens go off telling you it's safe," said Dick Dickey the pool manager.

"What about the tsunami warnings?" said one of the tourists.

"We get these warnings every time we get an earthquake!" said Big Dick. The visitors were at the pool out in the open when suddenly a violent thunderstorm came while the island was still shaking and moving; the heavy rain forced everyone to take cover under umbrellas and tents and the wind blew them away too!

Lightning struck a tree and another bolt struck a metal object on the pool area; the bolt traveled along the ground skidding on top of the water in the pool striking another tree setting it on fire! Everyone started screaming and running to hide anywhere inside.

The heavy rain put out all fires as the thunder was banging loud enough to pop you ears! The wind blew tables and chairs and every-thing on the pool deck was dumped into the pool; it looked like a trash dump the damage was so bad! People were thrown around like missiles and the wind was so strong it snapped trees in half.

The storm was over in five minutes then the sun came out and it was over. It looked like a war zone when it was over; the evening sun shined on a few broken windows in the hotel! Rushing mud came pouring down the mountain a few minutes later smashing palm trees and covered the pool in mud and debris. The storm left a trail of destruction!

The cruise ship Irene tour met with the tour guide at the Fado restaurant in the casino for dinner and he prepared them from what happened.

"Ladies and gentlemen. We had a very bad storm following a strong earthquake! We get earthquakes all the time here because we're on an island in the middle of the Atlantic Ocean. This one set off a tsunami warning and we had 8-foot waves! It was scary! We usually do not get tsunami warnings it's very rare! Hurricane Eric a dying storm picked up speed and gave us a shaking! We got caught by surprise! A thunderstorm that was so bad with 95 mile per hour winds and catastrophic flooding left a trail of destruction! Some people got caught off guard and were hurled like missiles across the pool deck but there were no serious injuries as far as I know, but after dinner you will need to go to your rooms and check for damage if your rooms have damage you can get another room. I will let you know if we have serious destruction and we might have to spend the next few nights on the ship because there is so much damage! It looks like the end of the world!" said Admiral Quonset Point.

Panicking people asked questions about the destruction in fear! The power on the island was out but generators in the bunkers brought power to the hotel. After dinner Nicole Nickelson, Patty McGroin and Dick Hurts went to the casino to gamble and to the night club. Willy Bird went back to the whorehouse for more action and it was closed so he went down to the beaches and everything was closed off from the storm-earthquake! Then he went to the casino and lost most of his money! Then he went to bed.

Willy Bird is in room 413 and he took a shower and he watched a movie on TV in bed. The movie was *The Perfect Storm*, a movie about a fishing boat that left Gloucester, Massachusetts and got caught in a hurricane. Suddenly he heard a siren going off and he looked out the window and he saw police lights flashing on top of the island's titty nipples! Another earthquake aftershock happened but he didn't feel anything. He dialed zero on the phone!

"Front desk, can I help you?"

"Hi this is Willy Bird in room 413. What are those lights flashing on the island's boobs?"

"We just had an aftershock, but it was very mild; there's nothing to worry about!" said the person at the front desk. Midnight Willy went back to watch the movie.

Then he heard someone laughing in the room and he looked at the alarm clock and the time was 12:23am. He got up out of bed and he walked around the room but found nothing. After the movie was over, he went to sleep. He heard a voice, "Get out!!" Quickly Willy got up and he heard the laughing again!

"Hey fellas quit fucking I'm trying to sleep!" He looked at the alarm clock and the time was 1:24 a.m. Then he turned over he turned off the lamp and went back to sleep. An hour later he heard a loud thump! Then the laughing again!

"Whoever is making these noises better cut it out! Or I'm gonna bust your fuckin' head in now stop it!!" Then he laid back down. Suddenly the alarm clock went off and the lamp lit by itself! He jumped out of bed and he couldn't find the off button on the alarm clock; the time was 2:25 a.m. and he pulled the plugs on the clock and the lamp, then he looked around the room and he found nothing and he went back to bed.

Just as Willy's about to fall asleep he heard a voice calling again, "Get out!!!!" He woke up from a sound sleep and he saw a bright bluish gray fog and it quickly formed into a person as Willy watched in shock!

"What the fuck is this!!!" Suddenly a pair of tits was suffocating Willy's face pinning him down on the bed and held him down for five minutes as Willy struggled to get off the bed! He did everything he could to break loose; finally, the ghost of Olivia released her grip formed back into a cloud and vanished into the mirror! Willy quickly left the room leaving his belongings behind and he ran down to the front desk screaming!

"Hey mister I have a fuckin' ghost in my room!"

"Really! You got to be kidding!" said the man at the front desk.

"No sir, why don't you go up there and see for yourself!? In fact, I'll go with you so I can get my shit!" said Willy. The hotel clerk and Willy went to the room and nothing was happening!

"Get your clothes and I'll give you another room," said the hotel clerk.

"Fuck that! I'm outta here!" said Willy. Then he grabbed his belongings and he packed his bags and he went to sleep on the beach for the night. He grabbed a big stick he found on the beach and he kept it with him.

"Come on ghost make my day I'll bash your fuckin' head in!!!!!" Then he laid his knapsack down on the beach sand and he went to sleep under a tree.

He had a dream about a hurricane hitting the island and he was running for his life! A giant wave swept him away out to sea luckily a coastguard boat spotted him and pulled him aboard and a sailor said to him, "What are you doing out here during Hurricane Elvis!?" Then a big wave came, and everyone went down buried in the ocean! Willy was screaming as a giant whirlpool tornado was drowning him and everyone with him!

He woke up in a hurry! It was a bright sunny morning and he got up and he went for a swim and then he laid in the sun before joining his friends for continental breakfast at the hotel.

Friday morning August 22nd around 9 a.m., Patty McGroin and Dick Hurts staying in room 535 got up took a shower and got ready for breakfast. Patty McGroin opened the window and she had a bird's eye view of the island's tits! She took a picture on her smart phone!

She said, "Dick, look at this! This island really looks like a naked lady in the water!" Later Dick and Patty went to Nicole Nickelson's room and they went down to get breakfast and they met Willy Bird there.

"Willy where the hell were you all night! Did you go to bed early!?" said Nicole.

"I was at the casino then I went to the club and nothing was happening, I couldn't find you guys, so I went to bed. That's only the beginning! I had a fuckin' ghost in my room! First, I heard laughing the lights were going on and off; I thought someone was screwing around until I pulled the plugs on the lamp and alarm clock after it kept going off! And I saw a weird cloud form into a woman with big tits pinning me down on the bed for five to ten minutes! I thought I was a goner! Finally, I broke free and I went to the beach for the night," said Willy.

"Holy fuckin' shit! Someone told me there was a ghost in this hotel!" said Nicole Nickelson.

"A ghost! You got to be kidding!" said Patty McGroin.

"Patty go to room 413 later tonight. Last night after the storm looking at the damage in the pool. I thought I saw a lady standing in the rubble, it was a faint glow, but I paid no mind. When my grandfather died, I went to his grave to put a flower plant down and I saw his ghost spirit standing over the grave standing in front of it! I said, 'hi Grampa I hope you go to heaven' then his vision went away, it's not the first time I saw ghosts!" said Willy Bird. The four of them told early morning ghost stories for two hours while eating breakfast as the rest of the tour listened.

"I never had any experience with ghost but when I was a kid back in Bangor, Maine, I swear I was overtaken by aliens! My friends told me it was a dream! I was in a group called the Webelo's, a group after Cub Scouts and before you get into Boy Scouts. I was with three other boys and the four of us went to a beach at Cockeagle Camp in Bangor. We wanted to go fishing and our scoutmaster told us not to go far because it was a new moon that night and it will be very dark. We went out in a rowboat paddling to the middle of the lake.

"Suddenly the moon started rising and it was bright and full but it got bigger and bigger and all of a sudden I could smell ether then I found by self and my three friends laying in a space ship naked and a bunch of aliens were doing tests on us, one alien working on me stuck needles all over me like acupuncture, they stuck a foot long needle in the head of my dick! I couldn't move I really thought we were going to die that night! I could not feel anything from what they were doing, it looked like we were under a surgical lamp like an operation room and these small looking fuckin' aliens with big heads small slanted eyes, ears like devil horns a small mouth with no teeth a skinny body arms and legs; you could not tell if they were male or female they all look the same!

"My friend next to me, the aliens stuck three-foot object up his ass hole and pulled out of his mouth and stuck the same object in the third person down his throat and pulled it out of his ass hole! The room was covered in blood all over the floor and walls! We all laid naked in this spaceship being tortured! They stuck needles of all sizes in our bodies!

"The fourth friend had what looked like carrots sticking out of his ears and needles in his nose and his balls were tied up hanging from a thin rope attached to a bar or pipe in the ceiling; his feet had a long needle sticking through them and wrapped around his feet and legs connecting to his balls! If this happened to me now, I would get a gun and blast every one of these mother fuckers away!!!!!!!!!!!

"Suddenly everything went dark and the four of us laid on the beach fully clothed found by our camp master. He said, 'where the hell were you all night? It's 3:30 in the morning!' I told him what happened, but he did not believe me! I called the local radio station TV and wrote to newspapers in Maine and contacted local media on my computer, and they didn't believe me. I was abducted by aliens when I was a kid but still to this day no one believes me! But it happened!" said Dick Hurts.

"That's not true you had a bad dream one night!" said Patty McGroin. Everyone laughed from Dick's story, but he believes his story is true. After breakfast the tour was on their own and most of them went to the beach for the day, others went to the pool or went shopping on the island. The damage from the storm-earthquake was cleaned up. A cruise ship pulled into port and tourists were getting off about 2 p.m. and a little while later when the ship emptied it caught fire and burned from stern to bow!

The whole ship was engulfed with flames as everyone watched on the beach! Fire boats quickly went to the scene to put out the flames and c130 aircraft arrived to help out. The flames were put out in a half hour and then the ship sank after that! The cruise ship Irene tour was at a barbecue at the beach all day until sunset watching the cruise ship disaster! A passing thunderstorm came also to help put the flames out.

A clam bake at the beach fed more than 1000 people. Fish, lobster, crabs, clams, quahogs, clam cakes, white and red chowder, hot dogs, hamburgers, potatoes, stir fry and all kinds of vegetables and beer, wine and the Q'klitores 190 proof alcohol and orange vodka. The party went well into the night. The rain came back around sunset ruining the sunset, but the beach parties went on. Police broke up sex parties on the beach.

Willy Bird, Nicole Nickelson, Patty McGroin and Dick Hurts were all together and they left the beach and went to the casino and night club.

Willy said, "Let's go to the casino. I only have $35.00 I need to win some money so I can go back to the whorehouse and get some more pussy before we go home Sunday afternoon."

"You do that will meet you at the club later," said Nicole Nickelson.

"Willy, why don't you fuck Nicole?" said Dick Hurts.

"She's too fat and ugly! She's not my type!" Dick shook his head and he went to the night club.

9 p.m. on Friday August 22nd, 2020 Nathian's rock house night club: located in the casino. The band playing was the Thundermist playing rock and dance music and the club was packed with people by 10p.m.. The club had stage and upper lights and a fog machine, neon tubes and lasers bouncing off of disco balls and everyone was dancing!

Willy came by to check out the club, he danced with one girl and he groped her, and she spun around and slapped Willy in the face and later Willy grabbed another girl and he was having his way with her!

She said, "Fuck off buddy!" Then Willy left the club and he met Patty McGroin and Dick Hurts in the casino. Willy put a 20-dollar bill in a dollar machine, and he pulled the lever and he won $300.00

He said to his friends, "I have enough money to get laid now!" Willy cashed out the money and he went back to the whorehouse!

When he got there, he said to the madam at the door, "Hi sweetie give me the best you got!"

"Go upstairs first door on the left and see the Hurricane!"

"No, I do not want the hurricane I want to fuck a chick!" said Willy.

The madam laughed and she said, "Go upstairs to the right and see Kim Young. It's 100 U.S. dollars please!" Willy paid the madam and upstairs he went looking for the girl.

"Are you Miss Kim Young?"

"Yes, come in," she said. In seconds Willy took his clothes off and he ripped the nightgown off the girl threw her down on the bed and he jumped on her and he started fucking her brains out!!!!!!!!!!!!!!! He was trying to drive the truck into the garage!

Willy said, "What's the matter Kim, how come every time I push in your toes crinkle up and when I pull out your toes straighten out!?"

"You didn't give me a chance to take my pantyhose off!" she said.

After Willy Bird was done, he left the whorehouse and it started to rain thunder and lightning, so he went back to the casino to play the roulette tables and he won $200.00. Then he went to the blackjack table and played at the crap tables and slot machines and he walked out with $850.00. It was three o'clock in the morning and he went to the club and it was closed so he went to get a room and he went to bed.

"Could you get me a room that does not have a ghost please?" said Willy. Willy was given room 733 one of the suites with his friends, Patty McGroin, Dick Hurts and Nicole Nickelson so Willy and his friends were talking and drinking gin all night until 6am. Patty and Dick slept in one room Willy slept in another and Nicole slept on the other side of the suite. There were no ghosts in here tonight.

"I fucked a hot bitch tonight an Asian!" said Willy.

"Let's get to bed, it's really late," said Dick. Saturday August 23rd. 11:30 a.m. Willy gets up and he looks out of the window and a helicopter was landing right between the island of Q'klitores's tits! Then he went to the bathroom staggering and he made it in time, and he threw up three times in the toilet!

"Is that you Willy, hurry up! I'm next!" said Dick.

Dick didn't make it he threw up in a wastebasket! Patty woke up and she was puking! But she made it to the toilet in time. Nicole got up and she got sick too! The four of them stayed in bed a good part of the day taking turns on getting sick! They all had a big headache drinking gin all night!

Later about 3 p.m. the four of them were lounging at the pool eating and drinking again, shots, beer, and mixed drinks! Then the four of them was part of a social group at the pool. Dick Hurts was shocked!

"Good afternoon my name is Dick Dickey, the hotel and pool host and we have a lovely group of people from Maine USA in the New England area. First, we have Willy Bird from Eaglemist, Maine and he's wearing a Boston Celtics jersey. Willy, tell us a little about yourself!"

"I work for Fed-Ex and I'm here on my dream vacation."

"Very good, next we have Nicole Nickelson wearing a Boston Bruins jersey on, tell us about you Nicole." said Big Dick.

"I live in Bangor, Maine with Patty McGroin and Dick Hurts and the four of us booked a vacation from Irene cruises to see the famous lady in the water island."

"Very good Nicole. Next we have Patty McGroin and what do you do for a living?" said Dick Dickey.

"I am a fashion agent with Nicole Nickelson we work together as clothes designers and fashion shows in Maine. My friend Dick Hurts is passed out right now and he's a lawyer. He's wearing a Red Sox shirt and I'm wearing a Patriots jersey; Tom Brady, the Patriots' quarterback, is my favorite player!"

"Very good Patty! Ladies and gentlemen let's give them a big hand!" said Dick Dickey. Clap! Clap! Clap! Clap! Clap!!!

"Once again welcome everyone to the island of Q'klitores. The cruise ship Irene tour will have dinner at the Fado Irish restaurant this evening at 7p.m., then a show after that tomorrow morning a continental breakfast will be served at 8 a.m. and all weekend cruises depart at 9am. Be sure to report to customs before boarding the ship thank you," said Dick Dickey.

It was a nice day at the pool and beaches for swimming and partying. Later it was dinner time at Fado. A ham dinner was served with mashed potatoes carrots and string beans laced in Guinness. The tour had eaten here before a few days ago. Dark bread dipped in wine and an ice cream cake for dessert and coffee. Irish music was playing, and Irish girls were dancing. Later the tour went to a Las Vegas stage show and it was boring for Willy Bird. He went to the whorehouse leaving his friends behind.

He got there and the madam said to him, "Looking for more action honey!"

"Yeah baby, give me a black one!" said Willy.

"I'm sorry I am the only one here, my name is Linda."

"You're the only one here, where is everybody?" said Willy.

"Everyone went home because we're getting ready to close for the night," said Linda.

"You're an old lady! What can you do!?"

"Mister I don't need an attitude! Do you want to get laid or don't? Let's not waste time, it's 100.00 U.S. dollars and let's go!" said Linda.

Linda took Willy to a room stripped butt naked and ready for sex. Willy jumped on her, forcing his way on her because she was a little dry.

He said, "What's the matter Linda don't you want to fuck!?"

"I may have winter in my hair, but I have summer in my heart!"

"Linda if you don't get some spring in your ass we will be here until fall!" said Willy. Willy roughed Linda up pulling her hair while he was fucking her brains out!!!!!!!! Then he left her there and he left the whorehouse and went back to the hotel pool, he stripped down to his underwear and he jumped into the pool for a swim, then got dressed and he went to a bar on the beach for a few drinks and talked to a few chicks.

Willy had a little too much to drink and a man came up to him and grabbed him by the throat and he said, "Leave my wife alone or I'll kill you!" Willy left the beach and he went back to the whorehouse and the Chinese-pantyhose girl and Linda the madam were there.

"Hey buddy, get lost you're not getting anymore!" said Linda. Willy was giving her some shit and Big Black Bubba the pimp picked Willy up by the throat and hurled him 10 feet in the air and he landed in a muddy patch of dirt. He got up and he limped away back to the hotel and he went to bed.

Willy staggered to his room and his friends said, "What the hell happened to you!"

"I was fucking around with the wrong girl I guess!" said Willy. His clothes were full of mud, he had a shiner black and blue on each eye where he got punched a few times! He had a big red mark on his neck where he got choked!

Linda told Big Bubba at the whorehouse, "He was Willy Bird I fucked him twice and he raped me, and he took advantage of me he was such an animal I thought he was going to kill me! He did the same thing to Kim!" said Linda. Bubba went to see Kim Young and she told him how Willy treated her.

Bubba said, "When sun breaks, I will go to the hotel looking for him and if I find him, I'm gonna fuck him up!!!!!"

"Willy you better get some medical treatment because you look bad!" said Nicole Nickelson.

"Willy who did this to you?" said Patty McGroin.

"I got into a fight at the beach and I was attacked by a big black dude at the whorehouse!" he said.

"Willy go down to the hotel clerk and tell them you need medical treatment and if I were you I would go back to the ship and stay for the night because whoever did this to you could be looking for you!" said Dick Hurts. Dick and Willy went to the hotel desk and the clerk contacted the hospital boat to come get Willy for the night. A helicopter arrived to take Willy to the hospital boat. Then the hotel clerk contacted Admiral Quonset Point. The phone rang at his room at 2:30 in the morning.

"Hello! Admiral Quonset Point speaking!"

"This is Lori White from the front desk. One of your clients got hurt bad and he's at the hospital boat getting treatment. Apparently, he got into a fight and he got roughed up!! Dick Hurts says that he may be in danger fearing someone may be looking for him."

"Lori tell Dick I will go to see him in a few minutes and don't let anyone know his whereabouts at the hotel," said the admiral. An hour later Admiral Quonset Point got a boat ride to the hospital boat to see Willy Bird.

"What in the hell happened to you!?" he said.

"I was out drinking and having fun and I guess I had a little too much and I was picking on the wrong girl and I got my ass kicked!!!!!!!!!" said Willy.

36

"Willy you are crazy! You always were, but you need to cool it! You're not in the United States, you're on an island in the middle of the Atlantic, and if you did something wrong, they could kill you and throw you in the ocean! You're lucky to be alive! When you get released in the morning you call me and I'll meet you at customs before we board understand because whoever is looking for you, finds you, you may not get out of here! The hotel clerk got threatening messages about you and the National Guard has placed you in protected custody. Call me when you get released, the ship is not leaving until you're on it!" said Admiral Quonset Point.

It was 7:30 a.m. This big black dude holding a big club came to the hotel lobby yelling in an angry voice.

"Where the hell is Willy Bird, the twin chopper rotor punk! Does anybody know who he is!? I'm gonna bust his fuckin' head in!!!!!!!!!"

"Excuse me mister you need to leave this hotel right now you can't be using that kind of language here now get out!" said Lori the hotel clerk.

"I need to see Willy Bird!"

"There's no Willy Bird here, now get out before I call the police," she said. A few people were in the lobby when this angry dude came in and he was still screaming as Lori the hotel clerk kept telling him to get out, but he will not leave! He was waving a big club and he broke a lamp with it! Finally, security arrived and held him at gun point and escorted him out of the hotel.

A woman outside told a guard, "Officer, there's a mad man in the hotel!" Big Bubba struggled with the police outside the hotel and he was outnumbered, and he was beaten by his own club by authorities and taken into custody by a golf cart trolley. Blood was pouring out of his head on the way! Big Bubba was taken to the hospital boat after his beating!

Sunday August 24th, 2020 the Irene tour is leaving today, and the continental breakfast was served about 8am. Muffins, bagels, orange juice pancakes and coffee. The tour went to customs before boarding the ship. Admiral Quonset Point and Willy Bird met at customs. The island police were there as well.

The police said to customs, "There is a rape charge against Mr. Willy Bird from two women, at the Tongue Kiss Cafe."

"Officer I paid for sex and they were over aggressive, and I had to defend myself!" said Willy.

"Here's what's going to happen we have to hold you in a detention facility before a court hearing deciding if you're guilty. If you're guilty you will serve 20 years in detention depending on the judge if not you will be on the next ship going to New York. We will get their story and yours in court. You must surrender your passport; the hearing will be at 9 a.m. tomorrow morning at the police and fire house," said the police. Everyone boarded the ship and Admiral Quonset Point made an announcement.

"Good morning did everyone have a good time here in Q'klitores? Unfortunately, we have a problem with one of our tourists and our trip to New York will be delayed until late tomorrow afternoon or evening, no one will be allowed to leave the ship. Please do not leave the ship!" said Admiral Quonset Point.

The next day Monday August 25th the court hearing, at police and fire.

"Everyone please rise before Judge Helen Kladova. Now you may be seated! The plaintiff Mr. Willy Bird versus the Tongue Kiss Cafe facility the defendant and the persons involved: Miss Kim Young and Miss Linda Eltoro," said the court sheriff.

"You ladies know that prostitution is legal on Q'klitores and some men are going to rough you up; and until I find a reason to prosecute

Mr. Willy Bird's counter claim of self-defense, Miss Linda Eltoro, let's hear your story," said Judge Helen Kladova.

"Your honor this man tried to kill me he was so rough; he was an animal! I had sex with him twice and he was very mean, because he could not get the one he wants. I run this whorehouse. First time I gave him the Hurricane and he was not happy with her the first time so I took him on and he was over aggressive; I was trying to calm him down because I'm 62 years old and I told him I may have winter in my hair but I have summer in my heart and he told me if I don't get some spring in my ass we'll be here until fall! Then he tried to stick his penis in my mouth forcing it down my throat and when I told him he needs to pay more money for a blowjob he picked me up and threw me down on the bed and left me there and he stormed out of the whorehouse!

"The second time he came back looking for more and I told him I was the only one available because everyone went home for the night. I gave him a second chance and he took advantage of me forcing himself on me when I wasn't ready, and he was acting like a wild animal!" said Linda.

"Miss Kim Young. What did Willy do to you?" said the judge.

"He forced his way on me when I was not ready, he didn't give me a chance to take my pantyhose off and he jumped on me he ripped my clothes off he picked me up and he threw me down on the bed and he forced his way on me like a wild animal!" Kim cried.

"Mr. Willy Bird, you were very mean to these girls and they deserve an apology, each one of them. In the United States you would be charged with rape and if these women have injuries you will be charged here in Q'klitores but because prostitution is legal on Q'kli-tores you're being protected from aggravated rape unless there are inju-ries to these ladies. Now I want to hear from you and why do you keep going back looking for trouble," said the judge.

"Your Honor, the first time I went to the whorehouse I was given a freak, all she did was blow on me she smacked me around with her boobs and she peed all over me. Her name was the Hurricane and she was terrible, so I asked for another and she gave me this Chinese girl and I screwed her just like I screw any other girls! Then I did Linda two times and she said I was mean the way I treated her, she's a prostitute looking for sex," said Willy Bird.

"OK we will have a recess until the jury comes with a verdict and the court will be in session later today at 2 p.m.," said Judge Helen Kladova.

A coin flip will determine if Willy will go to jail-detention or be charged and go back home! If it lands on heads, he goes home; if it lands on tails, he's in trouble!!!!!!!!!

At 2 p.m. the court was again in session.

"Please rise in honor of Judge Helen Kladova. Willy Bird versus Linda Eltoro and Kim Young. Please be seated," said the guard in the court room. Admiral Quonset Point was in the court room.

"Mr. Willy Bird several bruises were found on Linda Eltoro and Miss Kim Young has a fractured spine according to medical records. The jury has the verdict," said the judge.

The jury: "We find Mr. Willy Bird guilty in the first degree from aggravated assault on both women and second-degree rape on both women."

"Mr. Willy Bird you will serve ten years in detention on each charge for a total of 20 years in solitary confinement," said Judge Helen Kladova and she banged the gavel on her desk and the court was adjourned; the gavel fell off the stick and landed on the floor in the court room. Willy was taken into custody and a lawyer was there.

Admiral Quonset Point said, "Sorry Willy!" He left the court room and he went back to the ship.

The lawyer said, "Sorry Willy!" And he left the holding cell.

Another coin flip decides if Willy stays in jail or he escapes, if heads he gets away if tails he stays! The coin lands on heads and he has his escape plan later; the floor in the holding cell is dirt all he has to do is start digging. The jail is located in the bunkers; he's not there yet!

At 4:30 p.m. on Monday August 25th, cruise ship Irene left the island of Q'klitores and as it departed Admiral Quonset Point had a message.

"Ladies and gentlemen we are now departing Q'klitores on to New York without one of our tourists, Mr. Willy Bird will not be with us because he got into trouble on the island and we cannot bring him back, we wish him luck and pray for his safety!"

Meanwhile Big Bubba had his plan back at the whorehouse when Linda and Kim returned.

"Bubba what are you doing!?" said Linda.

"I'm going to the jail to kill Willy when it gets dark. I'm gonna bash his fuckin' head in and stuff his body in this drum and dump him in the ocean!"

"Come on Bubba, don't do that let him serve his time because if you get caught, we'll get thrown out of here!" said Linda.

About 9:30 p.m. an earthquake happened shaking the island knocking out the electricity and cracking the holding cell floor allowing Willy his escape plan. Bubba was hit by falling debris at the whorehouse delaying his attempt to kill Willy Bird, he ended up at the hospital boat with head injuries. The police and fire house were dark giving Willy a chance to start digging after the earthquake. Willy dug a pretty good hole in the dirt floor from cracks from the earthquake with a kitchen fork and his hands, escaping under the bars to get free.

He dug a hole deep enough to shimmy his way through from light shining through from the ships and he went out the door and he ran down the side of the mountain to the beach. He walked the beach and he took off his jail gown and threw it in a waste barrel and he covered it up with bottles and papers. He noticed a cargo ship bound for Miami and he swam to the dock where the ship was loading and he manage to jump over a conveyor belt to get aboard and he hid behind some boxes and he was never noticed and hitched a free ride to Miami. The ship left at six o'clock in the morning.

The policeman and the fire lady never heard or saw Willy escape they were too busy fucking in another room! Then about 7 a.m. they noticed Willy had escaped and it was a manhunt to find him and search dogs were called to find him, and all ships and aircraft were grounded to find this fuckin' guy! Military helicopters helped out while flying over the volcano looking for possible activity from last night's earthquakes and aftershocks. The choppers searched all day into the evening flying around the island looking for Willy Bird. Search dogs went in every building and bunkers sniffing out his whereabouts and the scent was picked up but no Willy Bird!!!!!!! The ships that left the island during the night were located but the authorities found nothing; Willy is long gone!

The cargo ship took three days to get to Miami non-stop. Willy hid up high on top of the crates and boxes to protect him from search dogs running below. He found boxes with chips and snacks to eat during his three-day hibernation and he also found boxes with bottled water. He took a blanket from one of the crates to sleep on.

Back on Q'klitores all ships aircraft and all moving transportation were grounded for a week until Willy was found; orders from David L. Sanberg the owner of the hotel.

"Dave if he jumped in the ocean to swim away, he may not last a day because of cross currents. There are no reports of him stealing a boat or boarding a ship unless security is not paying attention! All the boats hotel rooms and the bunkers were secured, and he was nowhere to be found. All buildings the mountain even the crater was secured, and we found nothing!" said Dick Dickey the hotel host.

"There's no question he's dead or he may have got away on a boat. We will find out soon when his body washes up on shore if the sharks didn't eat him, or his body will be found in the water," said Dave Sanberg.

The National Guard searched every building and the whole island from ground to deep inside the volcano 24/7 to find this Willy Bird! Water taxis searched all water ways for 200 miles inside international waters. No Willy!

The cargo ship arrived in Miami about 3 a.m. three days later! Before arrival Willy heard the announcement; the ship will be docking in Miami in 20 minutes. It was pouring rain and thunder and lightning it's not what Willy wants for his escape plan!

Willy waited a few minutes. The lightning stopped flashing and Willy had his eye on an anchor hole to make his leap. When he saw the city lights he made his move; he quietly got down where he was and he ran over to the hole and he leap frogged out of the hole 37 feet below landing in the water swimming in ten foot waves and he made it to a buoy and the storm started up again and he held onto the buoy rocking and rolling in the rough water. Willy watched the ship go away.

At 8 a.m. the sun came out and a passing boat came by and Willy was waving and hollering help!!!!!!!!!!!! A couple came to rescue him and take him to a beach. He only had underpants on hanging onto the buoy.

"Thank you so much!" he cried.

A man said to Willy, "What happened did you just break out of jail!?"

"No sir, my boat sank a half a mile away and I swam to a buoy hoping to get rescued and here you are! I was sleeping and I didn't have time to get dressed I had to abandon the boat and swim for my life!" said Willy.

"My name is Mike Mitchell and my girl Stacy Marks. I have a pair of jeans shorts and a Miami Dolphins Dan Marino Jersey you can have. Here's $10.00 to help you out a little."

"Oh! Thank you very much!" said Willy.

"What's your name buddy?" said the man.

"My name is Rockey; just call me Rockey!" said Willy. The couple dropped Willy off on Miami Beach.

"I have a phone if you need to call someone," said the girl.

"No ma'am I'm all set, thank you very much!" The boat left and the first thing Willy did with his $10.00 was buy sandals for his feet, $3.99 then he got something to eat and a soda. Now he has to get his life back.

Willy walked along the beach and he noticed a girl texting on her cell phone, and he asked her, "Excuse me miss do you mind if I could use your phone to call a friend, I'm in distress!"

"Sure!" she said. Willy calls from the girl's phone on Miami Beach. The phone rings in Dick Hurts' office and he picked it up.

"Good afternoon, Dick Hurts attorney at law."

"Dick, it's Willy. I'm here in Miami. I hitched a ride on a cargo ship and escaped, you know the story. Can you get me some help?" While Willy was talking on the girl's phone, she was reading a book; *Ground of the Devil* was the name of the book she was reading.

"Listen to me Willy be very careful you need to find somewhere to go for the next couple of days until I get the jet to come pick you up. When I get to Florida you will meet me where you are, and I will pick you up in a rental car and bring you to the airport and fly you back to Maine. Don't tell people your real name and when we get home you will have to get a name change because they will come looking for you because the boat you were on was notified. Find some chick to tangle with until I get there, you're very good at that," said Dick Hurts.

Willy gave the phone back to the girl and he said, "Thanks a lot, sorry I took so long. What are you reading?"

"I am reading a science fiction book *Ground of the Devil* by Richard Rezendes."

"What is it about?" said Willy.

"It's about a meteor that crashed into a small town in Connecticut and an indescribable creature comes out of it and it killed everything alive! It sprays fire it has a powerful stinger and scorpion-like pincers and it has 14 boobies and the animal is described as the devil from hell! It's a good book," said the girl.

"What's your name?" said Willy.

 "My name is Mary Maggy from Miami, and yours?"

"My name is Rockey Willis," said Willy Bird, using a fake name.

"Are you alone?" said Mary.

"Yes I was out in my boat and a storm came and my boat sank so I had to swim to a buoy and a boat came by to rescue me. I'm from Maine," said Willy. Willy and the girl hit it off all day at Miami Beach and she fed him sandwiches and drinks and had a long day at the beach until sunset.

*At the docks…

The cargo ship Willy snuck onto was notified by the National Guard on Q'klitores about the manhunt for Willy Bird. The ship radioed back to the island and said there was no report of someone sneaking aboard. The ship pulled into Miami at 3:17am. Search dogs came aboard to find Willy when the ship was unloading. The dogs ran around checking and left the ship.

*Back at the beach…

The girl Mary on Miami Beach fell in love with the lying Willy Bird for the next two days.

"What's your name again?" said Mary.

"My name is Willy, oh! Rockey Willis!" Later they had a candle-light dinner together, salad, Italian pasta, chicken, French fries, a bottle of wine and they smoked pot and then Willy did what he's good for! Fucking!!!!!!!!! Mary and Willy fucked all night at Mary Maggy's harbor view of Miami condo!

The next day Mary took Willy-Rockey shopping in a convertible sports car through downtown Miami, they had lunch and then went back to the beach until a thunderstorm chased them out before sunset and the ride was on at the condo, skin to skin. They were at it again!

Mary said, "You're a horny guy!" The next morning Mary and Willy-Rockey went out for breakfast in town. Mary's phone rang.

"Hello! Hi, may I speak to Rockey the man using the phone the other day?" said Dick Hurts.

"Rockey I'm at the airport I want you to meet me at Miami beach at 2p.m. I will call this number make sure you stay with the girl and I will give you the location where I will be," said Dick! Willy and the girl were at the beach after they got lunch. Willy-Rockey said to the girl.

"I have to meet with my lawyer at 2 p.m. and when he comes I need to have a few words with him so I need to leave but I will be in touch with you because I like you a lot and thank you for your help. He's going to call you in about 20 minutes. Just hand me your phone so I can direct him to where we are." Willy-Rockey waited and Dick Hurts called the girl.

"Hi is this Mary?"

"Yes, it is, would you like to speak to Rockey?"

"Please! Rockey I'm parked in front of the Prizzi's Pizza near the beach in a red car with Florida plates RSNY927."

"Oh! What a coincidence me and Mary just had lunch there!" Mary gave Willy-Rockey a ride to meet Dick!

After a brief meeting Dick Hurts took Willy Bird to the airport. While stopped in traffic at a light Willy saw a big black dude hugging and kissing Mary and he got in her car and drove off on the other side of the street.

"Look at that! I'll never call that cunt again! Let's go back to Maine!" said Willy.

At nighttime, Dick and Willy went to a McDonald's for a quiet bite before heading for the airport. Big Dick had a talk with Willy before flying off in his private jet.

"Willy, there's a worldwide man hunt out for you. If the island of Q'klitores finds out you got on a ship or plane when you escaped they will track you and find you in Maine, however if they believe you died trying to leave the island in a week you may get lucky! Have you ever seen the show, *I Almost Got Away with It*? If they rule you dead, you just beat the system! But you're not out of the woods just yet! If your picture comes out on the national news and television a positive identification you have some serious choices to make! Me being your lawyer here's what you should do:

Number one, join ISIS! Hide in a robe for the rest of your life and have your name changed; definitely change your name! We can go to an Islamic mosque get your name changed and get a new social security number.

Number two, just stay as you are and take your chances, but you have no license no identity because it vanished in Q'klitores! Not a good idea!

Number three, keep your name but you have to go to a psychiatric or mental hospital and claim that you lost your identity and claim sick disability; I will help you with that when we get back to Maine. You have choices to go back to Maine with me, stay in Miami, or run to Canada, but if you are on the local worldwide man hunt you have nowhere to go.

Number four, get rid of all your tattoos and shave your head and keep the hair off! Wear different clothes.

Number five, you can't travel anymore. If you are declared dead, you still have to change your name and get a new ID or just stay as you are with no identification!

"Let's go back home and will sort out what we have to do. You better pray Q'klitores declares you dead in a week, if that happens the manhunt is over, but you have a lot of work ahead of you! Enjoy your flight and let's go back to Maine!" said Dick Hurts.

Dick's plane leaves Miami. Two weeks later Dick Hurts found out that the island of Q'klitores declared Willy Bird dead! Willy checked into a mental facility in Bangor, Maine to get a new identity! Big Dick Hurts he's a good lawyer!!!!!!!!!!! *Thank god this mother fucker is finally out of this manuscript!!!!!!!!!*

Back in Q'klitores Saturday, September 20th, 2020 the Motor City Tour was leaving Detroit on a cruise ship heading to the island of Q'klitores in about a week. The cruise ship traveled through the great lakes and down the Mississippi river into the gulf of Mexico with a stop in Texas and Miami Florida through the Caribbean out into the Atlantic ocean with a couple of stops one in the Dominican Republic and Aruba before docking on the island of Q'klitores in the middle of the Atlantic.

Saturday September 27th, 2020 Motor City tour arrives on Q'klitores and it is show time! The show was at Nathian's Rock House and the club was packed. The band had about 20 people in it, playing and dancing. Songs and dances of Diana Ross and the Supremes. Gladys Knight and the Pips, the Four Tops, the Temptations, the Jackson 5, Smokey Robinson and the Miracles, Stevie Wonder, the Commodores, Marvin Gaye, Aretha Franklin and many acting performers.

Helen Kladova was running the show and it goes on Saturday and Sunday night. Songs like "Dancing in the Street" opened the performance. Nathian Jones played and the club erupted in celebration! "Celebration" from Cool and the Gang followed that, then "I heard it Through the Grapevine," "Little Bitty Pretty One," "Ooo Baby Baby," "Cloud Nine," "Love Potion Number Nine," "Baby Baby Don't Cry," "Mama's Pearl," "Ball of Confusion," "That's What the World is Today." "Endless Love," "My Cherie Amour," "Never Can Say Goodbye," "Being with You," "How Sweet it is to be Loved by You," "If You Really Love Me," "Cruisin," "Still," "Three Times a Lady," "Shotgun," and "Reflections."

And other songs. This band has actors like the real thing; it's a cover band that performs and dances and changes costumes to each set, there are two hours in a set. The first show was at 9 p.m. with an hour break and the second show came on at 11 p.m. and played until 12:30 a.m. and the crowd celebrated out of control and gave the Motown City live band a standing ovation for about 10 minutes. A DJ came on to play dance music for the rest of the night until 2 a.m.

Stage lights neon and lasers bouncing off disco balls and lights coming out of the walls, ceiling and flashing on the dance floor and strobe lights, spinning lights and police lights and a fog machine and blowing air coming from the dance floor. Blowing up girl's skirts until you see their panties.

Disco inferno was playing, and a pregnant girl was dancing wildly when suddenly her water broke, and people started slipping and sliding then the girl feel to the disco floor with her legs wide open and she delivered twins right on the dance floor! Boy-girl twins, the boy was white, and the girl was black. It was an embarrassing moment! The club was evacuated just before 2 a.m. and paramedics arrived to take the girl and her babies to the hospital ship. The ghost of Olivia appeared standing over her briefly then it disappeared! No one noticed.

The next day was Sunday and the Motor City live band did a brief matinee show right between the island's titties; ladies were dancing on the nipples! Then the band went for a tour of the island, the same tour cruise ship Irene with Admiral Quonset Point, went on. Then the band was invited to Benjamin's Steakhouse for dinner before performing tonight's show at Nathian's Rock House.

The club was packed again, and the Motor City live band put on another spectacular performance! They played the same songs in both sets and Helen Kladova did a comedy act to end the night. The shows were sold out both nights, but no babies were lost on the dance floor! The club closed at 1 a.m. The band members stayed in the suites located on the 7th floor.

Room 711 was an unfriendly room to six girls; everyone got undressed and went to bed at about 2:30 a.m. One of the girls woke to a loud growling noise and she quickly turned a light on and every-body's clothes were flying around the room and the girl saw Olivia's ghost dancing in the mirror and she screamed hysterically! Then the ghost disappeared, and all the clothes fell to the floor waking up the other five girls and it was 52 pick up!!!!!!!!!! The girls sorted out the mess, got dressed and left the room in a hurry! They went to the hotel front desk.

"We have a ghost in our room!" the six girls said.

"Oh my god! You're kidding! Let me get you another room!" said the hotel clerk. The girls got the best suite in the house room 764 a view of Mount Flow.

The ghost of Olivia visits this room too! The girls had their plan, they covered up all the mirrors in the room including the bathrooms and left some lights on and made sure there was no darkness in any room. One girl looked out of the window and she saw an orange glow pouring out the top of the volcano then it went away; she said to herself that's cool!!!

Then she went to bed; the time on the alarm clock was 4:02 a.m. Then the girls from the band got up between 11 and 11:30 and went down to the hotel comfort lobby for continental breakfast and the girls told their ghost stories and went to the pool for the day to rest up before leaving.

At 4 p.m. the Motor City live band left the island of Q'klitores and went back to Detroit. While the band was boarding the ship, the crowd went wild in celebration! The ship left the dock with waving fans.

A few hours later new tours were arriving and were greeted to a strong earthquake, a thunderstorm and waterspouts! Crying visitors thought it was the end of the world and the wind was whipping up and the rain came down so hard people were falling and swimming and trying to grab on to things before getting blown off the island. The wind was 130 miles per hour! It was the remnants of an offshore tropical storm! One of the tours got back on the ship and left the island in ten-foot seas. A few minutes later the sun came out leaving a mess behind! The clouds went from night to day in a matter of minutes! The tourist on Q'klitores!

4 THE NATIONAL WORLD CONVENTION!

Cruise ships from all over the world come to gather with world-wide leaders. Cruise ship Ding Dong Tours arrives loaded with Chinese and Chi Chung is the tour guide for this ship. A lot of these people do not speak English, some can't hear; translators and language interpreters arrived with them.

When the ship pulled into Q'klitores the Chinese tour got a good laugh getting off the ship and met with the hotel owner. David L. Sanberg and the tour got their rooms at the hotel and went on a tour through the hotel, the pool and the casino. Then they boarded the golf cart trolleys and went around the island the same as all the other tours.

This tour is a little different; now there's a road that goes up the mountain to the summit that begins near the pool and goes up to the crater. On the way up there were a group of naked men and women peeing on the vegetables.

"Ladies and gentlemen. Look here! The naked men and women stand over the tomatoes and pee on them every day for hours to make the tomatoes turn red and grow the size of bowling balls; however because of all the rain the tomatoes are not as big and rosy but the cucumbers are enormous!" said Chi Chung in English. The translators talk in Chinese.

The tour was laughing hysterically! Then the trolleys got to the summit and the tour saw the vagina shaped crater and they laughed and laughed! The translators and interpreters explained what they were seeing.

Later the tour went down the mountain and showed how the Indians and natives live. Went around the mountain showing all the buildings, boats the beaches and at the end of the tour the culture united national translations building is where the Chinese tour had to show their passports and visas and pay the island taxes. Doctor Raymound W. Hallowmostraphoniagalleriabarringtoncommonwealth was there to assist them.

"Just call him Dr. It," said Chi Chung.

While the tour was at the C.U.N.T. building checking in to customs, Chi Chung went to the whorehouse to get laid. He fucked Kim Young; the Chinese girl with the pantyhose. Chi Chung removed her pantyhose gently and he laid her down on the bed and he slid his sausage into Kim's slot gently! He was a real gentleman.

After leaving the whorehouse he met with the tour-translators and interpreters and finished the tour around the hands, the head ending at the island's tits where they took pictures. Later the tour did some shopping and went to the pool and the beach before a Chinese dinner tonight. Later in the evening the tour met in the food court for a tour before going to dinner.

"Ladies and gentlemen welcome to Lori's food court. We have several restaurants in here to choose from. Dunkin' Donuts, McDonald's, Chuck E Cheese and we have Charly's Philly Steaks. Now for our fancy restaurants. Popeye's Southern Fried Chicken, Dave and Buster's Gaming Eatery. Dave and Lori's Chowder House. The Parrot Fish Market. The fish is fresh everyday off the boat. Then we have devil's fried hot ghost peppers grill. If you like very spicy food. Then we have the Rice and Bean factory where we will be having dinner tomorrow night. Tonight, we will be eating here at the Long Wang Chinese Cuisine for the grand opening. The restaurant opens in about 20 minutes.

"Let me tell you a little about the Rice and Bean Factory it is our largest restaurant in the food court that connects to the Parrot Fish Market. The layout goes outside Mediterranean style and serves to all countries. There are two floors to this restaurant," said Chi Chung.

Translators translate the food court in Chinese and interpreters for the deaf. The tour was reading the menu while being serenaded with music, violins.

"A la carte: cum drop soup: the pee yu platter: hoo flung poo: suc sum tit: yung poon tang: no takeout orders accepted. Luncheon specials. Sum yung chick, served in a red wine sauce. Won hung lo in Chinese meatballs. Lik sum dik with mouth-watering beef sticks in a cream source. Chu sum twat dinner for party of 8 or more. Suc mi pork, a Chinese special. Fuc yu man, specialty of the house. Tung chow soup. Dinner combinations include smogg roll and fortune nookie noodles." Goo in hand, for those dining alone. Goo wee chick, sloppy seconds no extra charge! Cum tu soon, order early these go fast. Suk mi wang, traditional Chinese meatloaf. Sum dum chick, you get what you pay for. Fuc mei slo, not available after 10 p.m. Lik mi clit, a delicious lick smacking oriental delicacy. Cho kon it, not for the light threated, fuc sum now, for those in a hurry! Wai tu yung. Tung sum chick, a taste bud tingler! Sum gulp cum, low cal diet special. You cum suc mi platter. All menu at market price."

The tour got a good laugh at the menu; most of the tour had the you cum suc mi platter with soup-rice and salad. After dinner the tour went to a show and after they went to the casino. The next day Sunday November 16th, 2020, a church service at the international house of worship and many people were there from different tour groups.

"Good morning my dear brothers and sisters, welcome to the house of the lord, my name is Pastor In. Today I'm preaching end time revelations! First let us pray, sing some songs to begin our service."

After Christian songs, a couple of readings a prayer gospel and then the sermon, Pastor In continued.

"Today we are going to talk about earthquakes, volcanoes and hurricanes. As you know we have been getting several earthquakes on this island for years and some of them are mild and some have been quite strong lately! Where on an island in the middle of the Atlantic Ocean with a volcano and an area where violent hurricanes form. Everybody here knows this island is a ticking time bomb! The earthquakes we have been getting are a sign this volcano is ready to blow!

"The National Guard and Coast Guard officials have been monitoring this volcano for more than 50 years and it's the same old songs, moderate earthquakes! This volcano has been dormant since then.

"We have nuclear bombs stored inside this mountain along with heavy military ammunition; just think about it! If this mountain blows the destruction will be unbelievable! This island will be blown out of the water, but no one wants to believe; we're safe here staying in these strong military bunkers. You better think again because the number of earthquakes is a sign this volcano could blow one day with no warning! The storms we get here are strong enough to blow you off the island. If a hurricane gets trapped when this mountain goes up, we will be gone in a flash. If people tell you this island is safe it is not, we are on borrowed time! These revelations are going to happen soon.

This dormant volcano is getting ready to act up and our storms are getting worse. Will we be ready?" said Pastor In.

Just when the pastor finished his sermon the ground shook violently, and the church got damaged. Windows broke, pictures fell, and shingles started falling outside. The shaking didn't last a minute; everyone ran out of the church avoiding falling debris and gathered together outside in the pouring rain.

The pastor said, "Everybody don't panic, let's get outside in a hurry!!! Brothers and sisters, just like that! Heed these warnings we're getting more earthquakes! We must pray! Oh, ho! Lightning, let's get back in the church!" said Pastor In.

The rain came down in buckets and thunder and lightning; the church was flooded, and everyone was standing on chairs. The thunder was so loud everyone was blocking their ears and the wind blew things around in the church. The storm lasted just a few minutes and it was gone the sun came and the flooding went down.

"We must pray!" the pastor said.

The ground shook again, again and again! Up and down swaying back and forth, then it stopped. The aftershocks lasted about five minutes; it felt like the island was ready to fall in.

"Everyone don't panic we must exit the church and go where you need to go and stay out of buildings and away from falling debris. Keep praying!" said pastor in.

The church service was canceled, and all buildings were evacuated and everyone on the island met in front of the hotel. There was no damage in the hotel, but the earthquake was felt a little, but it was much worse where the volcano was.

"Ladies and gentlemen. My name is Sergeant Adam Santini. I just want to inform you about what happened. We had a pretty strong earthquake and a few aftershocks, and you need to stay out of buildings until we check for damages and see if there's any activity going on in this volcano. Just stay put and do not go down to the beaches in case of rising tides. The National Guard is flying over the volcano and if any activity is found you will have to evacuate. I will make an announcement when I hear more.

"Just stay out in front of the hotel and on the island until I give the OK to go in buildings or return to the ships. Food and soft drinks will be served outside the hotel and pool area. If you need to use the restrooms use the ones in the pool area. If we get more earthquakes, the bunkers are open to the public if you need to evacuate if so this process will last as long as it takes. We must wait for three hours before entering buildings. A volcano crew from NASA was called in for help in case there is a problem with this volcano. The crew will set up monitoring equipment TVs and computers in the cultural center and in the bunkers. Stay put or go to the pool area until I give the OK to go inside."

Sgt. Adam Santini boarded a helicopter to fly over the volcano and nothing was happening; there was no activity going on. Later toward evening hotel crew directed everyone inside, and it was a quiet night.

The island was in the dark until utility workers worked all night the get the power back on, on the island. The generators in the bunkers were turned on to restore power to the island. Workers checked for damages in the hotel before people could go back to their rooms.

The next day was recovery day before things got back to normal. More cruise ships arrived to get ready for the national world convention. The next day was Tuesday November 18th, 2020 and a Thanksgiving dinner was served in the meeting room where the world convention will be. Turkey, stuffing, mashed potatoes, turnip, carrots, sweet potatoes, squash, green beans, broccoli, soup and salads, etc. Apple, blueberry and squash and pumpkin pie for dessert. Coffee and tea for drinks. Wine, red and white, was served during dinner; the meal started at 2p.m. and lasted all day into the evening.

The next day the world leaders went on a tour of the island and went to the food court for their meals. Dave and Buster's opened and the world leaders had dinner there, played video games then went to the casino.

The next day is the convention. Thursday, November 20, 2020. The worldwide national convention took place in the convention event center conference room the room with a large mahogany wood table seating about 300 people from all over the world. The Chinese spoke first in Chinese and then translated to English talking about politics and the economy. Then former U.S. president George W. Bush spoke about the United States and he was slushing with his speech because he was drunk, and he threw up in a waste basket! His speech was over, and he left the room. Other countries had their speech. Then the hotel owner spoke.

"Ladies and gentlemen. My name is David L. Sanberg the owner of this hotel and I also run the island of Q'klitores, this island is not under a nice name, but it is what it is. The looks of this island as a naked lady in the water and the slit on top of Mount Flow gives out the name because it looks like a woman's vagina and I thought I would make a resort out of this island from changing the naked lady in the water hoping it would be a big hit! I was right we are very successful, and we are doing very well here except for a few issues. Being in the middle of the Atlantic we get the worst storms, we have been bumped by several hurricanes over the years and we get tropical rains almost every day, then we get moderate earthquakes from time to time and third we have a volcano. We had a strong earthquake the other day and we watch this volcano very closely, but we have not had any activity here in more than 50 years, but we are an earthquake prone area.

Don't worry we are safe I recently hired NASA to come to monitor this mountain every day. Our next speaker please," said David L. Sanberg.

"Hi my name is Sgt. Adam Santini and with me is Dr. Raymond W. Hallowmostraphoniagalleriabarringtoncommonwealth. He has a very long name and he likes to be called Dr. It! Him and I run the political part of this island, we make the rules and give instructions when we need to. Dr. It is the counselor and MD on the island. I make the decisions here. We have a democratic island here and we all work together.

"The world is in turmoil threatening for world war three. The United States and Russia are heading back into the cold war and the peace agreement with North Korea is not working, they're still launching nuclear missiles and one struck South Korea on November 14th, just a few days ago; luckily it didn't detonate because we'd be in world war three right now. Another missile touched down north of the big island of Hawaii about 350 miles, leaving the U.S. on edge. Former president Bush was here earlier was about to talk about this and he got sick and he had to leave.

"The problem in the world is not getting better and the more things get out of hand the worse it's going to get! This is why we're here. The United States brought this island testing nuclear weapons back in the late 1970s and 80s because of the threat of the Gulf War and we had two Iraqi wars. Then the testing stopped and David L. Sanberg brought the island and made it a resort here and he built it up. But he's part owner, the U.S. military owns the other half. If we have another war, things may change in a hurry because we will have to take over! He makes the money bringing in the tourists and the military is here to protect them."

While Sgt. Adam Santini was giving his speech, the room shook and the lights blinked on and off! Everyone was screaming hysterically!

"Be calm ladies and gentlemen it's only a mild tremor, we get these all the time there's nothing to worry about!"

As Sgt. Adam Santini continued his speech there was a big earthquake! The island raised up 10 feet sending 300 people off their feet and the tables and chairs and everything lifted off the ground with them! The chandeliers fell and smashed on top of them; lamps fell and several people were hurt, broken bones and cuts all over them! The volcano backfired, instead of erupting it erupted under the sea floor sending a shockwave under water; it was a low wave tsunami moving water 600 miles per hour toward the south Atlantic, no one knows what happened! The National Guard and medical teams rushed into the damaged hotel to rescue hundreds of injured people taking them out in stretchers. Helicopters landed to take the injured to the hospital ship. A Brazilian cruise ship was crossing the south Atlantic Ocean heading for Portugal with 6000 people aboard, and it was a beautiful day and a calm cruise. Everyone was enjoying the cruise. Suddenly the sound of thunder and a loud roar and the ship was vibrating!

The captain saw a huge wave get bigger and bigger crossing over a sandbar and he said, "Mayday, mayday, mayday!!!!!!!!!" in Brazilian language.

The wave struck the ship in such a force it broke into pieces, killing everyone aboard! The Brazilian ship was struck broadside by the 600 mile per hour wave! A nice cruise went from calm and relaxing and then *bang!!!!!!!!!!!!!!!* No one knew what happen—like night and day. The ship and bodies were spread across the ocean like a bunch of bowling pins being knocked down; then the ship sank quickly in pieces!!!!!!!!!!!! The great white sharks were invited to an open buffet leaving the ocean in a pool blood with swarming great whites eating the bodies. Then thousands of seagulls came to join the feast!!!!!!!!!!

Large waves later hit the coastlines from South America to Africa, leaving damage to boats and low line areas; it looked like Sri Lanka during the 2004 day after Christmas tsunami!

Back on Q'klitores, the island was damaged, and the hotel was seriously damaged. Everyone raced outside when this violent earthquake struck. The people saw injured bodies being removed from the hotel in a pool of blood. NASA was flying over the volcano looking for the eruption.

"Everyone please be calm and gather near the island's boobies! My name is Vincent Tino the NASA head volcanologist. Everyone must evacuate at this time go back to your ships and all ships and boats will need to leave the island immediately! We had a possible volcanic eruption, but we don't know for sure!"

The visitors were led to their cruise ships and all the boats and sea transportation left the island within a few minutes! All the injured—about 300 people—being transferred lined up in whirlybird helicopters and were taken to the hospital ship and left the island leaving the National Guard and the NASA volcano crew behind. Military ships stayed docked on the island and the volcano crew was flown in by helicopter. While the island was evacuating NASA was flying over Mount Flow looking for activity. The hotel was a mess and it would have to be knocked down and rebuilt. The Indians and natives were rescued by helicopters.

5   THE VOLCANO

The NASA volcano crew and the military has a big mess to clean up. What happened!!!!!!!!!!!!! Friday November 21st, 2020, NASA was setting up monitoring equipment in the bunkers the only safe haven on the island of Q'klitores. The hotel and all the buildings are damaged. Adam Santini who was injured from the conference room collapsed but not hurt as bad, and the island doctor left before the earthquake. The two of them met the crew and took them down to the bunkers to set up monitoring equipment and computers and aboard military ships.

"My name is Sergeant Adam Santini, and this is doctor Raymond W. Hallowmostraphoniagalleriabarringtoncommonwealth. Just call him Dr. It!"

"Oh my goodness, what a long name! My name is Vincent Tino the head volcanologist for NASA. And my crew. Amy Amitriptyline and this is Linda Lincoln who will be monitoring the TV and computer screens and call in updates and news reports. This is Jay Domers and Paul Arts who will be bringing the equipment up to the crater with Richard Dennis the chopper pilot. If more helicopters need to be used

Jay, Paul or myself can fly helicopters or airplanes."

"Vinny what do we have? Did this volcano erupt? What happened!?"

"Sergeant, we have no reports of any activity in this mountain, it is my job to make decisions, but we do have a report that a strong undersea earthquake struck this island sending a shock wave tsunami that sank a Brazilian cruise ship with 6000 people aboard and everyone is feared dead! We don't know for sure the full details! The Brazilian ship was heading to Portugal when the wave hit," said Vincent Tino.

"Vinny, we need to set up a meeting with the National Guard later today when you finish getting reports here in the bunkers. Finish setting up and will have this meeting when you're ready!" said Sgt. Adam Santini.

Amy Amitriptyline and Linda Lincoln was watching the news on TV when the generators were giving the TV and monitoring equipment power.

"Good evening this is the world network news. We have breaking news: the so-called lady in the water island suffered a strong earthquake late Thursday afternoon injuring 377 people when the island was rocked 10 to 15 feet out of the water, luckily no deaths were reported. The earthquake was an 8.8 on the Richter scale deep under the ocean six miles south from the lady in the water. There is a volcano on that island but there were no reports of an eruption.

"The shockwave triggered a tsunami in the south Atlantic that struck a Brazilian cruise liner killing all 6000 people aboard. The wave was estimated to be 111 feet high traveling at speeds of a jet plane! The death toll could rise if these waves hit the coastline.

"The lady in the water island reported several strong earthquakes there lately causing some serious damage. The island was evacuated, and the National Guard and NASA is there in case the volcano erupts! The injured were transferred to hospitals off the island. This is Victoria

Tiverton reporting on World Network News!"

Amy and Linda cried while watching the terrible news on TV. The military men and women and NASA saw the news as well! John Nicolini a news reporter for NASA arrived late. He was the man holding the meeting. The meeting was held up until later in the evening until the NASA crew was finished monitoring the volcano. Richard Dennis flew over the crater and Jay Domers and Paul Arts were taking readings while flying over the volcano and John Nicolini was getting the reports.

At 11:11 p.m. on November 21st, 2020. The meeting was held in the bunkers with the NASA crew and the National Guard. John Nicolini was the speaker.

"Ladies and gentlemen. My name is John Nicolini the news reporter for the NASA volcano crew. I'm sorry it took six hours to find out if we had an eruption on Mount Flow! We have no activity up there! There's no magma in the magma chamber. This volcano has not erupted since 1969. Yesterday's earthquakes raised fears but according to my reports there's nothing up there. If we get another earthquake, we better get the hell out of these bunkers and get aboard ship in a hurry! If the ground shakes again we all need to evacuate.

"We have monitoring equipment aboard the ships in case this mountain blows. I have the Spudweb robot to go up the mountain crater to take samples of earthquakes and magma and readings to prepare for a possible eruption. The same one used on the movie *Dante's Peak*. Jay Domers and Paul Arts will go up with Richard Dennis tomorrow morning taking Spudweb with them and it will be places 10 feet in Flow's vagina and bolted to rocks on a flat surface. The robot will stay there for a while so we can get data from it 24/7. The machine will operate in all kinds of weather. We also can get weather reports from it and it's stable like the ones used on Mars! If a strong earthquake happens and knocks it off course this thing will still work. When Spudweb is hooked up it will get readings on all our equipment. If something happens the equipment will make a beeping sound with lights flashing. That's all I have to say. Thank you," said John Nicolini.

"Ladies and gentlemen. Our job is to be in touch with NASA and pay close attention. We need to get out if this island shakes again and let NASA do their thing. Right now, we do our regular duties and let them do theirs. A crew will gather in the morning to start cleaning up! We have a lot of work to do until Q'klitores shakes again and if so! We're out of here no if ands or buts!!!!!!!!!!! Let's go to bed now, this meeting is over," said Sgt. Adam Santini.

The next day November 23, 2020. Around 9 a.m. the helicopter landed to take Spudweb up the mountain with Richard Dennis the pilot with Jay Domers and Paul Arts.

The chopper started its engines, the rotor went *wop, wop, wop, wop, wop, wop, wop, wop, wop*! And the little propeller in the back went, *ginny, ginny, ginny, ginny, ginny, ginny, ginny, ginny, ginny*! Then the helicopter lifted off and flew over Flow's vagina and a rescue basket lowered Spudweb in her slot and Paul and Jay bolted it into the rock on a flat surface and put a tent over it bolting the tent corners into the rock tight so the wind wouldn't blow it away! Then the men set the computer on Spudweb to get data. The workday went perfect. Then Paul and Jay waited for the helicopter to bring them back.

November through March is the rainy season and most of the work was done in the rain on Q'klitores.

There were no earthquakes or volcanic activity for days; Spudweb kept getting weather updates. TV news arrived on Q'klitores reporting what happened on the November 20th earthquake, World Network News.

Heavy utility trucks were brought in by military ships to knock down damaged buildings and resurface the land. The National Guard took down and rebuilt the barracks. Food ships came in to bring food to feed everyone left on the island and workers put the food in giant refrigerators and freezers located in the bunkers. The generators in the bunkers kept the food cool or frozen. The hotel was knocked down and the buildings around the volcano got a little damage and most of them got saved but a few took a hit! The hotel will have to be rebuilt.

The military and NASA celebrated Thanksgiving and Christmas together. Christmas trees were set up aboard ship and one big tree in a family room in the bunkers. The holidays were celebrated in the bunkers, aboard ship and on the beaches.

After the holidays the crew started moving what could be saved from the damaged hotel and storing it in the bunkers. New entrances were built to get in the bunkers. January 2021 was a quiet month for NASA, no activity, just weather reports. The military was still cleaning up and rebuilding the island.

February was still quiet. NASA keeps monitoring the volcano and the military is building up the island. March was the same and workers started the construction to rebuild the hotel. Mid-April 2021 is still quiet, not one earthquake!

Now almost four months the island of Q'klitores was safe for tourists to come back. David L. Sanberg came back to check on the hotel construction and a Courtyard Marriott is being built much smaller than the first hotel. The foundation and the wood frame structure were already built but the hotel would not be finished until June.

Jay Domers, Paul Arts and John Nicolini were in the crater checking Spudweb to make sure it's still working, and the robot was fine, just getting weather reports. It showed rain and storms for the last four months almost daily. Spudweb showed the magma chamber was empty with no lava in the volcano; it was quiet.

Early May 2021 the island was getting back to normal, the naked lady in the water was fully rebuilt and stores were opening and all that was lost was rebuilt and opened to the public. Security cages were built at all entrances to the bunkers. The island's titties had new nipples! Late May the Indians and natives came back to their homes that were all rebuilt. All the ships came back, the emergency boats arrived.

Cruise ships started coming back and the island has a nice recovery; however, the hotel and surroundings will take some time. The old pool was rebuilt, the hotel has five floors and 40 rooms on each floor. The food court will be built in a separate building with the same restaurants, the casino is another building with two floors with tables and gaming on the first floor and slot machines on the second floor. Nathian's Rock House will be in the hotel with the casino show room. Benjamin's Steakhouse and Fado will be in the hotel. The buildings will surround the pool connecting to the mountain. The hotel will be named: David l. Samberg Courtyard Marriott. The new convention center will now be an outside tent.

June 2021 the hotel and the casino were open and some of the restaurants in the new food court. Tourists started coming back. The Indians and natives were growing vegetables again on the mountain side and boats were bringing fresh food every day. Cruise ships had to remain on ships until all the rooms in the new hotel were ready. The hotel was full almost every weekend.

July 2021 Q'klitores was getting busy. A concert on the island's stomach packed with people and a rock band was playing and everybody was dancing. Thundermist played first with a laser show coming from the island's titty nipples flood lights and fog machines! The second band was called the Backbreakers playing hard rock and blues and the concert ended in a fireworks display on the night of the 4th of July!

A little while later right after the grand finale a severe thunderstorm rolled in with heavy rain clouds to ground lightning and a 50 mile per hour wind sending everyone running for cover! The fierce storm lasted about 10 minutes and a lightning bolt struck the island's titty nipples connecting one to the other and flew off striking an antenna on top of the hotel.

Another bolt struck the middle finger connecting to the other middle finger on the other side of the island, and then straight down between the island's tits and hitting the ground sending more flashes of lightning blinking on and off like a strobe light during a 50 mile per hour wind! This went on for five minutes and then it was over, and the island was flooded! The Fourth of July evening was over, and everyone went inside.

The next day the temperature reached 105 degrees, and everyone was at the beach. An offshore storm brought in big surf.

August 2021 the resort was open for a year and on the 20th was a one-year celebration. Food ships arrived with food vendors for the anniversary festival and bands were playing and the full casino was open. A meeting was held on that day between the military and the NASA crew in the hotel.

"Sgt. Adam Santini we have some bad news but it's not enough to lose sleep over. My name is Vincent Tino the NASA volcanologist supervisor, I know we must have met before. The bad news is the magma chamber is filling up again and it's half full. Amy Amitriptyline and Linda Lincoln are watching it closely, if we start getting earthquakes again, we will need to put this island on alert. This does not mean this mountain is going to blow up!

"I have reports that this mountain backfired last November. Final evidence we had a reverse eruption. This volcano erupted under the ocean floor sending a shockwave across the Atlantic that sunk a

Brazilian cruise ship that killed about 6000 people. The blast killed more than 7000 overall! This volcano has not erupted since 1969, however this strange phenomenon that happened on November 20th, last year raises concerns! This island rose up about 10 feet and several people broke bones and luckily no one died. But the earthquakes we've been getting lately may be a threat that this mountain is ready to go at any time.

"I don't mean to scare you people, but the magma chamber had no lava in it yesterday and today it's half full. This is why we're here to monitor the situation. If the magma keeps rising, we may be in trouble, because we will be getting more earthquakes and a greater threat this mountain is ready to blow! The magma is stable right now and we're not in any danger; just because the magma chamber is half full and just floats around it may go down again but we're watching closely."

"Vinny, what do we do!?" said Sergeant Adam Santini.

"Sit and wait, maybe nothing will happen. This volcano has gone through nuclear explosions over the years and nothing happened. The only concern I have is why the magma chamber is filling up again! I want everyone to go about their business and don't worry, until earthquakes start happening again. We have not had an earthquake in eight months. We will be watching this volcano!" said Vincent Tino.

The crew was getting reports from Spudweb and everything was quiet. A military helicopter flew over Mount Flow and nothing was happening in her volcanic vagina! Island tourists were at rest after the big meeting. The rest of the month through September things were quiet, there were no earthquakes and the magma chamber was still half full and not changing.

October 10th, 2021 Q'klitores had a mild earthquake and people started panicking! The NASA volcano crew saw no changes. The rest of the month was quiet, but the island lost a lot of business due to the mild earthquake.

November 2021 the island was having their annual national world convention and it was held in an outdoor tent that holds more than 150 people. Ding Dong Tours cruise ship arrived first from China.

A new group with Chi Chong got off the ship and they saw a vision of the Virgin Mary on top of the mountain and one said to another in Chinese, "Look, look up there, it's the devil!"

The other one said, "No, that's the lord giving us a warning! Something's going happen; I don't know what it is, it might be a good thing or something real bad is going to happen!" one man said to the other, in Chinese.

Later they checked into the hotel before the convention later in the week. The two who saw the vision shared the same room together, they were in room 213 overlooking the island's titties! Cheech is the one who thought the vision was the devil and Chang is his roommate.

Cheech was looking out the window and he said in Chinese, "Chang, come look at this, Titty! Titty! Titty! Wow!!!!! Big ones!!!" They got a good laugh.

Cheech went into the bathroom and he said to Chang speaking in Chinese, "Here is the washroom, a sink, toilet, bathtub and shower but what's this!?"

Chang had to think about it for a while and he said, "It's to wash your back side!" That's what Crocodile Dundee said!

"I know what it is! It's for women to flush out their pussy!" Chang said in Chinese. The men laughed!

Later in the day they went on a tour with their tour guide Chi Chong; the same tour he went on last year. After they were served a Thanksgiving dinner at the outdoor tent where the convention would be held. It was a beautiful day. It was about 80 degrees and a light wind. After dinner the tour guide Chi Chung went to the whorehouse to get laid, but it was closed.

Two days later, the worldwide national annual convention was held at the tent and this year there were only 45 people and it was a peaceful day sunny and nice. The meeting talked about what happened last year; most of the injured made a full recovery.

While the convention was going on, the NASA volcano crew was at full swing checking data to make sure everyone was safe. The mountain was quiet. The magma level in the chamber was still half full and stable.

This meeting was talking about the world going into a recession and world leaders talked about avoiding this happening so a world war doesn't break out. Tom Brady is running for the United States president and he talked about greenhouse gases, the dangers in dirty politics, big storms and football.

After the meetings the group was invited on a fishing tour. The fishermen caught tuna, swordfish, marlin and all kinds of fish, squid, shrimp, crabs and lobsters etc.

Then a great white grabbed onto a catch and leaped on one of the fishing boats and almost bit this lady as she screamed hysterically fighting off the shark! The shark got a good grip on the big fish that was caught and it went after the woman and a fisherman fought the shark with a fishing pole with a hook at the end of it so the woman could get away; she was not hurt.

Then the great white leaped up on the boat charging at more people and other fisherman came out with shot guns to kill this shark; the shark went wild and it tried eating the boat while it was getting shot at! The shark was eating the smokestack and *Bang! Bang! Bang! Bang! Bang!!!!!* The shark was blasted in a million pieces! The boat was covered in blood and everyone got inside while the fishermen were firing away at the shark. The remains of the shark slid off the boat and more sharks joined the feast in the blood-filled water eating the dead shark's guts! Everyone laughed and cheered!

Then the fishing tour was over, and the catch was cooked in giant fire pits on the island for everyone to eat. The Chinese tour brought some of the left-over fish aboard ship before leaving the next day. The fish fry lasted well into the evening until the rains came chasing everyone out so the Chinese could steal the rest of the fish.

The next day Ding Dong Tours left early in the morning because a strong storm was coming. The cruise ship went around the oncoming storm and they were OK. The storm hit Q'klitores with thunder, lightning, strong winds and heavy rain. Then it was quiet. All the military ships are back in port but not many cruise ships as the island is getting ready for the Christmas season.

Wednesday December 1st, 2021. The military, the natives, and Indians were putting up Christmas trees and decorations around the island. The first tree was a 30 footer with colored lights set up on the island's bellybutton, two trees with all white lights were set up on each titty-nipple and on each middle finger and a tree with colored lights was set up on top of Mount Flow. Two more trees were set up on each side of the pool with orange lights. And a 20-foot tree with colored lights was set up in the lobby and two trees with green lights were set up in the casino. The ships and boats were decorated with Christmas trees and decorations.

A week later was the island's Christmas bazaar. December 10th, 2021. The night before, Vinny Tino was outside walking around drinking a bottle of Heineken and as it started to rain suddenly, he saw something bright forming into a figure on top of Mount Flow. He looked up and he saw the Blessed Mary with her arms out covering the volcano.

He said to himself, "Wow, that's a cool Christmas decoration!" Then the vision disappeared and went dark; the Christmas tree on top of the mountain was the only view. The rain came down harder, then a flash of lightning and thunder!

He went inside the hotel and he met with the owner at the hotel banquet room bar and he said, "David I was outside looking at all the Christmas trees and decorations and I saw this amazing light on top of this volcano of the Blessed Virgin Mary and then it went dark; it was beautiful!"

"Vinny, we have a ghost here and her name is Olivia! She was seen in the last hotel and her vision appears in the middle of the pool deck standing near the mountain, almost every night, usually about 2:30 in the morning. She haunted my last hotel, but she has not been seen in this hotel, nor has she been seen in over a year. Since last year's earthquake her presence has not been seen," said David L. Sanberg.

"What did this ghost look like?" said Vincent Tino.

"It's a girl with big boobs and she's been known to smother people in their beds and appear in mirrors and jump out at people! Most of the time she appears in the pool area," said David.

"The vision I saw, looked like the lord coming down to protect us then she went away!" said Vinny.

"It sounds like some kind of a warning, maybe Mount Flow is going to erupt!" David L. Sanberg joked.

The two talked about ghost stories until the bar closed at 2 a.m. Later Vinny took a walk out to the pool area drinking a beer, it was still raining, and he waited to see something, and he saw a faint vision of a woman form near the mountain. Then it disappeared! He didn't finish his beer and he left! He went into the bunkers to check data from the volcano and it was quiet, and he went to bed.

About 4 a.m., David L. Sanberg went outside, and he looked up at the mountain and he saw a mist that formed the Blessed Virgin Mary, but he could barely see it! He kept looking at it and it went away! He said to himself, "OK Olivia, stop playing games; you're scaring me!"

At 5:30 a.m. the computers and data screens started beeping and strobe lights were going off singling activity in the volcano. David L. Sanberg the hotel owner was sitting the lobby when suddenly he heard rumbling while he was reading a book and the chandeliers rattled and the island was shaking and moving a little bit then it stopped. He realized we just had an earthquake; it was the first pretty good shaking in about a year! He said, "Oh, no! Not again!"

Vinny Tino woke up out of a sound sleep hearing the beeping sounds and saw the lights on the monitors. He got up to look and the volcano was quiet. The rest of the crew got up to investigate what happened and then the lights went out and the beeping stopped. The crew was sleeping in the bunkers and they never felt the earthquake, but they know we had one! Vinny Tino and John Nicolini were checking the data from Spudweb and it reported a 3.3 earthquake and the magma chamber went down.

"That's good news, no worries here!" said John Nicolini and everyone went back to bed. The next day Vinny got the crew together to spread the news from what he saw last night. Saturday December 11th the Christmas bazaar was going on and cruise ships arrived to buy items and food. The NASA volcano crew had a meeting with Vinny Tino in the bunkers while the Christmas bazaar was going on.

He said to his crew, "Good morning crew. Last night I saw a strange vision on top of Mount Flow, and I thought it was part of a Christmas display before it went dark. It looked like the Blessed Virgin Mary with her arms covering the mountain. I was told it was a sign of some kind of a warning like something might happen and last night we had an earthquake for the first time in about a year. I don't know if it's evil or the lord is telling us to leave."

"Vinny, it's a sign that is not good. I think the Virgin Mary appeared to warn us that something may happen in this volcano," said Linda Lincoln.

"I want Jay and Paul to call for a helicopter to go up on the mountain and search the crater for sulfur vents and if found we may have activity in the mountain. Right now, we have no activity on the monitors but to be on the safe side let's go up there and look around. Me and John will check the island for possible damages," said Vincent Tino.

Him and John Nicolini went to police the grounds and Jay Domers and Paul Arts went up in the helicopter, the rotor kept going *wop*, *wop* and the propeller in the back kept going *ginny*, *ginny*! And lift off! The chopper flew over the crater and smoke was seen in a few areas and the chopper flew around a few times before lowing Jay and Paul in a safety harness deep inside Flow's vagina and they had tools to take samples and they found a lot!

Jay radioed to Vinny on his walkie talkie. "Mr. Tino, we have activity up here! I am finding several sulfur vents and we need to get some air tanks and masks to get down in deep. Spudweb is not showing any strong gases yet but these sulfur vents are quite active and there is a strong odor!"

"Jay call Ricky to come pick you and Paul up and get out of there as soon as possible!" said Vinny. The chopper came to get them.

Later in the day, Jay and Paul took samples outside the crater and around the mountain then they met Vinny and John Nicolini back at headquarters and Amy Amitriptyline and Linda Lincoln were checking for activity; beeping sounds and lights on the monitors did not go off because the activity in the mountain is not an earthquake. A few hours later Spudweb was picking up the sulfur vents' activity in the mountain.

Sunday December 12, 2021. A meeting was called, and John Nicolini met with David L. Sanberg in the hotel. Many people gathered together to hear this meeting.

John said to him, "Mr. Sanberg. We found sulfur activity in the mountain and we found several vents and heat rising in the crater. It is not anything to panic but it is a sign that something may be happening in this volcano. The magma level is very low that's a good sign, but if we get another earthquake or if the magma starts rising, we will need to put this island on alert!" said John Nicolini.

"David, I don't know if you saw the movie *Dante's Peak,* we need to follow the same protocol that was in that movie. Right now, samples are being taken and we are finding positive results. Just one more big boom—we better evacuate!" said Vincent Tino.

The next day Jay Domers, Paul Arts and John Nicolini went up in the chopper to the summit with protected gear and oxygen masks and lowered in a safety basket deep into Flow's vagina! The three men were at the bottom of the crater and worked their way to the summit taking samples and they got the same results Spudweb was reporting. Nighttime a loud rumble of thunder set the monitors off raising concerns. The crew went to work to find the problem; the mountain was quiet; it was only a bad thunderstorm. The thunder was so loud it shook the island waking everyone out of their beds in the hotel. It was boom after boom after boom! The storm was over in five minutes. *It was the volcano acting up with sonic booms coming from air pockets deep inside the crater; at the same time there was a strong thunderstorm and lightning struck Spudweb knocking it out!* The lightning blew its transformer out!

Vincent Tino saw what happened. He said, "Hey crew, we have a problem. Lightning just struck Spudweb and blew it up! We're going to have to go up there and reset it tomorrow. No way should lightning do damage like that! Spudweb has a lightning detector; it had to be something else, there was a lot of pressure in that crater to blow Spudweb up!!!!!!!" said Vinny.

The electricity was knocked out from the storm and the big booms. Then the generators kicked in to bring the power back. More storms rolled through during the night and the next day was sunny. More cruise ships came in with holiday vacationers. The volcano crew went to the monitors to check on Spudweb and it reset itself and it was working, and it reported falling rocks inside the crater.

"Good news crew, Spudweb's working again but I don't like the falling rocks it's reporting! Jay and Paul call for a helicopter get protective equipment and go up there to make sure Spudweb's alright. Be very careful while you're up there!" said Vincent Tino.

The crew went up there and John Nicolini went with them. It was very warm inside Flow's vagina instead of wearing jackets they had to take them off. It was 75 degrees outside and Spudweb was reporting 122 degrees inside the crater. *That's not good news!*

The crew checked on Spudweb, why it blew up and how it reset itself hours later. Then took more samples and found a burning smell in Flow's vagina! The crew walked down the mountainside looking for cracks before going back to headquarters for a meeting with Vincent Tino.

Friday December 17, 2021. Vinny was watching them on the web monitors.

Meeting: "Good afternoon crew, the magma chamber is completely empty and Spudweb is reporting a temperature of 145 degrees at the bottom of Flow and 122 degrees at the summit and it's 78 in the outside temperature. That's not good news. It is unusual for a temperature that high when the magma chamber is empty! The lava went somewhere! If pressure builds up from heat, we could be in trouble. When the magma chamber level raises that builds heat threatening an eruption. If the chamber goes down or empties the volcano cools and it's not a threat. But that's not the case here because heat should not be rising when the lava cools; it went somewhere! Right now, the mountain is safe but pressure is building and we have to watch it closely. The sulfur vents are not pushing out ash they're just steam vents," said Vinny.

"Vinny, I see water boiling deep in the crater," said Amy Amitriptyline.

"Holy shit! Something is going on in this mountain! There is something hot down there! I'm not going to worry about it right now it seems to come and go like it does in all volcanoes. This mountain has not erupted in more than 50 years, but it is showing signs we could get an eruption soon. Let's go to dinner!" said Vincent Tino.

The next day John Nicolini was writing up a report about the activity in the mountain and sending the information to NASA in Miami. At 7 a.m. he went to the hotel to get breakfast and on the way, he saw the vision of the Virgin Mary on top of the mountain and smoke was coming out of the top. John took pictures. Then he developed the pictures and they did not come out right. There was no vision of the blessed Mary or smoke from the pictures he took.

He told Vinny what he saw and Vinny said, "I saw the vision too, you're not seeing things! It might be a sign this mountain may be ready to erupt!"

The crew was checking the monitors, and everything was quiet in the mountain. The pictures John Nicolini took were sent to NASA in Miami. The pictures showed a mountain on a nice sunny morning.

The next day was Sunday December 19th, 2021. Everyone was in bed when the ground started shaking. John Nicolini woke up and saw the strobe lights flashing on the Spudweb monitor and a rumbling sound and a vibration.

He looked at the monitor computer and Spudweb was reporting small earthquakes in the mountain and he said, "Vinny come look at this! It looks like the magma chamber is full!"

"Holy shit! That's not good! It doesn't mean this mountain is going to erupt but it's getting hot and we will be getting more strong earthquakes! We need to put this island on alert before something bad happens here. I will call Sgt. Adam Santini to call for an evacuation," said Vincent Tino the head volcanologist.

At 5:37 a.m. a loud boom was heard, and the mountain erupted! The boom was so loud it felt like the island was going to blow apart!!! People were knocked out of their beds in the hotel, the Indians and natives started running down the mountainside and the volcano crew was busy writing up reports in an office away from the monitors just before the eruption. The first boom was felt in the lower bunkers where the crew was safe, just before the eruption.

"Vinny did you feel that!" said John Nicolini.

"No what!" said Vinny. Then the second boom!

"I felt that!" said Vinny.

The ladies went to the monitors screaming, "The mountain's erupting!" The crew watched in shock as Mount Flow blew ash out of the top of the mountain!

"Everybody we have to get out of here in a hurry before this fuckin' mountain blows apart! Let's make our way to the left-hand hallway and exit the middle finger and it will get us on our ship," said Vincent Tino.

Panicking people started running to the cruise ships from the hotel and Sergeant Adam Santini announced on a loud speaker, "Ladies and gentleman you need to run for your lives and get aboard ship as fast as you can and get out!!!!!!!!"

Then a violent eruption; fire lava and a pyroclastic flow started pouring out of the mountain and down the mountainside so fast a lot of people didn't make it! Some people made it aboard ship after the first eruption, but it was too late in the second eruption! The second eruption happened so fast the rest of the people never had a chance.

David L. Sanberg and the hotel crew made it to the bunkers before the second eruption safely. The second eruption Indians, the natives and people running for their lives ran for the beaches to avoid getting burned but the pyroclastic flow moved so fast it overcame the island and killed everyone! People were on fire running for the water and the ones trapped on the island were fried in a matter of minutes.

All the structures on the island including the hotel burned to ashes in a few minutes! Military and tourist cruise ships were able to escape the island just before the second eruption. The remaining ships docked in Q'klitores were damaged. The lava flowed halfway down the 1695-foot mountain and everything in its path was burned to ashes! The pyroclastic flow covered the island and burned everything!

The volcano crew was able to escape the second eruption by minutes! Their ship left dock as soon as they got aboard and watched the eruption cover the island as the ship was pulling away. The people that made it had time to get to their ship and it left dock just before the second eruption.

Lightning appeared in the pyroclastic flow while it was roaring out of the mountain it was so hot; about 600 degrees! The Christmas trees burned like twigs they disappeared in seconds. Hot steam blew the nipples off of Q'klitores's tits and hot volcanic water sprayed out like a geyser!

Three days later the dust settled leaving burnt bodies and dead animals scattered everywhere! Everything burned to the ground and hot water and steam was still pouring out of Q'klitores's tits! Smoke and ash was still flowing out of Flow's vagina and the lava at Flow's clit dried up! Several people were still trapped in the bunkers and they were shaken up, but they were OK.

The NASA volcano crew monitored all the activity aboard one of the military ships heading to New York. Newspapers read across the globe: 56 people die and several animals as Mount Flow erupts for the first time in more than 50 years on the lady in the water in the Atlantic Ocean.

Friday December 24, the day before Christmas, the military and the hotel owners had one big mess to clean up! Military ships, aircraft carriers arrived in Q'klitores with heavy earth movers to push all the ash and the dead off the island to the beaches. Vultures came out of nowhere by the thousands to feast on the dead; seagulls and seals came from the ocean to join the feast. The volcano crew came back to the island to check on the volcano coming in by helicopter and it quiet down after flow blew her load! The hotel crew and the owner of Q'klitores were able to evacuate and the island once again was a dead zone!

PART 2
EMMA GRACE'S WRATH!

6 HURRICANE EMMA GRACE

From Christmas Eve through the summer of 2022 the island of Q'klitores was cleaned up and David L. Sanberg sold the island back to the military and the NASA volcano crew was back monitoring the volcano. The military and NASA were the only people on the island living in the bunkers, only to evacuate again because of a strong hurricane brewing.

On August 20th, 2022, tropical storm Emma Grace formed off the coast of Africa. The storm clouds were almost as big as the United States and lots of damage was done already!!!!!!!!!! Lightning struck homes villages, boat mariners killing people and thousands of animals before crossing into the Atlantic. The storm had 60 mph winds that dumped 30 inches of rain and duckpin bowling ball sized hail burying and flooding villages leaving a trail of destruction before heading out in the Atlantic Ocean and strengthening rapidly!

That's enough of the naked lady in the ocean—Q'klitores, Flow's volcanic pussy exploding comedy and Willy Bird's missing in action! Let's get down to business because Emma Grace is really going to blow her load!!!!!!!!!!

The weather channel flew planes out to monitor this storm from Miami Florida and bring back news and data. The planes found a double eyewall and the planes flew in both of them to get data. The storm gets its name first: Emma Grace! Then the storm formed in one super eye and gained strength and moved north toward another storm: Tropical decaying storm Dick. Emma Grace swallowed it whole! And she weakened. Then Emma Grace stalled near Portugal made a loop back toward the African coast as a strong tropical storm heading back to land as a huge weak storm, so the weather channel U.S. planes related the data back to the weather channel in Atlanta, Georgia. The planes—c130s—flew back to Miami and the result was a dying tropical storm and weakening. The planes never got a report on the devastation Emma Grace left in Africa before forming in the ocean!

At 9:59 p.m. on August 20th, new data from the weather channel came in and the storm is getting much stronger and has three eyewalls in it! The winds are now 105 mph. The storm was moving slowly across the Atlantic. A fishing boat was out pulling in tons of tuna in a calm ocean from one of the Caribbean islands on a partly cloudy night under a bright half-moon and the boat was heading into danger! For hours into the night the fish kept flowing packing the boat with plenty! The sun came up shining through pink clouds.

"Hey fellas the sky doesn't look good maybe a storm is coming. Pink sky in the morning sailors take warning but in the evening it's sailors' delight," one fisherman said to another!

"Let's keep going we can get more fish; when the sea is calm such a storm is far away!" said the other fisherman. The day sky darkened, and rain was coming as the fishing boat was cruising along. Two hours later the sun came out and it was a peaceful ride in the ocean, but few fish were caught then a sea breeze. The boat captain picked up speed when suddenly he saw a big wave coming.

He said, "Oh my blessed mother of god! Mayday! Mayday, Mayday!!!!!" he hollered over a loudspeaker. Then it was all over before you can blink your eyes! The wave swallowed the boat and buried in the ocean!

On 2 p.m. August 21st, 2022 the military flew planes off aircraft carriers in Q'klitores to fly into Emma Grace and the weather channel sent C-130's to get updates. The storm had three eyewalls formed into one huge stovepipe vortex and the winds picked up to 160 mph now a Category 5 hurricane. The planes flying through the eye recorded a giant tornado moving across the ocean and the storm aiming at the island of Q'klitores!

The military ships evacuated the island in a hurry going through the Caribbean Sea to the U.S. coastline. The military vessels docked in Miami and the volcano crew set up cameras on the island and set up computers and TV monitors in the bunkers to record the oncoming hurricane. Then flew off the island in a military whirlybird helicopter with monitoring equipment aboard and they're going to New York. Before nightfall news reports were heard in Miami about the storm on the weather channel.

"Good evening we have breaking news: Hurricane Emma Grace is a catastrophic EF5 hurricane with 195 mph winds with gust of 220! This storm is a killer! Hurricane Emma Grace is located off the coast of Africa and heading straight for the Caribbean islands and the path of this storm may make a direct hit in Cuba and continue toward the U.S. coastline in less than a week. Whoever is in the path of this storm faces instant death!

"The famous lady in the water island the U.S. practiced bombing during the Gulf War that was recently made into a resort until an erupting volcano destroyed the resort in November 2020 is in great danger! The storm is scheduled to make a direct hit on this island between noon and 3 p.m. The island has a volcano with nuclear warheads stored in storage facilities in the mountain and if this volcano erupts in this storm will be catastrophic! This is Lisa Lipator reporting on the weather channel."

Other people watching the local news showed the devastation from Emma Grace at a Miami Dolphins preseason game against the Jacksonville Jaguars on a Thursday night game at halftime. It was 14 to 6 Miami at the half when the news came on the video boards in the stadium.

"Warning we have breaking news on WMIA TV here in Miami a major hurricane is coming, and we are in danger! The storm started in Africa killing more than a thousand people, thousands of animals and drowning villages under 30 feet of water and reported hail bigger than grapefruit! This storm had three eyewalls and the cloud base is almost as big as the United States and it's heading straight through the Caribbean. Stay tuned to WMIA TV news and we will have updates every hour and let you know what this storm is doing. This is Karen Wells WMIA news." A few minutes later it started pouring during the game and it ended with no scoring in the second half and the Dolphins won 14 to 6.

The next day, Monday August 22nd, 2022 at 1:34 p.m., a military helicopter was ready to evacuate Q'klitores as Hurricane Emma Grace was coming and a huge thunderhead appeared and a bolt of lightning struck the top of the mountain and then a loud crack of thunder then the rain: a blinding rain!

The pilot said to the co-pilot, "It's time to go!" The helicopter lifted off leaving the island with nobody there. The chopper got away safely.

Just after 2 p.m., the Virgin May apparition appeared on top of Mount Flow covering the mountain it was bright then it faded away!

A brief calm and a few seagulls and sea birds landed on the island as the sun came out briefly.

It was a steady calm then at 2:23 p.m. Hurricane Emma Grace hit Q'klitores with 180 mph winds and a vortex sucked the inside of the volcano's core until it erupted and exploded in a million pieces, the mountain and the island was blown off the face of the earth out of the ocean! The nuclear bombs exploded with such force the lady in the water disappeared in seconds! The blast sent a mega tsunami across the Atlantic! And a ring of fire above the stratosphere that burned for days the heat dried the storm up temporarily!

Cruise ships and cargo ships were hit by these mega waves and sank with no warning as far away as the Antarctic Ocean. The waves hit icebergs lifting them and throwing them over snowy mountains in the Antarctic, that's how much energy this blast had! Big waves struck the coast on both sides of the Atlantic. 50-foot waves struck the north coast on Aruba, flooding half the island and damaging hotels and boats and a golf course was flooded. Big surf hit all of Europe all the way to the east coast of the United States all the way to the Canadian Maritimes. The blast was severe setting the sky on fire for days putting the world in global fear. A newsflash came over Times Square in New York City on the big screen as thousands of people watched!

"Good evening this is World Network News broadcast all over the world. Michael Anthony reporting. Mega hurricane Emma Grace struck the South Atlantic islands with 180 mph winds with gusts as high as 220 hitting a volcanic island with nuclear bombs stored there causing a mega explosion. When Emma Grace struck an erupting volcano, the blast triggered a 10.4 mega earthquake due to the nuclear bombs exploding! The mega blast set the sky on fire up past the stratosphere setting off a worldwide fear. No planes or rockets may fly that high to put the flames out! The fires will have to burn themselves out.

It will help when high rising thunderstorms arrive, but the blast was so hot it appears that Emma Grace may have dried up. It will take several days before the dust falls from nuclear fallout.

"The bad news is not over, the blast trigged not only a 10.4 earthquake but a 100-foot tsunami from one coastline to another from east to west sinking cruise ships and ocean liners the death toll may never be known! A 10.4 earthquake is the worst ever on earth; strong enough to split the earth in two! All marine travel crossing the Atlantic Ocean will be canceled until the blast zone settles. No vessels will be allowed to travel out of the Caribbean Sea.

"According to the Merchant Marine Coast Guard, the fire in the sky is caused by the height of the blast going through three atmosphere zones and it is unknown on how long it will burn. Cold air from space will push the nuclear fallout and fires back into the atmosphere eventually! The weather channel has reported that Emma Grace was blown into space from the volcanic nuclear blast drying up until the fallout. When the dust settles Emma Grace may start up again and move on its path because the change of the blast zone will start spinning when the debris settles back down. The fires will not burn out until the atmosphere levels change. It is a scary scene in the middle of the Atlantic and hope for rainstorms in September brings relief! Michael Anthony WNN."

All TV stations covered this unusual event across the world, and it looked like the world is coming to an end and people were on edge! Three days later the U.S. military flew planes out to monitor the blast area. The sky was still on fire and the planes flew under the burning ring about 200 feet wide in a complete circle.

The military dropped samples from the planes into the blast zone where Q'klitores once stood under the ring of fire. The fire above changed color the higher it rose and now the color of the flames is blue. The sample readings were volcanic ash and nuclear debris falling back down to the ocean.

The crew in the planes was wearing protective clothing to avoid getting burned. The planes had their own icing unit to keep the planes cool going through the hot zones. The temperature was still 200 degrees just below the boiling point and the planes hit severe turbulence because of the heat until flying out of the blast zone. Other planes flew around the blast zone and a thick fog started forming for miles and temperatures went to normal out of the blast and rain and thunderstorms were forming around the fog zone working into the blast ring.

A few days later more clouds started forming then a few thunderstorms started forming with high cloud tops and pulling air down toward the sea pulling down the nuclear fallout and volcanic ash and finally the fires went out in the upper atmosphere when cold air shifted and Emma Grace started up again! The spinning motion from the fallout and volcanic ash reformed Emma Grace it was a giant tornado over Q'klitores spinning out of control in place for a day or two then she moved toward the Caribbean islands at a high rate of speed and went on its attack!

Military and weather planes monitored the storm when it reformed and followed it 24/7! The planes reported the data back to the Weather Channel. It was a storm with straight line winds coming straight down taking the volcanic ash and nuclear fallout with it and then started spinning before moving away.

It was September 14th, 2022. News reports came on radio and TV stations to prepare for the coming of Emma Grace!

"Good evening this is Vennessa Goldstein from the Weather Channel. We have breaking news: Hurricane Emma Grace has re-energized and heading toward the Lesser Antilles at a high rate of speed and could be a danger to the Caribbean islands. The storm is heading into open ocean with 180 mph winds with gusts as high as 220! The wind shield is more than 200 miles wide and the cloud base is about 2000 miles wide. That means tropical storm winds can wrap around the center 1000 miles away! Beware this storm is the biggest hurricane ever in the Atlantic and the lowest air pressure ever reported on earth.

"The 1998 Hurricane Gilbert was the worst Atlantic storm in modern times but this one is much bigger and maybe more dangerous! Emma Grace formed off the African coast on August 20th, and it caused catastrophic damage before the hurricane formed. Two days later this storm hit a former nuclear storage facility on a military island during a volcanic eruption and blew the island and volcano apart and the blast was so severe it set the sky on fire for about two weeks over the blast site. The blast triggered a 10.4 earthquake and a mega tsunami sinking ships and killing thousands of people! Coastlines from Brazil to South Africa were leveled!

"The storm dried up from the blast but when the dust settled from the fallout the heat from the fallout refueled Emma Grace and right now the Lesser Antilles and the Caribbean islands are in great danger! Those areas must evacuate right away!

"The track of this storm takes it through the Caribbean Sea. The following areas will be affected: The Dominican Republic, Cuba, Puerto Rico, all the Caribbean islands and Florida pay attention because this storm is moving so fast and could arrive on the east coast in less than a week. This is Vennessa Goldstein reporting on the Weather Channel."

People watched the news reports at home, in bars and meeting places in Miami. The Miami police went riding around calling on loudspeakers warning people about the coming storm.

Tollgate military island, West Indies. Tollgate Island has a lot of tall buildings and was the capitol city of Warwick; another volcanic island with an active volcano, and Emma Grace is coming! Ships and aircraft evacuated. The island was empty except military police evacuating the island and they hid in bunkers until the storm passed. People were bused to cruise ships and aircraft evacuating the airport from the city and around the island. It was a cloudy humid day, and everyone evacuated Tollgate safely.

Then about an hour later Emma Grace hit Tollgate with 195 mph winds and ripped the island apart! The buildings were ripped slate clean from their foundations and blown off the island into the ocean! Everything standing was blown off the island and gone! Airplanes and boats that remained were gone! The only thing standing was the Mount Tollgate volcano still erupting! *At least there were no nuclear bombs in this volcano!*

Tollgate military Island was leveled; all the homes and buildings are all slate slabs! The big city of Warwick was gone; nothing there!!!!!!!!!! The military island police heard the loudest noise up above hearing glass breaking, smash, booms, bangs and crashes and the violent suction of wind and very loud thunder! Triggering a 4 earthquake! The storm lasted four hours before exiting Tollgate Island.

The crew came up from the bunkers after Emma Grace passed and they saw the massacre; nothing there! It was at night, so they did not investigate long because there was lightning. The crew went down in the bunkers to call for help and they got no signal just walking around with flashlights. There is no power on the island, they have to wait until help arrives.

Emma Grace is now heading for the Lesser Antilles looking for another volcano to suck out of! The storm winds weaken to 120 mph winds after giving the city of Warwick on Tollgate Island a good blowjob!

Daytime the police crew came up from the bunkers on Tollgate

Island and they could not believe what they saw; the entire island was blown off the map!

One cop said to another, "Oh my fuckin' god! This city of Warwick is gone there is nothing standing, we have no vehicle to get out of here, no boats there's nothing here! What kind of a storm hit us! Is it something from out of space or were we blown up by our sister island, Q'klitores! We may have been hit by a nuclear bomb from this storm! No hurricane is going to wipe out an island like this! The only hope we have for getting out of here is a military aircraft comes to get us or yell help from a passing boat!"

"The only thing we can do now is find a signal; other than that, is hope some of our men come to get us! Let's walk to the beach and see if we can find something there?" said the other cop. When they got to the beach there were 20-foot waves smashing up against the rocks washing dead fish, seals and whales up on the rocks with blood pouring down on the rocks and laying in seaweed.

A few minutes later they heard what sounded like a helicopter and two of them landed to get them. The rest of the crew evacuated! Then Emma Grace hit the Lesser Antilles Islands right over a volcano and sucked the life out of it like she did on Q'klitores but this one did not erupt, Emma Grace sucked all the dirt and rocks out of the crater and threw it on the island's village smashing every building in sight, the storm fired volcanic rocks like missiles destroying the island. *It's a good thing everyone evacuated two weeks ago on cruise ships.*

Then Emma Grace hit another island destroying buildings ripping trees out of the ground tossing debris, rocks, sticks and anything blowing around like missiles! Then she searched for another volcano to suck the life out of it, but there were none; just high mountains and Emma Grace blew through them at 130 mph, taking trees and villages with her! *Emma Grace sucks and she blows!*

Then she hit the main island with 140 mph winds uprooting villages and throwing debris bouncing off the mountains and tossing her blow job out into the ocean! The main island looked like the others; wiped slate clean! No buildings no nothing!

Then she decided to take on one more island with three volcanoes before she pays a visit in Antigua. When Emma Grace hit the fourth Lesser Antilles island the volcanoes there were much bigger than her favorite one on Q'klitores! There were two active volcanoes Emma Grace went to visit and there was a bad storm on both active volcanoes side by side. Downdrafts and blowing snow slowed Emma Grace down because the storms winds blew in against the oncoming hurricane.

The sky was sunny when Emma Grace blew through a much higher mountain range. Her blow job was no match for the fourth island's trade winds! Emma Grace winds down to 50 mph until she goes back out on water. Lesser Antilles four won this one, its tall mountains were too much for Emma Grace!

Then she turned her attack on Antigua West Indies and the winds picked up to 70mph. She decided to attack this island with no one there because it has a nice volcano for Emma Grace to suck out of! She parked right over the crater and spun like a top, throwing debris everywhere! Mud and rocks the size of medicine balls were tossed like missiles all over the island smashing everything in its wake!!!!!!!

Emma Grace was not strong enough to make this volcano blow its load, so she gave up and she went to visit Antigua! All the islands in the Lesser Antilles evacuated long before Emma Grace came. The residents will be in for a big surprise when they return!

Antigua did not evacuate because Emma Grace weakened; when the storm was coming the wind was down to 60mph, so the government on Antigua didn't take the storm seriously. The storm was back out in water gaining strength! And Antigua was not ready. It was near dark when big waves started crashing the beaches.

Nightfall about 10 p.m. the waves were between 15 and 25 feet coming ashore; a cargo ship was lost off course from the oncoming storm and smashed into a boat marina crushing boats until it crashed into a village! The cargo ship pushed boats and buildings in land and smashing them into pieces! People were killed and property was destroyed! A large village port was crushed as people woke out of their beds, coming out of bars and going out in the open only to be pulled out to sea and drown! Emma Grace had 85 mph winds pulling everything out to sea after it smashed a good part of the island! The cargo ship that was pushed to shore by the large waves destroyed everything in its path!

Jesus Christ! Why does Emma Grace hate Antigua so much!! It's not done yet!

Two hours later a rogue wave about 60 feet high split the damaged cargo ship into pieces and slammed it into a resort area crushing hotels homes and businesses. Airplanes were tossed around like toys and the airport was completely destroyed! The waves buried villages and drowned everybody in there!

Emma Grace went looking for a volcano on Antigua but couldn't find one. A tornado hit a hotel and a nearby village and tore it apart! The night was the end of the world on Antigua as Emma Grace left a trail of destruction! People and animals laid dead in its path! Cruise ships and boats were damaged, and the island was destroyed!

Then Emma Grace went to visit Saint Kitts with 110 mph winds and found two volcanoes here! *Emma Grace loves volcanoes!*

The storm stalled over one of St. Kitt's volcanoes trying to suck it alive! The wind uprooted rocks and dirt from inside the first volcano and tossed it across the island damaging buildings and heavy rains flooded the airport in a field of mud! Airplanes and helicopters were crushed up like a pile of metal from Emma Grace's 180 mph gusts! The plane hangars and the main terminal were leveled!

The winds and a mud cloud moved across the island in a form of a tornado and hit the other volcano wrapping around the second volcano before lifting up in the storm cloud and the sun came out. The eye passed over the second volcano and Emma Grace moved on! *She was not interested in sucking out the second volcano she wants open water to pick up speed and she did just that!*

The second part of the storm was in open ocean and Emma Grace is now a deadly Cat 5 with 210 mph winds and heading toward the Dominican Republic, Puerto Rico, Haiti, Jamaica and Cuba and making directly for Miami! This storm left a trail of destruction on the island of St. Kitt and the Lesser Antilles islands! The next target St. Lucia then St. Thomas.

What's the problem? Emma Grace don't like Catholics! She wants to level all saints!

Emma Grace is now targeting St. Maarten, as these islands are getting a late start evacuating loading up cruise ship and flying out. Emma Grace hit St. Maarten with 150 mph winds and 50-foot waves leaving cruise ships stuck in port packed with people! The ships were rising up and down while docked; it was too late to leave the island and it was a big panic as people watched buildings get blown away being tied up to poles aboard ship to avoid being tossed around. Everyone aboard the stranded cruise ships were screaming and crying! The wind was so strong buildings were lifted off their foundations and blown to pieces, the storm blew through St. Maarten in five minutes leaving a trail of destruction!

Then it hit St. Lucia destroying villages, hotels and smashing boats, then Emma Grace hit the mountains leveling everything in its path!

Then she blew into St. Thomas with 135 mph winds going through the mountains; of cause she's looking for another volcano and Emma Grace found one a big one too! The storm scooped up the mountain-side of an active volcano that slowed Emma Grace down that spared St. Thomas major destruction as she sucked the inside of the crater out before the eye passed over the volcano that pushed the storm back out to sea. A waterspout hit a boat marina smashing a few boats and became a weak tornado striking the island's fishing port and village!

7   THE AFTERMATH

Cruise ships just got away in time heading to the Gulf of Mexico to safety as Emma Grace slowed down to 80 mph when it struck the high mountain range on St. Thomas. Cruise ships followed a line from several Caribbean islands ahead of Emma Grace to the west coast of Florida but battled 30 to 50-foot waves! The waves knocked people and ship crew from side to side causing several injuries.

One ship made it through the Caribbean Sea between Jamaica and the Dominican Republic when it left early but several cruise ships that didn't evacuate in time got a rough ride.

Emma Grace weakened crossing the high mountains in St. Thomas allowing aircraft and rescue boats back to the damaged islands. Later Emma Grace moved back out into open waters as a Cat. 1 hurricane with 80 mph winds and it moved slowly toward Puerto Rico aiming for Punta Cana Dominican Republic. Navy and coastguard helicopters flew out to the islands to assess the damage.

A military helicopter landed on Tollgate Island and the crew could not believe the destruction! The capitol city of Warwick was gone and most of the island was flooded with nothing there! Military and weather planes flew over the islands Emma Grace hit! Antigua got the worst of it; they did not get out in time and several people died there. The planes and helicopters send back reports of the damage to TV and radio stations in Miami.

"Good evening this is breaking news on the weather channel! Victoria Goldstein reporting. Hurricane Emma Grace hit several islands in the Caribbean leaving a trail of destruction! Four islands in the Lesser Antilles were leveled, the damage was unimaginable! Villages were leveled and those islands were completely destroyed! St. Maarten, St. Lucia, St. Kitt, were leveled, hotels, villages boat marinas and beaches are unrecognizable! Luckily these islands evacuated.

"The storm finally slowed down after striking St. Thomas mountain range, but a waterspout and a couple of tornadoes damaged a resort. Emma Grace seems to pick on volcanoes striking Montserrat.

"Antigua was not so lucky! Tourists did not evacuate in time being struck by 60-foot waves pushing an ocean liner into a village killing several people and a good part of the island was destroyed! Cruise ships were trapped on some islands because of a slow start on evacuations from thousands of people in a scary situation as huge waves battered cruise ships delaying departure from the islands; several injuries were reported! Dutch minister Conney Cooley stalled evacuations because the storm has weakened, and Antigua took a big hit.

"Hurricane Emma Grace is back out in open waters at this time moving slowly with 80 mph winds but she's building and predicted to strengthen and become a powerful hurricane once again. Keep tuned into the Weather Channel with updates all night long, this is Victoria Goldstein reporting."

Restaurants, bars, businesses, ball games, everything stopped to listen to the updated news on this very powerful hurricane! Weather planes and military aircraft were sent out to monitor this hurricane once again; Emma Grace is now targeting Punta Cana, Dominican Republic.

The next day the volcano crew from NASA flew back to where Q'klitores once stood dressed in protected clothing from nuclear fallout poison. Military whirlybirds being followed by a fuel plane and aircraft carrier dropped down boats and subs to find the island and nothing was found! The crew searched where the bunkers might be and the area was unrecognizable! The crew can't tell if they were in the correct area it was just ocean; the crew picked up radiation in the area, but it might be somewhere else! The military and NASA crew spent two days looking for any signs from the lady in the water and found nothing; not even a lead to where the volcano was, no debris nothing was found!

The crew came from New York to find the island of Q'klitores only to be disappointed! That's how bad the blast was; it wiped out everything!

The crew flew to the nearest island to regroup and fuel up before going back to New York. They landed on Tollgate Island leveled by Emma Grace and the island looked like a pile of rocks and bricks and trees with the leaves and rock ripped off of them and gas lines were burning where the city of Warwick once stood. Sea birds flooded the beaches feeding on the dead sea life. The area smelled like the dead! Then the NASA crew left Tollgate Island to fly back to New York. The military from Q'klitores stayed behind to investigate Tollgate Island and cleanup was done so the military could move back in and start building the island back up. *It's going to take years!*

Weather planes and military aircraft started looking for life and assessing the damage on the islands Emma Grace destroyed. Military ships arrived to find possible survivors on these islands. Aruba and Carriacou were struck by big waves and were searched by French and

Dutch military officials. Buildings were destroyed and people still there started looting! Military patrols sprayed pepper spray to stop the looting and arrested them. Hospice boats went to each island looking for survivors and all the islands got out in time except Antigua and St. Thomas. Helicopters spotted all the damage left behind flying over and all the islands Emma Grace hit, and they were all flooded by giant waves and could not land. Military and rescue boats arrived looking for bodies and some that did not evacuate were all dead! Military boats and tugboats helped cruise ships get out of Antigua and some ships were damaged and some were stuck on sand bars.

One ship cruise ship *Victoria* caught fire while being tossed around in the big waves and hundreds of people were lowered in lifeboats just like the *Titanic* into the giant waves everyone had life jackets on until military boats rescue them. A few people leaped to their deaths as the ship exploded and sank!

Military choppers landed on Antigua after the flooding went down, and rescue boats to scoop up the dead! Hundreds of people were found dead and a cargo ship that washed out a village and a resort was resting on rocks split into with oil pouring out of it! The cruise ships left before the hospice boats and helicopters came to remove the dead so the rest of the island can finish evacuating! Still hundreds of people were waiting in line to board ships to get out!

Another storm was coming, and a bolt of lightning struck the leaking oil on the shipwreck that triggered a huge explosion killing more people! People started running to get away from the flames and jumped into the water to safety and they had to swim a far distance to get rescued! The fires burned for days and the people who were trapped burned to death! Rescue workers could not get near the flames to rescue them and the hard rains were not putting the inferno out from Hurricane Fucka!

Finally, the rest of the cruise ships were able to get away from the second hurricane in time following Emma Grace until getting to land safely. The ships were traveling through the Bermuda Triangle trying to avoid Emma Grace and newly formed Fucka. The ships will arrive at the Virginia navy facility not before traveling through more large waves as people panicked in fright!

Some cruise ships went through the Caribbean Sea ahead of Hurricane Emma Grace into the Gulf of Mexico and docked in a large port in Galveston Texas over 50 cruise ships from the Caribbean islands that were struck first from Emma Grace. The late arrivals went to Virginia Beach navy facility.

When the first group of cruise ships arrived in Galveston everyone had to go through customs and bussed to a closed area with vacant buildings for years. The tourists were taken to an old vacant city, Oldtown, Texas. The facility was used for war practicing years ago; even nuclear bombs were tested here in the 1950s and during the cold war. Ghosts were reported being seen here. Tents were being set up for extra bedding and the facility was run by the National Guard and Texas Rangers! One cruise ship at a time departed and boarded waiting buses and the National Guard and Texas Rangers directed about 500,000 people from more than 50 cruise ships to get in line and get on the buses. Texas Rangers gave the hurricane evacuation people instructions when the bus was filled. National Guard troops passed out sandwiches and cold water as the tourists were boarding the buses.

"Ladies and gentlemen, welcome to Galveston national evacuation port for hurricane and national disaster relief victims, Galveston, Texas. My name is Officer Clayborn Roots and we are going to evacuation living headquarters in Oldtown, Texas about 93 miles from here, it's an old city in the middle of nowhere! Sit tight and enjoy the ride."

Officer Toots is the Texas Ranger on the first bus.

It was getting dark when the buses arrived, and the place looked like a ghetto! The buildings had no windows and no lights.

"What the fuck is this?" someone said when the first bus arrived.

"We will be here for at least a couple of weeks until cleanup is done in the Caribbean Islands and Hurricane Emma Grace is gone. It's dark out here so be careful where you walk there's a lot of loose rocks out here. Everyone follow the flashlights and you will be directed to a tent to receive bedding, canteen and a jail jump gown for temporary clothing and you will be given a tag that has a number on it and that's the building you will be going too. When you get there, you will be directed to rooms to sleep. Tomorrow morning you will be directed to a military mess hall where breakfast will be served. These buildings have no air conditioning, no heat and no windows! I know a lot of you may be upset but it's better than drowning where you came from! There will be no looting or breaking the law because Texas Rangers don't play in the Lone Star state; good night!" said Officer Clayborn Roots.

There were snakes and scorpions and thousands of rats running around during the night in Oldtown Texas! When everyone was going to their buildings they smelled like urine and bug spray. The buildings get sprayed every day to keep the night critters out so visitors can sleep. Each building had about 40 empty rooms and six people slept in each room and there were about 80 buildings so some people slept in tents. Six port-a-johns were set up along each building and tents. People waited in lines to go for a piss or shit in these crowded port-a-johns. Some peed up against the buildings at night!

During the night a passing thunderstorm moved through with flashes of lightning to bring much needed light! The visitors can really see where they're at! Many people didn't sleep at all last night in this smelly stinking old city. They saw rats running everywhere, snakes swimming across the ground and scorpions crawling everywhere! People were screaming and crying! It was a noisy night in Oldtown.

The next day it was raining, and this evacuation facility looked worse than a rotten jail! Thousands of people went to the military mess hall for breakfast and ham, eggs and home fries were served with orange juice and coffee. A medical doctor spoke while breakfast was being served.

"Good morning ladies and gentlemen, my name is Doctor Raymound W. Hallowmostraphoniagalleriabarringtoncommonwealth, from the lady in the water island in the south Atlantic before being evacuated during a volcanic eruption in November 2020. Then I came to Miami for research working as a health counselor and then transferred to Galveston, Texas, still a doctor and a health counselor and I also have an office in Dallas. You may understand that I have a very long last name and it may be hard to pronounce so just call me Dr. It!" Everyone laughed! Then he continued.

"I realize that this place is not the best place to be but our cruise ships need to get more people because hurricane Emma Grace has picked up speed with 120 mph winds and threaten to hit Punta Cana, Dominican Republic head on and evacuate them people and bring them to Miami. Then the ships will come back to Galveston to get you and bring you back to your islands. If you feel that you want to leave get a bus or call for help you have the right to do so! The only thing is you have to remain in the United States until Emma Grace passes; this is a very bad hurricane sucking all the water out of the Atlantic Ocean.

"You will be given a pass to enter anywhere in the U.S. if you have family or relatives. If you have a passport you can go anywhere! If you want to walk off these grounds right now go right ahead. We will not stop you or shoot you like Jonestown; just leave if you want. If you have money to change you can change your money at any bank. The National Guard will help you with phone calls; you can use a credit card and you have to wait in line if you do not have a cell phone. If you have a cell phone, please help others. We might not have much here in Oldtown, but we do have cell phone service, we have good cell towers here.

"If you do not have anything to leave; you're stuck here until your cruise ship is called then you will be bused to Galveston to get to your ship. Harthorn Tours please report to your bus to go back to Galveston and go to your ships and you will be going to Miami and flown back to St. Thomas, St. Lucia. When more islands open up you will be told to go to your buses.

"Meanwhile it's hot here and we have no AC and the lakes are dirty and filled with alligators and wild animals just like in Africa. The wild-life is dangerous here so people you must stick together to keep the wild animals at bay. If you need pepper spray, bug spray or anything to keep these creatures away you can get them at the National Guard tents, any needs you go there.

"If you need to bathe and wash yourself, cold water pools are set up at every tent, you're allowed two baths a week in these pools they are not to use for swimming. Men, women and children will have to bathe together. Hotel towels and wash cloths and soaps will be available. All bathing will be monitored, and you may have to wait for hours in line to use the pools, sorry for the inconvenience.

"If you're looking for a place to cool off, go back to your buildings to stay out of the sun or when it rains go out in the rain to cool off and you can bath as well. The only problem when it rains, we get a lot of thunderstorms here just like the Caribbean, and we get tornadoes here as well this is why Oldtown looks like this! Stay out of the lakes, there's no swimming here because you will get eaten!

"We have ball fields here if you want to play baseball or football. We have a couple of basketball courts, tennis courts. We have a swimming pool, but it was destroyed by a tornado another one will be built next summer. The buildings are tornado-earthquake proof; we do not get earthquakes here very often and when we do, they're mild. That's about it!

"Enjoy your breakfast you will have two meals a day here at the mess hall. From 5 a.m. until 11 a.m. breakfast will be served, it's the same food every day. Dinner will be served beginning at 4 p.m. until 10p.m.; if you do not arrive during those times you do not eat. Dinner is family style chicken, salad, chicken soup, pasta with red sauce, French fries and chicken. If you want steak you will have to kill one of our wild animals here! If you have any questions, I will be here every day from 5 a.m. until close. If you need medical treatment just go to any tent to get help. If you need to go to the hospital you will be air lifted by helicopter or treated in our tents. Once again, my name is Dr. Raymond W. Hallowmostraphoniagalleriabarringtoncommonwealth, just call me Dr. It!"

"Good morning, my name is Franko Cooper the head of the National Guard evacuation team and Dr. It is the head medical doctor and counselor for the Caribbean islands. We will work together to get you where you need to go. Some of you will be flying back to the islands and some will be bused back to Galveston. Hurricane Emma Grace is heading to the Dominican Republic with 120 mph winds and more people will be coming here from Punta Cana. Just relax and find something to do until your ship is ready to go back. Me and Dr. It, will have white night meetings nightly from 6 p.m. until 10 p.m. here in the mess hall for people who need help."

"Mr. Cooper are you a preacher? What the hell is white night? What are we, in Jonestown!?" said someone in the crowd.

"No sir, it's not like that, we do not wake people up during the night to have meetings. When you come in at dinner time after 6 p.m. Dr. Hallowmostraphoniagalleriabarringtoncommonwealth calls meetings for counseling, by the way just call him Dr. It! It's shorter than his 40-letter last name. Enjoy your breakfast," said Franko Cooper.

Later some people left on their own; National Guardsmen guarded the gates with shot guns just like Jonestown but there was no violence. People walked eight miles to get out of the Oldtown compound to get help. There was violence inside with rapes, fights and people getting arrested. A few thunderstorms came with heavy rain to calm things down. The evacuations will be here for a while until this hurricane passes.

Meanwhile a meeting took place at Paramount in Dominican Republic and a speaker was getting the island ready for this powerful hurricane. She spoke in English and Spanish.

"Good afternoon my name is Ann Garcia the head of moving controls: we have a major hurricane coming right for Punta Cana the most popular resort in the Dominican Republic. Emma Grace is a powerful storm with 120 mph winds, and it will arrive by tomorrow night. You may get cruise ships out of Santo Domingo as soon as possible if you want to evacuate. Those in Punta Cana, you need to leave now!"

8   THE SECOND COMING

Monday September 26th, 2022 Emma Grace was supposed to strike around 9 p.m., the sky was clear and seas were calm and people walking through the resorts throughout the hotels and on the beaches no hurricane yet!!!!!!!! The storm was gaining strength and heading for Santo Domingo with 145 mph winds. By 2 p.m. the next day the storm still had not come and the sky was clear.

Ann Garcia did not evacuate much sooner because the storm's not here yet. The cruise ships left Santo Domingo in time going to Texas. Two days later the storm was still at sea stalled between two fronts and spinning and weakening. All the tourists never left Punta Cana.

Friday evening September 30th, 2022 Emma Grace shot out of its rut and slammed into Punta Cana with 160 mph winds at 11 p.m. A group of people were playing cards in a hotel lobby at 11:02 p.m. when a gust of wind blew the front window in and glass was flying everywhere! People got cut and tables were blown over and soon later people were getting sucked out of buildings and ended up in the water just like that! Flowing in the ocean in 15-foot waves and trying to survive swimming to shore trying to fight against a rip current;

some people were killed instantly!!!!!!!!! Roofs were ripped off, water was sucked out of a pool and people and building debris was thrown around like bowling pins! The damage was incredible!

A few minutes later the eye passed over and it was calm. There was pretty good damage and the back end of the storm has not arrived yet!! People came out to check out the damage and were frightened because the back end was about to arrive soon! The sky cleared as the eye passed over; people came out to see the damage and saw the big waves coming and crashing on the beach; bigger than normal! It was a half moon and the sky cleared.

People were at a party at the Palace Alliance Resort drinking Blue Moon beer drafts and absolute vodka martinis and smoking vapor cigarettes and a band was playing at 12:34 a.m. on the 27th. A loud roar and soon later the wind blew so hard people were blown every-where! Tables, a bar, windows and roofs ripped away; and the hotel and club were ripped apart in a matter of minutes! People screamed for their lives and found themselves being thrown around in the waves and pulled out to sea as quickly as they can think! The winds were so strong it was hard to swim against the surf and many people died trying to fight the current!

Emma Grace is now getting really nasty as she sucked people out of resort hotels and huts, bars, and washed them out to sea to their deaths! Hotels were blown away in 160 mile per hour winds and the Punta Cana resort was torn apart; buildings, resort huts, casinos, hotels, bars and beachfront condominiums and apartments were ripped away like matchsticks in a trail of destruction! Everything was flattened! The hurricane went on and on tearing everything apart. Boats and ports were blown away and the wind tossed boats and sea life up against the mountain sides so the vultures can come down the mountains to eat the dead! Cars trucks and buses were tossed around like toys and tossed like missiles through buildings and busted up in a million pieces. The area looked like a junkyard full of metal!!!!!!!!

The storm then struck the Punta Cana airport with 190 mph winds and tossed planes around like toys in a sheet pile of metal until it was unrecognizable! Airplanes, helicopters, hangers and terminals were busted up, like accordions!

Then the storm left Punta Cana and head for Santo Domingo destroying a village! Killing more people and destroying the city leaving a trail of destruction then it retreated back to Punta Cana to finish the job. Emma Grace destroyed every hotel one by one!

First Hotel Hilton, people were hiding in tight areas to protect them from the wind and Emma Grace started ripping the hotel apart piece by piece! The roof was torn off and a woman was holding onto a pole as the wind was trying to pull her away and her feet were dangling in the air, when suddenly a strong gust pull her from her grip and took her away! A man was under a bed holding on when the storm blew a wall in and sucked the man up into the vortex! He saw an angel flapping its wings while he was flying gently through the vortex with lightning bolts all around him and he landed on a picket fence that nearly cut him in half and he was killed instantly! A group of hotel guests were holding onto poles and heavy furniture to avoid getting blown away, but it didn't work the hotel was blown off its foundation and thrown in the ocean! Boats were tossed around like toys and smashed up like match sticks!

The Hyatt Hotel; a man woke up out of a sound sleep when he heard a sucking wind and he went to the window and he saw a boat flying through the air and it crashed into the hotel and blew his window in and he tried to get out of the room safely then he saw the hotel breaking apart! The floor under him was gone and he saw water and big waves and he found himself out in the water being pulled out to sea holding onto hotel debris and he was washed up onto a beach and then the wind went from 150 mph to a dead calm as the eye was passing over and the sky cleared and the moon was shining. He felt a bump on his head surviving this ordeal! He saw lightning all around him and he walked along the beach and he saw all the destruction!

"Holy shit! I can't believe I survived all this!" the man said to himself! He saw dead people being washed ashore and fish flapping around on the beach when the lightning was flashing.

Caro hotel guests there saw fish flying through windows hitting people; swordfish, marlins and baby sharks crashing through windows and a seal was thrown through the front entrance knocking people over like bowling pins during the hurricane before the eye passed over! The seal bit this girl on the leg and hotel workers were hitting the seal with chairs until a security guard pulled out his gun and shot the seal dead! Minutes later that hotel was blown away and everyone went with it!

Then another hotel was torn apart and blown into the water. More hotels and tourists' cities were taken by the wind like dominoes! When the eye passed over just after 3 a.m. Emma Grace left a trail of destruction and the resort was in darkness and a few cries for help then everything went quiet! Huge waves hit all of Punta Cana's resorts and coastline as the back end of Emma Grace finished the job!

Then she went inland to target Santiago City during the wee-hours and weakened when she was going through the mountains! 30 to 50-foot waves washed Punta Cana away! A resort on a mountainside was getting ready for the storm and a bus outside people were boarding at 4 a.m. to evacuate. A giant squid crashed through a plate glass window and landed in the lobby of the Santiago Palace and it slid across the lobby floor and its eight arms tried to grab on to walls and stuck there! The giant squid tossed furniture around and knocked people over sending everyone running and screaming!

One lady cried, "Help! Help! Help! Help! Help! The aliens are coming to get us!!!!!!!!"

People ran outside to get on the buses to get to higher ground. The wind was blowing hard and Emma Grace arrived in Santiago leaving a giant squid in the palace lobby!

The manager took a picture of the creature and he said to another guest, "Holy shit! It looks like a giant squid or some king of octopi! But a giant squid is not going to crash through a window on an 8000-foot mountain and go on an attack, we're being invaded by aliens! Let's get the hell out of here and get on the buses!"

The buses left the resort and went to higher ground. Emma Grace's winds weaken to 60 mph wind as she crossed into the Santiago Mountains and headed to the city and the island of Hispaniola and then hit Cuba! Emma Grace stalled in the mountains and she dumped more than 50 inches of rain and catastrophic flooding drowning villages and killing hundreds of people; the sudden deluge came with no warning!

The flooding buried parts of La Ramada sinking boats destroying and washing away villages! Laharas washed cities and towns away in the Dominican Republic. Mud and water washed down mountainsides from Emma Grace's heavy rain! The storm stalled in the mountains before she made her next move in Hispaniola and threatened Jamaica. Planes and cruise ships evacuated Jamaica, Cuba, the Bahamas and Puerto Rico when Emma Grace hit Punta Cana. The ships docked in Miami from those islands and planes landed at Miami international airport and military bases and the crowds of people were taken to shelters and stadiums to escape Emma Grace. The next day news reports came out on every TV and radio station about this destructive hurricane!

"Good afternoon we have breaking news! Hurricane Emma Grace

has picked up speed from a category one to a category five with 190 mile per hour winds and leveled Punta Cana and hit Santiago, Dominican Republic before weakening in the mountains. We have several reports of fatalities and catastrophic flooding and the death toll may never be known!

"The storm has 70 mile per winds and heading to Hispaniola and it is unknown where Emma Grace will strike next. The storm's track takes it right between Jamaica and Cuba and threatens to strike Miami dead on and continue into the Gulf of Mexico. The good news the storm has been downgraded to a tropical storm but is expected to become a hurricane again once she comes back out on water!

"This storm is the worst one ever! The destruction and the fatalities! Emma Grace is worse than Katrina, take my word! Worse than Winter Storms Cialis, Lavetra, Sustango and Viagra! You must take this storm seriously! 37 feet of snow from Winter Storm Viagra is no match for what's to come!

"The Punta Cana resort was completely destroyed; every building was leveled to matchsticks! The damage was like a bomb has gone off, the area looks as bad as Hiroshima and Nagasaki everything has been blown away! Now the storm is flooding the rest of the Dominican Republic threatening a world ending situation.

"Large waves have hit almost all the Caribbean islands causing damage to boats and low line villages. This storm caught the Dominican Republic by surprise and many people did not have enough time to evacuate. Planes are flying in the storm and we will have updates 24/7. When you're told to evacuate you better leave because this hurricane is an end of the world type of storm, it is really bad!!!!!!! This is Lisa Dogg reporting on the Weather Channel."

Airplanes and helicopters flew over what once was Punta Cana, blown away like Tollgate Island, and a trail of destruction all the way to Hispaniola where Emma Grace is going next! It was a trail of wood, bricks, rocks and dead bodies, humans and animals! Giant vultures and eagles scooped down the mountains to feast on the dead! One vulture grabbed a dead hippo by its legs, and another grabbed the neck and a group of vultures ripped the dead hippo apart and finished the job. Eagles and other animals came to the death buffet! Ground troops saw the animals and birds eating the dead! The ground troops arrived from boats and landing helicopters trying to get a count of the fatalities.

It was a sunny hot day before ground troops got to the Santiago mountain range calling in reports to the United States about the damage when suddenly they heard a loud roar like rolling thunder then a wall of water came out of nowhere like pyroclastic flow from a volcano and buried them alive in seconds!!!!

One man said, "Oh my fuckin' god, mayday!!!!!!!" Then it was all over in seconds!!!!!!!!!!!

The crew disappeared in rushing water from Lahara! Helicopters flew over watching the horror below and nothing can be done about it, bodies and animals were washing away! Emma Grace was heading for Hispaniola dumping heavy rain and thunder and lightning and the town of Alves was getting ready to evacuate and the police ordered everyone to an open field speaking in Spanish over a loudspeaker. Interpreters were there speaking in English.

"Ladies and gentlemen, we need to get away from buildings and go to an open field and follow to the river a bad hurricane is coming! Boats will be waiting for you at the river."

The storm arrived missing the mountains and hitting the valleys. First came the rain and hundreds of people were walking through flooding water in the field and people started running when lightning started flashing like a strobe light hurrying to the river to get on the boats to safety! Then strong wind and then the sky cleared as the eye was passing over. There was no radio contact no electricity! The boats quickly got out of the river heading out in the ocean toward the Gulf of Mexico. About 15 boats got out of the Hispaniola jungle safely but the monkeys and animals were screaming and making all kinds of noises sending a message that something bad is coming! Out to sea all the boats followed one another in a single line.

A vision of the Virgin Mary appeared above the sun and the boats met a cruise ship out at sea to rescue everybody. The boats put down their anchors as each boat emptied when people got aboard the cruise ship to safety leaving the boats behind.

Then a huge thunderhead formed, and it looked like the devil! It was coming fast with rolling thunder then the sky darkened quickly! The clouds had a face of a wild animal with black eyes, pointy ears and horns popping straight out and a mouth open with no teeth and lightning was flashing in this mouth! Then *boom*! Followed by a loud boom, then thunder so loud then the wind picked up and the rain came down in sheets and wild lightning as Emma Grace was gaining speed.

The wind picked up to 110 mph winds racing toward Cuba. The cruise ship with the evacuation from Hispaniola was fighting huge waves at sea from the hurricane as the back end of Emma Grace came out of nowhere to haunt shipping in the Caribbean. The ships at sea had to take other routes to avoid this storm playing a chess game! The storm formed a huge vortex. Emma Grace is strengthening and gaining speed now a category five with 145 mph winds and making a run at Cuba.

News reports in Miami during a football game, the Dolphins were playing the Carolina Panthers in Miami when the Panthers kicked a 45-yard field goal to tie the game at 24-24. It was a successful field goal with eight minutes left in the game. The ball cleared the uprights leaving the stadium and the ball never came back, the ball was never found. Then an announcement came over loudspeakers in the stadium and the game was stopped.

"May I have your attention please! At this time, we need to evacuate all of Miami because Hurricane Emma Grace has erupted into a Category 5 and it's heading for us! Please evacuate this stadium at this time and police will direct you to transportation. Buses and taxis will arrive. Thank you," said a stadium official.

People evacuated in a hurry; it was like a big panic racing to buses and taxis. Some people fell over running to the buses! Traffic jammed highways and gas stations were running out of gas and people were getting stuck on highways and there were some accidents. Stranded people started running for their lives trying to evacuate! It was a mad, mad, mad, mad, world! Grocery stores were running out of food, water, batteries, flashlights, everything!

The hurricane is about ready to hit Cuba with 150 mph winds. First water was being sucked out of the harbor leaving boats on dry land and people and animals started running uphill to higher ground because of a tsunami warning as sirens were blasting all over Cuba.

Then the waves about 25 to 30 feet high slammed to shore smashing boats into pieces until they were a pile of splinters and the waves destroyed villages and smashed buildings and a mini mall was covered in water and buildings were mangled! Gas lines erupted and fires burned a town to the ground. Airplanes flew in the eye of Emma Grace and it was so wide and so big you can see the storm clouds wrapping around in circles as the storm is getting even stronger!

Now at 175 mph winds Cuba is getting ripped apart! Homes and buildings were blown off their foundations and roofs ripped off! Fish was sucked out of the water and thrown in fields and in damaged neighborhoods. Big waves tore up the shoreline as damaged ships washed up on shore and spilled oil and fires started until it was a huge inferno and there were explosions! Some small islands were washed away by the waves and boats and ships destroyed.

People who went to higher ground hid for cover in caves to protect them against the wind. Horses, birds, wild pigs and deer joined people up in the mountains in caves. Heavy rain wind thunder and lightning roared across Cuba leaving a trail of destruction! There was no radio TV or news, or no contact of any kind cell towers were down there was no electricity it was a race for survival; those who went to higher ground survived and those who did not evacuate will be killed! That's how bad this storm is!

Then the eye passed over and the worst is about to come! It was sunny and calm for a little while and planes were flying in the eyewall. A few minutes later thunder sounded, and the second half of Emma Grace is on the way! The sky darkened like nighttime and the wind picked up and hail poured down the size of baseballs covering the land followed with strobe light lightning and thunder so loud that it could move rocks! Then the storm passed leaving total destruction and death!

Miami is its next target. Emma Grace slowed down to 120 mph winds and stalled off the Florida coast. Examining Miami waiting to give south Florida a good blow job! News from the president came over all TV and radio stations.

"Good evening. All residents of all of Florida must evacuate immediately! Emma Grace will be here shortly! This storm is very dangerous; it has killed thousands of people and it left catastrophic damage across the Caribbean, Dominican Republic and Cuba for those who plan to stay you may not make it out alive! You have less than a day to get out before it's too late!" said the president of the United States.

Ships and all land transportation left Miami in time. Some people stayed behind living in skyscrapers and a meeting was going on before a helicopter landed to pick them up to get out.

Suddenly a waterspout appeared out in Biscay Bay and it was a big one! Scooping up fish sky high in the air and a shark came crashing through a plate glass window on the 34th floor in the meeting room and landed on a big table sending everyone out of the room in a hurry in a state of shock! The shark bounced around the room trying to get out and it was stuck there! And it died there. The shark made so much damage it crashed into a wall and made a big hole and would stay there for days.

"What the fuck was that! A shark!" one lady from the meeting cried.

"Yes it was it must have been picked up from the storm there's a very powerful hurricane coming!" said another guest from the meeting.

"A shark being thrown through a window on the 34th floor!" said the lady. The group couldn't believe what happened.

A waterspout scooped up fish from all sizes including sharks and dumped them in neighborhoods. Fish landed in streets; parking lots even thrown through windows! The waterspout became a tornado when it crossed over land. The people from the meeting went to the roof of the shark feared skyscraper to a waiting helicopter and they saw the giant tornado moving toward downtown Miami with fish and sea life wrapped around this tornado! The helicopter couldn't take off until the tornado left.

One man said to the helicopter pilot, "Franco we had a marketing meeting in the conference room here at the Ultrasun Skyline Apartments and a shark came crashing through the window into our room on the 34th floor; that's right a shark!"

"Roger, that's possible! A waterspout that size can suck up fish out of the ocean and carry them for miles and dump them everywhere! It has been known tornadoes can carry just about anything for hundreds of miles away! This is not the first time this has happened, but it is unusual that a shark would go through a window on the 34th floor but strange things happen. Now let's get aboard the chopper and get out of here Emma Grace is coming!" said Franco, the helicopter pilot.

The helicopter lifted off the Ultrasun skyscraper and flew away. Many people could not enjoy the fish falling from the sky because of the evacuation from Emma Grace. The power from this hurricane had the energy to form deadly waterspouts and tornadoes to lift giant fish and scoop up animals as big as cows. Traffic was leaving Miami north toward Daytona Beach on the Florida turnpike when thunderstorms were developing, and fish fell out of the sky landing on the highway and on cars.

A woman was driving when suddenly an alligator fell from the sky and landed on her car and she screamed hysterically! Then the alligator fell off and she ran it over and it was *thump-thump-thump*! As she drove over it! She was hysterical! A big truck finished the job running over, the same alligator smashing the alligator like a pumpkin!

A wild boar fell from the sky and landed on a police car smashing the windshield and landed on the cop's lap and he crashed into a ditch and the police car landed on an alligator. The policeman has triple trouble! The wild boar tried biting the policeman and he was pushing the head away to avoid getting his head bitten off; the wild boar took a chunk out of the policeman's shoulder but he managed to get his gun and shot the wild boar right in the fuckin' head and killed it! Then he pushed the dead wild boar out of the car and a huge alligator grabbed it and ate it, then the alligator lunged at the policeman and he fired the rest of his rounds from his gun to kill the monster alligator!

The policeman had to get out of his car and get up to the road;

another alligator was trapped under his car and the injured cop had to swim in swamp full of alligators and snakes to get to the road sitting in the middle of the road in a pool of blood from the wild boar attack. People driving by didn't even stop to help! The police lights were still flashing, and he called for help and more police and a rescue came to get him before another alligator was ready to eat him!

This evacuation route is turning out to be a disaster! The road ahead has the following obstacles! A fish-fall from thunderstorms, alligators, wild boar, snakes, hail the size of baseballs, deer, some flying cows, wild horses—not to mention tornadoes and heavy rain to go with it! It was bumper to bumper for hundreds of miles going through all these obstacles!

The front end of Emma Grace is arriving in U.S. waters not far from Miami and she's coming fast and she's blowing a big load! Driving out of Florida was a challenge going through storms and driving over wild animals! The storm base was several miles wide and you can hear it roaring miles away and it was a scary panic!!!!!!!!!! Newscast on radio and TV warned everyone to evacuate.

"Good evening this is the WMIA news in Miami Florida. Everybody must evacuate in a hurry! Hurricane Emma Grace is coming right at us; we have less than seven hours to get out of here! This storm is worse than Katrina with 175 mile per hour winds, worse than Hurricane Andrew and the track of Emma Grace takes the storm directly over downtown Miami expecting catastrophic damage before 7:30 a.m. tomorrow morning. If you do not leave you may not survive!

"This storm has spawned many waterspouts and deadly tornadoes sucking up fish and tossing sea life and animals miles away. We have reports of sharks being thrown into office buildings in downtown Miami! Emma Grace has killed thousands of people in the Caribbean islands, Dominican Republic and Cuba. This storm has blown up volcanoes and has wind well over 200 miles per hour and 200-foot waves sinking ships and has the potential to suck water out of the ocean and dump it on you in minutes!

"Emma Grace dumped 56 inches of rain in less than one hour in Hispaniola, killing more than a thousand people. The island did not have time to evacuate as Emma Grace buried everyone alive! When Emma Grace struck Santo Domingo and the Santiago mountain range, it slowed down to a tropical storm until she caught Hispaniola by surprise, and she picked up rapid speed in a hurry as soon as she got back out on water and she became a killer and she's getting worse! If you think you can stay put, you'd better think again! If you saw the movie, *The Day After Tomorrow* it is that bad. This is Kate Kiss, reporting, WMIA news."

9   *THE END TIMES*

On Sunday, October 2nd, 2022 the bands started hitting Miami with heavy rains. Thunderstorms with several waterspouts and tornadoes started touching down striking homes and businesses and flattening them; the destruction was incredible! It took less than a few minutes for several tornadoes to make homestead Florida looked like the end of the world; the lightning flashed like strobe lights for hours!!!!!!! The rain bands started at 5 a.m. followed by the destruction minutes later! A tornado touched down in Fort Lauderdale struck a long tank and it exploded like a nuclear bomb and burned for miles torching towns and cities homes, buildings and everything it its path making it look like the entrance to hell! Luckily the areas evacuated long ago; ones who stayed to ride it out in this area were killed! Tornadoes and waterspouts tossed alligators and snakes around like missiles everywhere!

A group of college kids decided to ride this storm out while the destruction was going on north, triggering a 3.5 earthquake from the long-tank blast! It was *Boooom! Booooooooom! Boooooom!* Over and over for a half hour then it went quiet.

There were more than 50 kids having a hurricane party on a big yacht in a Miami boat yard. The college kids were drinking, smoking pot, doing drugs having sex orgies and dancing the night away and running around naked! It was dancing, music and a DJ playing. The college kids braved the 80 mph wind gusts. Women were standing at the bow of the yacht showing off their titties as they were flapping in the wind just like a bird in the pouring rain and flashes of lightning and rumbles of thunder! The college kids were getting rowdy enjoying the party. Police told them to evacuate and get out in a hurry a long time ago, but they refused and rode it out!

Then at daybreak the wind died down and everything got quiet and the sky cleared, and the sun came out. The eye is now passing over and the kids were celebrating and cheering.

"We made it! We rode it out. Hey!!!!!!!!!!!! All you suckers evacuated what hurricane! Emma Grace is a pussy! It's over baby! It's over!!!!!!!!!"

Then the party quieted down and the kids enjoyed a pig roast and downing Jack Daniels shots and resting bare-assed on the yacht in the sun. Then about 45 minutes later they heard a roaring sound and clouds started to appear, low clouds started covering the sun and the party goers were falling asleep when suddenly the water was disappearing and the roaring sound sounded like a whistling sound and water gurgling and the clouds were thickening. Some of the kids got up got dressed and they left.

One kid said to another, "The tide is getting very low this storm might not be over, let's get out of here!"

About a third of the group got off the yacht as the water was going out but the rest stayed and were asleep. Then the yacht fell up against the dock and things were falling on people.

A big fishing hook fell on this girl and it tore her tits off! Part of her body was ripped open and she later died from the accident lying in a pool of blood!

Crying kids saw the horror and that was not all; all the water in the harbor was gone! The yacht was almost laying on its side and the drunken remains and the injured had to get out and get upright on the dock and a group of kids went to the marina building to get back on land.

The wind started to pick up and the partly sunny skies clouded up with dark clouds and the whistling roar was still heard—it had not gone away—then a mountain of clouds appeared and then a wall of water coming fast! The kids could not tell if it was water or clouds until it was too late. The wave was about 100 feet high and it was coming fast!

The wave was curling over and the college kids yelled, "Run, run, run!!!!!!!!!!!!!!!!!!"

The tidal wave overtook them and washed everyone away in seconds! Then the wave struck buildings in downtown Miami smashing windows, burying boats in the harbor and leveling store fronts and strip malls! The result looked like the 2004 Sri Lanka day after Christmas earthquake! The harbor looked like a sea of splinters; then a second 100-foot wave turned everything upside down leaving a trail of unrecognizable destruction!

Downtown Miami was buried under 20 feet of water 10 miles away! Not to mention two more waves 100 feet or higher moved the destruction into downtown floating out into the Everglades and into the Gulf of Mexico and then came the back end of Emma Grace with 200 mph winds which leveled buildings, ripped roofs off smashing windows and pushed the ocean into downtown leaving unimaginable flooding! Almost every building in downtown Miami looked like a bomb hit it! The blown-out windows made the buildings look like a lost dead city!

It was all over by 8 a.m. on October 2nd. That's how fast this storm came through! The 50 or more college kids who decided to ride out this storm made a big mistake because they're all dead!!!! Emma Grace slowed down to 140 mph winds; still a category five, after smashing the tall buildings in downtown Miami; it was the worst storm ever!

Emma Grace made a direct aim at Houston, Texas before making a last second turn and went on the same track the 2005 Katrina took! Now New Orleans may be next! Hurricane Emma Grace is stalled in the Gulf of Mexico and building and getting stronger again.

At 7:53 a.m. when Emma Grace left Miami it spawned several tornadoes and waterspouts to create more destructive damage in record numbers! There was floating crumpled up metal and splinters in the receding water building a pile of debris about 30 feet high up against buildings! Lightning struck homes down and dug craters in the ground and tornadoes finished the job ripping everything apart!

Then the sun came out and finally Emma Grace was gone! Tidal waves struck the keys leaving a trail of destruction! It will take weeks before waters and flooding get back to normal in Miami.

Back at Oldtown, a meeting took place in the mess hall with the few evacuees left.

"Good morning. The weather outside is sunny and beautiful here but Miami was just leveled! That's right! Leveled by Emma Grace! Every building and boat was destroyed and this bitch is heading for Houston dead on! It didn't take 20 minutes for Emma Grace to leave a trail of destruction in downtown Miami and South Florida and now this bitch is in the Gulf of Mexico waiting to strike its next target and she's strengthening. We need to be ready! Pay attention to news reports because no one is going anywhere until this bitch dies! Once again, I'm Doctor Raymound W. Hallowmostraphoniagalleriabarrington-commonwealth. I will keep getting updates on this storm, just be calm and wait. Just call me Dr. It!"

Later news reports came from the president on all national TV stations as people watched in bars and restaurants at home and workplaces. On the Gulf of Mexico coasts from Florida to Texas and north to New Orleans and residents in New Orleans watched!

"Good afternoon we have breaking news from President Tom Brady!"

"This morning super storm Emma Grace has struck Miami, leaving total devastation with big waves, strong winds, tornadoes and heavy rain. The damage is unbelievable! Our military and city staff did a good job with evacuations in Miami and all of Florida. Whoever did not evacuate is probably dead! Highways and air travel were jammed but most people made it out in time. The problem now is where is Emma Grace going next!

"This storm is a killer. I want to warn you this storm has killed thousands of people in the Caribbean islands, Dominican Republic and Hispaniola before making a mess in Miami. This hurricane is worse than Katrina and any storm on earth this storm had the energy to move mountains, throw sharks into high rise buildings and blow cities off the map; nothing like this has happened in the modern era! Miami was hit by six mega waves before the strong wind—the tornadoes came to finish the destruction! The waves are estimated at 50 to 100 feet destroying boats and buildings.

"Heed my warning: everyone on the Gulf Coast from Mexico to New Orleans must evacuate at least 200 miles from the coast. We will have updates on where Emma Grace is heading. President Tom Brady reporting WWN News."

A football game was playing at the Superdome between the New Orleans Saints and the New England Patriots and the score was 0-0 with 1:11 to play in the first quarter when suddenly the game was held up and the players left the field and then an announcement came over the loudspeaker.

"Good afternoon ladies and gentlemen President Tom Brady ordered an evacuation due to Hurricane Emma Grace! Sorry for the inconvenience! Everyone must evacuate now!"

People left the Superdome and buses and cruise ships were ready for evacuations in New Orleans. Several cruise ships boarded thousands of people and went up the Mississippi River hundreds of miles away; some ships traveled all the way to Canada and stayed in camps and bunkers for safety. Other ships took New Orleans residences to military bases and airports. The same along the Gulf Coasts in Texas went to Oldtown with Dr. It!!!!! And Mexico.

On Monday October 3rd, 2022 at 7 a.m. Emma Grace was in the same spot grinding away! Then she started turning north in the same exact position as Katrina with 180 mph winds taking aim at New Orleans! The storm stirred up 60-foot waves and hit an oil rig with a gust of 230 mph and tore the rig apart and the winds ripped the oil rig out of the water like tearing up a piece of paper and sank it! An oil tanker stuck out at sea anchored survived Emma Grace as she moved on over open water.

Then about 9:07 a.m. news reports warned all residents in New Orleans, Mississippi, Alabama, Florida and Oklahoma to evacuate 200 miles inland.

"We have breaking news on WNEO TV channel 10. Hurricane Emma Grace is heading for us just like Katrina! You must evacuate now! Anyone in New Orleans you have to get out now we do not want to have another Katrina you have to get out now! This storm is worse than Katrina!!! You must leave now!"

Early evening on October 3rd New Orleans was a ghost town only streetlights were lit as everyone was gone; only a dog was walking in the road. Rain bands started arriving in New Orleans from Emma Grace still 250 to 300 miles away and moving slowly toward New Orleans with 160 mph winds after striking three more oil rigs and lightning struck one of the oil rigs setting off a huge inferno at sea. In New Orleans the rain started then thunder and lightning. The lightning was so bright it lit the city of New Orleans up like daylight. A few minutes later it got windy and a tornado touched down! The twister hit an apartment complex and leveled it!

Armored trucks went through the streets of New Orleans during the night, National Guard making sure everyone evacuated. Then they left town. Heavy rains and thunderstorms ruled the rest of the night in New Orleans. A helicopter landed at the Superdome to make sure everyone was out. The Superdome was locked, and the helicopter lifted off before the heavy rains and storms arrived! A military jeep was riding down a road and spotted a dog and he stopped to get the dog, the dog was barking at the man and he went to grab the dog, the dog bit him on the hand so he left the dog there and he took off.

Daybreak the sun came out and clouds were in and out with tropical rains and some thunderstorms. A few hours later the wind started as the front rain bands of Emma Grace arrived in New Orleans and lightning flashes turned into clouds to ground lightning bolts! Tornadoes touch down and waterspouts cross Lake Pontchartrain. The front end of Emma Grace covered a wide area from Panama City, Florida to Galveston, Texas! The hurricane is expected to hit New Orleans dead on; the new flood levies built after Katrina are ready to challenge Emma Grace!!!!!!!

Weather planes flew into the eye getting reports and data and sending it back to the Weather Channel. Newscasts came on the Weather Channel as people watched the news in Times Square in New York City!

"Good afternoon, this is Crystal White reporting on the Weather Channel. We have breaking news: New Orleans I hope everyone evacuated! Emma Grace is going to make a direct hit in the speakeasy sometime between 4 a.m. and 7 a.m. on Wednesday October 5th, 2022. This storm is a Category 5 with 180 mile per hour winds with gusts as high as 230 and she is 300 feet wide! Emma Grace leveled Miami on Monday and the damage will not be known on how bad until Emma Grace strikes land! She destroyed oil rigs in the Gulf of Mexico with 150-foot waves! When this storm hits land it will be catastrophic! God forbid anyone trying to ride this storm out will be killed! This storm is much worse than Katrina!

"The evacuation route is 200 miles from any source of water inland, that includes all of Florida, Georgia, Mississippi, Alabama, Oklahoma and all of the Texas coastline and anywhere along the Gulf coast; expect devastation!

"We have more breaking news! Miami was devastated by Emma Grace from tidal waves and powerful winds. Several buildings in downtown were destroyed and boats were crushed like they went through a wood-chipper! This is Crystal White reporting. We will have updates, 24/7 on the Weather Channel!"

At 4:07 a.m., a tidal wave slammed into downtown New Orleans about 100 feet high and the dark city disappeared until the water went down. Another big wave covered the first one and it was all water! At 5:45 a.m., Emma Grace's winds came to finish the job! It was a giant tornado going across the land! The storm moved so fast it hit Kentucky, Memphis TN, where she weakened from a cold front and the front pushed Emma Grace still a strong hurricane over Georgia, South Carolina, then she hit North Carolina then back out on water and out to sea missing New England and became a tropical low before striking Canada and it stalled out in the middle of the Atlantic for days and weeks. Before Emma Grace hit the Carolinas, it stalled in Atlanta, Georgia dumping record rains; that is her track.

After Emma Grace hit New Orleans the sun came out and the water washed back into the Gulf and New Orleans looked like a bomb hit it; everything was leveled, there was nothing standing, except the Superdome! The sun came out at 7:30 a.m. on October 5th and the sky cleared. The water rushing in and washing out leaving a trail of destruction! Then Emma Grace met the cold front to slow this fuckin' bitch down!!! But she dumped record rains in Kentucky and Tennessee. The city of Memphis was buried in 10 feet of water and lightning struck buildings and tornadoes came to do more damage! *Emma Grace is a demon!* The front pushed Emma Grace over Georgia and she now wants to pick on Atlanta.

Friday October 7th, 2022 President Tom Brady flew over Miami to assess the destruction, while Emma Grace was giving Atlanta a good blow job! The sky was half gray and half blue before Emma Grace moved into downtown Atlanta with a strong tropical storm with 70 mph winds and gusts over 100 during tornado touchdowns and the rain to follow. The unexpected city of Atlanta was unprepared; it's only a tropical dormant storm they say!!!!!!!

A meeting took place at the Atlanta city hall outside and the city mayor was ready to give a speech to thousands of people. Before the mayor took the mike, the crowd looked up in the sky and saw gray and dark clouds coming like thunderheads and a vision of the blessed Virgin Mary appeared above these dark clouds and the sun shining on the other!

A woman said in the crowd, "Look up in the sky the Virgin Mother is warning us that something bad maybe coming!"

Then the mayor spoke, "Good afternoon ladies and gentlemen. We have a big storm coming, the remnants of Emma Grace! She's only a dormant tropical storm still dangerous with 70 mile per hour winds but we do not have an evacuation plan unless the storm has 100 mile per hour winds or greater. If you feel that you need to evacuate leave right now because this storm is less than an hour away; it's thundering right now! You don't need to panic it's only a 70 mile per hour gale! We're going to get strong winds, heavy rain and thunder and lightning and it will be over and out of here, that's all! But we do have a tornado warning because she's still a tropical storm.

"If you need shelter go to St. James Church or the new stadium. This hurricane was the worst storm on record! If you think Katrina was bad this one is 10 times worse. Emma Grace has killed thousands of people and the Caribbean islands, Dominican Republic, Hispaniola, Cuba and downtown Miami was leveled! I need to cut off now because of lightning find somewhere and get inside there's no need to panic!" said the mayor and he went inside city hall.

A few minutes later the rain came straight down then constant thunder and lightning followed by baseball size hail hitting people in the head as a mad rushing crowd of more than a thousand people had to run for cover in all directions. Cars started crashing into one another and people were getting run over! Then a tornado tore the roof off St. James Church where people went to take cover and the wind blew the walls in. A second tornado touched down in a mini mall shredding it to matchsticks and the wind blew people down the city streets of Atlanta! The wind was so strong some people being blown around lost their clothes! Lightning struck a steeple from another church and the wind blew the church steeple through the air like a missile and tossed it at a house and it went through the house and out the other side and it broke into tumbling splinters being swept in the wind.

A man was holding on to a telephone pole and a bolt of lightning struck him dead! Another lightning bolt struck a barn until it caught fire and caved, and a horse was fried from the lightning strike. While the storm was going on the city was flooded in 6 feet of water and the wind was blowing so hard it looked like the city of Atlanta was in the middle of the ocean!

The mayor looked out his window at city hall and he could not believe what he was seeing! People being blown down city streets like a bunch of bowling pins in the wind then the rain started coming down in sheets and he saw a cow flying through the air crashing into an office building near by then he saw a black funnel moving through the sky.

He said to himself, "God, my Jesus! Is it the end of the world?!" Then the wind started blowing out windows! The mayor went under his desk and stayed there!

He heard his co-workers bitching, "We should have evacuated long ago! Now we're stuck here, the whole fuckin' city of Atlanta is flooded, we're getting some serious overtime for this bullshit! We don't know if we're going to get out of here alive!"

A half hour later the sun came out and Emma Grace is gone leaving Atlanta a flood zone for weeks! Then she moved on to South Carolina and North Carolina as a weakening tropical storm but she's still dangerous! When the flooding was over several dead bodies laid in the streets of Atlanta; dead bodies floating in the water from drowning from Emma Grace's fury!!!!!!!!!!!!

Let's give Hurricane Emma Grace a rest for a while and get to her destruction in Miami!

It was Friday October 7th, 2022. Airforce One with President Tom Brady aboard flew over the destruction in Miami! The damage was incredible, windows blown out of buildings, roofs ripped off and boats in the harbor laying on their sides and destroyed and dead bodies from the college hurricane party and fires burning below from broken gas lines, and flooding!

"The damage is so bad we can't send the ground troops in there for weeks until the flooding recedes, it's impossible! What kind of a storm was this; it looks like the end of the world?!" said President Tom Brady.

"Tom what did you do to Miami, I know the Dolphins had your number when the Patriots played in South Beach, but you didn't have to do this?!" the pilot joked.

Then the helicopter flew over Miami Beach and the National Guard was there not letting anyone in and stopped boats from going into the harbor; the beach was a mess with debris! The Airforce One helicopter flew over the buildings and downtown was flooded with wood and glass floating in the streets and flowing out into the ocean and fires burning. It was a beautiful day to view the destruction in Miami; the sun was shining. The helicopter flew lower over downtown Miami and there were dead fish floating below in the flooding and some were smacked up against buildings and some went through buildings. The president could not believe the damage. A smashing freighter had to come in and crush the damaged boats and remove the debris before work can be done to downtown.

"Could take months or years to clean up Miami!" said President Tom Brady.

"There will be plenty of work here in Miami for people looking for work!" the pilot joked. The president laughed. Then Airforce One flew up the Florida coast to view more damage until reaching New Orleans to view its damage and it looked like a pile of wood floating in the water; all you could see was the Superdome and a few buildings.

The president said, "Oh my god! This storm is a lot worse than Katrina; I just hope everyone evacuated!"

Later the helicopter flew back along the Florida Gulf coastline and saw damaged boats and some homes from Pensacola all the way back to Miami by the big waves! The president never got a report on what happened in Atlanta because the storm was still going on there. Tropical storm Emma Grace left Atlanta under 20 feet of water before departing. Then the storm moved over parts of Georgia and South Carolina dumping heavy rain and spawning tornadoes, she still had 50 mph winds crossing the Carolinas. Emma Grace still packing a punch as she crossed into North Carolina before going back out into water; a cold front pushed Emma Grace far out to sea splitting the storm in two however she became a hurricane before being caught up with the cold front and downgraded to a tropical low over the Bermuda Triangle and she rested dormant for a while. The front part of the storm reached Long Island, NY before dying out as a nor'easter in the Canadian Maritimes.

Is Emma Grace gone; nobody knows!

Monday October 10th, 2022 reality sets in and President Tom Brady does a fly over Atlanta to see the flooding and dead bodies floating in the water and damaged buildings from tornado damage! Airforce One flew over the Carolinas it was not as bad, then reports started coming in on the death count!

"Good afternoon this is World Network News, tropical storm Emma Grace has finally left the United States, but she left a message of the end of times!

"Emma Grace struck Miami with total devastation and we have a report of 56 people dead! The storm hit Miami with 185 mile per hour winds with gusts over 220! Miami Harbor was leveled, and several downtown buildings crumbled setting off gas lines and fires! Lightning struck a nuclear power plant in Fort Lauderdale killing at least 100 people; the count there may never be known! A tank ruptured and more than 1000 people are missing! 13 more people were killed along the Gulf coast from tidal waves. 100-foot waves buried Miami and

150 feet ones when Emma Grace struck New Orleans and there were no reports of deaths there.

"New Orleans was buried under 50 feet of water and the city was destroyed! They did a good job evacuating learning from Katrina, good job New Orleans! New Orleans was hit with 200 mile per hour winds before moving up as far as Tennessee meeting a cold front weaken Emma Grace into a tropical storm but she hit Atlanta with more than 20 feet of rain, baseball size hail and several tornadoes 45 people were reported dead and hundreds missing! The storm hit the Carolinas with heavy rain and spawning tornadoes before the cold front pushed it away.

"Emma Grace began almost two months ago off the coast of Africa blowing up a volcano, islands in the Caribbean were destroyed at least 220 people were killed in Antigua and over a thousand people were killed in the Dominican Republic and more than 5000 are missing! Punta Cana was completely destroyed. 500 people died in Hispaniola where Emma Grace dumped 50 inches of rain and dangerous lightning strikes! The storm hit Cuba killing 55 people and more than 300 were reported missing and Miami was its next target. This storm blew up mountains, nuclear plants and killed an estimated 20,000 people. She was the deadliest and most costly storm on earth ever!!!!!!!! This is David Dunkin' on World Network News reporting."

10   *BACK TO RECOVERY*

I t was Tuesday October 18th, 2022. Cruise ships arrived in Galveston, Texas to bring the evacuated back to their islands. Buses arrived in Oldtown to pick up thousands of people. Many people in evacuation zones left long ago but thousands more arrived from other islands and buses were busy coming and going every day. Until one day everybody has to leave because Emma Grace is dormant.

Cruise ships were leaving Galveston every five minutes; 100 ships and boats left for the Caribbean. When cruise ships arrived in Punta Cana D.R. the resort is no longer there the Dominican military was removing the damaged building and scooping up the dead. Dead bodies by the hundreds were wrapped in white blankets and put on trucks to be buried in an open field so the vultures can come to eat the dead! The evacuated residents were placed in tents until homes and hotels can be rebuilt. Some hotels survived the storm and people came in a mad rush to get housing.

In Hispaniola it was devastated; the whole island had to be stripped of debris before they can rebuild! Flying vultures already ate the dead! In Santiago and Santo Domingo camps were set up for people to go, some people in the Dominican Republic walked hundreds of miles to get better service. The dead were removed to open areas so the wild animals that remained had something to eat and the ravens and vultures arrive to finish the job! Not many people did evacuate in the Dominican Republic that is why so many people died! In Cuba it was a wasteland when cruise ships arrived and everyone in Cuba has to start over.

The best thing Emma Grace did when she struck Cuba is hit the jail and everyone escaped, some died doing so and the prisoners took over the country after the evacuations; they were smart not to leave now they're all free! The prisoners had to fish, eat berries and fruits to survive. When the hurricane blew the roof off the jail the prisoners escaped like a bunch of running rats! Prison guards were shooting at them as they ran as fast as they could in the jungle! The guards shot and killed a quick 20! The guards removed the dead and buried the bodies! The rest of the prisoners are gone! The wind was too much to get them all and the prison guards left the island during Emma Grace.

The rest of the Caribbean islands went through the same bullshit as everyone else! Welcome back tents set up for housing just like in Oldtown, Texas outside port-a-johns and beds in caves. *The island natives had to live with the bats in the caves!* The island of Antigua had a lot of dead people here trapped under a damaged ocean liner and it's going to stay there! The stench of the dead was terrible, and it attracted all kinds of animals seagulls sea birds and vultures eating all the guts! Hundreds lay dead on a beach. Destroyed buildings had to be rebuilt; the resort the ocean liner crashed into was wiped out! The result set in with thousands of mosquitoes biting people all across Antigua; restaurants, hotels and homes were blown away! People had to live in caves with the bats! Most people stayed on cruise ships for weeks until they find a safe place to go.

Military planes and ships arrived at Tollgate Island to start rebuilding. Military and weather helicopters flew over the Caribbean islands. Ships and boats went looking the area where the island of Q'klitores once stood and the famous naked lady in the water was never found and the mountain is gone. Billions of U.S. dollars of damage in the Caribbean islands and Florida the eastern seaboard, and New Orleans.

Cruise ships that evacuated people in Miami and New Orleans were held in military ports up the Mississippi River until cleanup could be done. Ocean liners and heavy freight ships arrived in Miami and New Orleans to remove the smashed harbor and clean the debris in downtown. Camps in Alabama on the Mississippi River where the evacuations were, were given instructions. The National Guard troops held the meeting.

"Ladies and gentlemen, we have updates from Miami and New Orleans areas hit by massive tidal waves and 200 mile per hour winds from hurricane Emma Grace. New Orleans was devastated, only the Superdome and a few city buildings remain, everything else was destroyed! The good news the new levies from Katrina held up and the flooding is going down. The favorite speakeasy area is unknown. When all the flooding goes down you can go in there get your belongings if you can find them in residential areas on foot; good luck!! New Orleans is unlivable there is nothing there. You will need to find somewhere else to live or remain here in the camp, living in tents!

"In Miami there are some residential areas available to return in about two or three weeks. Downtown was demolished! Roofs were ripped off buildings and windows broken in and the city is a mess. There is no more harbor in Miami every boat and dock was destroyed by 100 foot waves from Emma Grace. 150 foot waves buried New Orleans. No lives were lost in New Orleans, but some died in Miami.

"Tod Choice from WNOL radio reported wind gusts of 340 miles per hour when Emma Grace struck New Orleans! This storm was 10 times stronger than Katrina and if you want my opinion, I doubt anyone in New Orleans and downtown Miami will not be going anywhere for at least a year. The city of New Orleans will need to be rebuilt and it's going to be a while for downtown Miami to get back to normal. You will need to make phone calls and make arrangements to find other places to live. New England will be a good place, Maine or New Hampshire away from the hurricane zones!!!!!!!!!!! My name is Sergeant Richard Rich, Mississippi military police."

Thousands of people stayed in tents and bunkers until they leave to go elsewhere. New homes were built along the Mississippi River to house the evacuation. Water trucks came into New Orleans to suck up as much water as possible and go to treatment plants. Heavy earth tractors came in to push the debris together for miles and set it on fire burning all the wood structures. Anything left standing that could not be saved was mowed down. Steel was loaded onto freighter ships to be melted down. Dead fish dropped in from Emma Grace were eaten by animals. Thousands of animals were found dead, torched by military workers.

The burning was seen from downtown New Orleans and near the Superdome. The Dolphins had to play their home games in Tampa or Jacksonville and the New Orleans Saints had to play their home games in Alabama or Oklahoma. Atlanta was flooded and the Falcons had to play their home games in the Carolina Panthers stadium or share with the Jacksonville Jaguars, because Georgia stadium was damaged.

In Miami the debris was move and pushed out to sea by tugboats to be burned or drowned! Earth tractors were brought in to downtown to clear the streets to get to the buildings. Office furniture was thrown out of windows in damaged skyscrapers and windows pushed through to get ready to rebuild.

Fire and rescue crew went in to clean out damaged buildings up a stairway to the 34th floor because of the smell of rotten flesh in one of the buildings.

Pushing in a door and part of a broken wall one man said to another, "Oh! My god, we have death up here!" He opened a door to a conference room and a dead shark lying across a table partly crashed through a wall.

"Jesus Christ, Mark look at this! How in the blessed mother of god can a shark be tossed from the ocean at this height from a storm!!!!!!!!!"

"Holy shit! You got to be kidding Tommy! Let's get out of here before I puke! Let someone else do this job, fuck that!!!!!!!!!" The rescue team went downstairs to report what they saw to a co-worker.

"Harry you're not going to believe what we saw in a conference room on the 34th floor!" said Tommy.

"I heard; a shark! We have a crane coming to remove it! That's not all, more buildings had fish and boats! Thrown through windows! We were hit with 100-foot tidal waves and waterspouts with 300 mph winds not to mention Emma Grace's great blow job! This fuckin' storm turned the ocean upside down! That explains why we had flying sharks and boats here in Miami!

"Did you hear what happened in New Orleans? The entire city was blown off the face of the earth just the Superdome and a few buildings remain the rest of New Orleans was blown away! Emma Grace hit New Orleans with 200 mph winds with gusts over 300! And 150-foot waves washed the city away! Atlanta had 50 inches of rain killing about 1000 people and some of the ocean washed almost 200 miles inland when New Orleans was hit! Emma Grace has gone out to sea and weakened.

"This storm is the worst ever on earth; nothing ever like this has happened worse than any natural disaster! Worse than any earthquake, volcano, typhoon or any tornado! This storm is the beginning of the end of the world! Now the recovery from this may not happen in our lifetime. I believe it's over in Miami the recovery here is going to take years! You guys go to another building until I get a crane to remove the flying great white!" said Harry. His name read Harry Hitchcock on his name tag on his shirt.

A truck with a long crane reached up to the 34th floor where the shark was and workers dressed in chemical war clothing with gas masks to come in and wrapped rope around the slimy stinking shark and it was pulled out of a window smashing a wall to get it out of the building! The ropes slipped from the crane and the slimy shark fell 34 stories to the ground and splatted in a million pieces! It was blood, guts and shark debris and blood splatted everywhere! What a mess that's going to be to clean up! Workers going by were getting sick. The shark guts stunk so bad even the vultures were flying away!

The buildings were littered with broken glass damaged furniture and mold. Water trucks were sucking all the water off flooded streets and damaged trees were mowed down and earth tractors cleaned the streets.

Another storm was coming with lightning strikes setting off fires and spawning tornadoes helping the clean up! A bowling alley was destroyed by a tornado and bowling pins were flying around like missiles and bowling balls rolling down the streets and raccoons were chasing the bowling balls! Bowling pins and dead fish laid in city streets and sea birds, rats, raccoons, foxes, snakes and alligators came to feed on the dead fish. Alligators even ate some bowling pins and pythons anacondas and other big snakes swallowed some bowling balls; alligators and other animals played with them!

In New Orleans big rats and rodents ruled the land. Large animals of all kinds took over the remains in New Orleans after the flooding went down from the sea and the land. Horses, pigs, deer, wild boar, snakes, birds, hippos, elephants, big crabs and ravens, vultures as big as airplanes! Bobcats, cougars, fisher cats, and all other animals enjoying the dead fish feed from Emma Grace making the speakeasy a little Africa! *All we need is lions, tigers and hyenas and it will be a complete success!!!!!!!!!!!*

Later even bears came in chasing all the animals away for a big feed for many of them! The bears dominated the fish kill and ate other animals as well! *We need more bears to come in and finish the job!*

In Atlanta, animals arrived in the city all the way from New Orleans to feed on the dead and the bears followed as well. Animals never seen before in Atlanta as bears roared like crickets in the night. Atlanta looked like the afterlife; people with bones from the dead laid in city streets and the bears were eating them! People there left the city as a ghetto and the animals and ravens and vultures took over; it looked like the end of the world. In North Carolina a Christian church service was heard talking about the end times and recovery.

"Good morning brothers and sisters, welcome to the New Hope Assembly Church. My name is Pastor Cam Newton. Today's sermon: We are going to talk about the end times and back to recovery. We just experienced the worst hurricane on earth! This storm leveled Miami and New Orleans with 150-foot waves and 300 mph winds, and it killed uncountable people and blew away buildings and moved mountains! And bowling ball size hail! What is this world coming too!? Fish and sea life being pulled from the ocean from giant tornadoes and tsunamis and thrown into skyscrapers! Nothing impossible like this has ever happened!

"Right now, we are in god's rapture because the end of the world is very close when you see storms like this. At this time god is taking his people and when it's over the ones left behind will be with the devil! Before the devil walks the earth; something else may happen! We have to pray to be with God and his rapture may not be over yet!

"On September 11th, 2001 when the World Trade Center, the Pentagon and Washington D.C. were attacked with our airplanes and thousands of people died was the beginning, and global warming causing these storms!

"This storm spared North Carolina with heavy rains and torna- does; god is not ready for us yet, but I believe the devil owns the world right now. Hurricane Emma Grace went out to sea downgraded to a tropical storm but she's still out there and she may not be done yet! This storm blew mountains out of the water and across the Caribbean islands, turning the ocean upside down and flooding landscapes bring the sea life out of its environment into the unknown. Atlanta drowned to death and the sea life took over, now after the flooding withdraws land creatures comes in to take over from mice and rats to bears. Life after people; the animals will take over from the land and the sky! New Orleans looks like the African plains, right now!

"My brothers and sisters, this is a sign the end times are here. Now back to recovery will be under the devil's rule! I don't mean to scare you but it's a fact! You are seeing it right now! To overtake this evil you have to rebuild and it takes years; you keep moving forward and you don't look back, as soon as you turn your back the devil will get you; you keep moving and don't stop!!!!!!!!!! We need to read the bible and praise god until he returns," said Pastor Cam Newton.

.

11 IS SHE COMING AGAIN!?

Hurricane Emma Grace seems to be gone as she crossed into dry air and she's parked dormant over the Bermuda Triangle with passing clouds rotating but not doing much of anything but it looks kind of strange to viewers as fishermen watched.

In the Bahamas, an old man and his grandson went to a soccer game and the Bermuda intense fire was playing the Bahama island mission and the mission won 1-0. The next day Grampa and his grandson went fishing in the Bahamas and it was a partly cloudy day and the water was spinning forming a whirlpool clockwise and black bottom clouds were rotating counterclockwise.

They looked up in the sky and the old man said, "That's strange! The clouds are turning one way and the water is spinning the other way!"

The boy said, "Grampa the fish is coming in let's get our poles out and let's go fishing!"

While they were fishing about 20 minutes later, Grampa fires up a cigar, the grandson asked, "Grampa can I have a cigar?"

Grampa said, "Can your dick touch your asshole!?"

The young boy said, "No Grampa."

"Then you can't have a cigar."

Twenty minutes later Grampa opens a can of beer. The young boy asked, "Grampa can I have a beer?"

Grampa says, "Can your dick touch your asshole!"

"I told you no! Grampa!"

"Then you can't have a beer." 20 minutes later the young boy opens a bag of chips.

Grampa says, "Can I have some of your chips?"

The young boy said, "Well Grampa, can your dick touch your asshole!?"

"It sure can!" he said.

The young boy says, "Well good, then go fuck yourself, these are my chips!"

Grampa said, "Watch your mouth young man if you want to keep fishing."

The young boy was quiet, and he caught more fish than Grampa. 20 minutes later it started raining and thunder and the old man and the boy went home with lots of fish. 20 minutes later heavy rain and thunderstorms formed as Emma Grace is starting up again and 20 minutes later strong winds started picking up and fishing boats had to come into port. Nighttime it was a rainy night and windy and fishermen were at a bar telling jokes, drinking beers and eating pub sandwiches, as the wind was howling outside.

A man introduced himself to the bartender while drinking a beer. He said to a female bartender, "Hi there, my name is Jack Daniels."

"Pleased to meet you Jack. My name is Heather Hunt."

"Heather do you want to hear a joke?"

"Sure Jack, bring it on!"

"A family is at the dinner table and a boy asks his father, 'How many kinds of boobs are there?'

"The father, surprised, answers, 'Well son, a woman goes through three phases. In her 20s a women's breasts are like melons, round and firm. In her 30s and 40s, they are like pears, still nice, hanging a bit. After 50 they are like onions.'

"'Onions!?' the boy asks.

"'Yes. You see them and they make you cry.'

"This infuriated his wife and daughter. The daughter asks, 'Mom, how many different kinds of willies are there?'

"The mother smiles and she says, "Well dear, a man goes through three phases also! In his 20s his willy is like an oak tree, mighty and hard! In his 30s and 40s, it's like a birch, flexible but reliable. After 50, it's like a Christmas tree!'

"'A Christmas tree?' the daughter asks.

"'Yes, dead from the root up and the balls are just for decoration!' said mom."

The bartender Heather laughed hysterically! Then Jack Daniels ordered the drink Jack Daniels and he told her another joke:

Before marriage:
Man: I have been waiting for this day.
Lady: Do you want me to leave?
Man: No!
Lady: Do you love me?
Man: Of course.
Lady: Will you ever cheat on me?
Man: Never in my life!
Lady: Will you ever hug me?
Man: Every chance I get.
Lady: Will you hit me?

Man: Are you crazy?

Lady: Can I trust you?

Man: Yes!

Lady: Sweetheart.

After 25 years of marriage: Now read from bottom to top.

Heather read the joke backwards and she said to Jack Daniels "Go fuck yourself," and she walked away, and she stopped serving him. Then Jack went over to his friends telling jokes and playing pool and having fun, everyone was having fun in the bar when suddenly the wind outside was blowing so hard a window blew in and the roof tore off and people went from having fun to holding on and running for cover, just like that!

People ran out of the bar in the heavy rain and wind running to their cars then hail as big as baseballs hitting people in the head some of them ran back into the bar to hide under tables that did no good, the tables were blowing around and people. Then the hail came down so hard it filled the bar under three feet of hail because the roof of the bar is gone! People were bleeding from being hit in the head by the hail, the ones that made it to their cars survived disaster.

Then lightning and thunder then it stopped. People scrambled through feet of hail to get out of the bar, they grabbed some bottles of booze on the way. The lightning was striking everywhere sending fear to get to safety. A dog ran to hide under a tree and a lightning bolt struck the tree and killed the dog.

"Jesus Christ, is Emma Grace starting up again?!" Jack Daniels said to one of his friends, drinking a bottle of Jack!

The storm was so deadly it came so fast then it was gone, and the sky cleared up and the stars were out. Everyone went home except the bartender Heather as she drank everything, she could get her hands on while she was soaking wet from the weather. The storm destroyed the bar and she helped herself to whatever was left over. Then she passed out until daylight.

She woke up and she puked several times from all what she drank last night. Heather staggered to the road and she saw destruction like a tornado had gone through. She was shocked!

The police came down the road and the cop said to her, "Lady you have to leave the area due to storm damage during the night."

"I know my bar got damaged the roof is gone and the windows were blown out!" Heather staggered down the road and she was intoxicated, and the police drove her to safety because her car was buried under falling trees.

Police drove around and the sky started turning colors from blue to green and orange and gray, then yellow then back to blue and passing clouds going one way, other clouds were going the other way, then drifting down to the ground and back up and it formed a round circle with a clear sky in the middle and black bottom scary clouds formed around the circle. Lightning flashed inside the clear opening; the lightning was barely viewable and then it got brighter and brighter than it was flashing constantly like a strobe light and getting so bright to a point that you can't look at it. Bright enough to blind you if you keep looking at it!

The cop pulled over and he got out of his car. He wiped his eyes for a minute then he had another look and he had to turn away because it was so bright then lightning bolts started striking the ground followed by loud thunder and then heavy rain came down. The policeman put sunglasses on, and he drove away in a hailstorm all the way to the Bahama police station.

He said to another policeman, "Did you see what I saw out there!?"

"It's only a thunderstorm, a pretty good one is going on out there!" said the other cop.

"Yeah Jerry, it's a good one alright! The sky started turning all kind of colors then the clouds started dancing like people square dancing and lifting and boiling over like a burning torch and it formed a circle with blue sky and the sun shining. Then all of a sudden lightning appeared until it looked like a strobe light bright enough to burn you to death and then comes the lightning bolts then the rain came out of nowhere, and hail as big as baseballs! I swear the aliens or something from the Bermuda Triangle is coming to get us! I was never so scared from this experience! Not even Vietnam was worse than this!" said the cop.

Jerry the other cop looked out the window and it was a dark gray sky and it was raining and thundering.

He said, "Officer Cornbean, are you on drugs!?"

Officer Jerry didn't believe Cornbean's story; meanwhile he got a call. Jerry drove his cruiser out to a beach to a boat fire. He stopped on the side of the road to call for help. Then he got out of his car and he walked down to the beach. His lights were flashing as he waited for a rescue and back up help.

Suddenly a yellow mist formed a thick cloud and it lowered down on the beach where Officer Jerry was, and it smelled like sulfur from a volcano like a strong odor of gas! Officer Jerry ran out of the way and a vicious bolt of lightning shot straight down to the ground and blew a big hole in the ground on the beach about 30 feet wide and 20 feet deep! Officer Jerry could feel the heat from the lightning strike!

The bolt was a bright white with a yellow color on the outside and it was about a foot wide. It was *zap* you can hear the strike. Then a cloud of black smoke came out of the crater the lightning strike made! Then the yellow mist and cloud disappeared leaving a big hole on the beach!

A rescue, fire truck and a couple of police cars arrived at the scene. When help arrived Officer Jerry told them what just happened.

The other cops said, "We have been hearing a lot of strange things in the Bahamas lately since Hurricane Emma Grace about gas smells and strange thunderstorms, we are in the Bermuda Triangle; a lot of strange things happens here!"

The rescue team and fire department went out in a rescue boat to put out the boat fire, no one was aboard the boat. *The boat was struck by lightning!* Officer Jerry went back to the police station and he told Officer Cornbean what he saw.

"Officer Jayson Cornbean, you are right something strange is happening. When I got a call for a boat fire at Closeland Beach I saw this strange ugly yellow cloud come out of nowhere and it smelled like a strong odor of gas when a violent bolt of lightning struck the beach and blew a hole in the ground big enough to swallow a house! No thunder, just *zap!* I can feel the heat from the lightning strike! Then a ball of black smoke came out of the hole and then it was gone, just like that! We need to contact NASA or some kind of volcano crew to come to Bahama Island to investigate what's going on here because we could have a volcano ready to erupt here," said Officer Jerry, Bahama Island police!

More fuckin' shit is happening here in the Bahamas!

A woman was washing her car outside her house and she can smell gas and she got her cell phone to make a call then her house blew up! The explosion blew her home to matchsticks on a beautiful sunny October day, in seconds! The debris fell everywhere, and the girl was screaming hysterically! Her refrigerator flew high in the air like a missile and it came down landing on a dog walking. The dog was killed instantly! The rest of the belongings from the home were blown to pieces. The girl called the police and they could not believe what happened! There were no reports of gas leaks in that area. Electric and utility trucks investigated the gas leak and there was none.

A soccer game was going on at Bahama Island high school and the score between the two teams was 0 to 0. The ball was being kicked around near the goal when suddenly the ground opened up in the middle of the field into a huge sink hole about 30 feet wide and 20 feet deep! Everyone went running for cover running to the school screaming hysterically! Clouds formed rotating around in circles and started getting thicker and it started raining and then it stopped and cleared up again.

Police and the fire department arrived at the scene and school buses came to evacuate the area. The NASA crew came from New York to investigate the area and they set up monitoring equipment in the school to see if Bahama Island is volcanic. NASA and the Bahama Island police met at the high school a day later.

"Good morning officers my name is Vincent Tino the head volcanologist of NASA and my crew, John Nicolini, news reporter, Jay Domers and Paul Arts will be working the investigations and this is Linda Lincoln and Amy Amitriptyline whom will be on the computers and monitors to see if we have volcanic activity here. We need to set up in this school to find out what is going on here. We also check for radioactivity and methane gas vents."

"Pleased to meet you my name is Officer Jerry and he's Officer Cornbean, and this is Lori Langs, the school principal."

"Pleased to meet you. You can set up equipment in the library," said Lori Langs.

Later dump trucks with gravel, rocks and dirt filled in the big hole in the soccer field. The crater on the beach was left alone and the area was closed off. The NASA set up base in the school while Jay Domers and Paul Arts used a Spudweb robot like they did on Mt. Flow from the lady in the water volcano. They found radiation in the sky and methane gas deep underground and in the ocean.

John Nicolini went with the Coast Guard flying helicopters over several areas in the Bahamas testing for activity. Amy Amitriptyline and Linda Lincoln were getting reports from John Nicolini, Paul Arts and Jay Domers all reporting radioactivity, methane gas and sulfur.

The next day, Monday October 24th, 2022, the NASA crew stayed up all night getting reports that a warning was issued by the National Weather Service that Hurricane Emma Grace may be beginning to start up again. 8:29 a.m. A helicopter landed in the soccer field at Bahama Island high school and John Nicolini got out of the chopper and he went into the school; school was in session and John went to the library where the crew were and the police was called into a meeting and John Nicolini came in with the report; the library was closed to the public until NASA leaves.

"Good morning, I have the same reports as everyone else. We have no volcano here or any known active volcanoes on the Bahamas but what we did find is radioactivity, methane gas and sulfur poisoning in the atmosphere! We don't need to be alarmed about it nobody is dying because of bad air, but we are part of the Bermuda Triangle. We have methane gas in the ocean under the sea floor that causes air bubbles to rise and it has been known to sink ships, get in the atmosphere and choke aircraft causing planes to crash. Methane gas can also cause land explosions and sink holes! This event is rare, unfortunately we had a few bad things happen here this past week. The sulfur and the radiation we found raises fear and more bad news tropical storm Emma Grace has started up again off the eastern

Bahamas and heading for Bermuda and will be upgraded to a hurricane by tomorrow morning. We need rain here to clean the air and limit gas eruptions.

"On August 22nd Emma Grace struck a volcanic island in the eastern Atlantic where nuclear bombs were stored there and the volcano was erupting at the time when Emma Grace hit with 200 mph winds and blew the island and the volcano out of the water and the nuclear bombs helped trigger a mega explosion that dried up the storm but set the upper atmosphere on fire for two or three weeks! Then the hurricane turned into a super killer and tore the Caribbean apart, the islands, and nearly leveled Miami and New Orleans was completely destroyed! Atlanta drowned. The storm has killed more than 20,000 people and she's been out there for over two months.

"Now the strange things that happened here may be caused by the remnants of this storm Emma Grace, still radioactive and maybe the reason why she was so violent. This is the storm of the century! It's a storm that comes around once every 10,000 years. In modern times this storm is the worst of all time. In 2019 Hurricane Forion demolished all the Bahamas and you guys were spared from Emma Grace, you got lucky here, but hidden danger may still be lurking, while she was dormant.

"We found radiation and sulfur in the air from this storm. Methane gas will cause the sky to turn colors and the mixture of radiation and sulfur will cause strange and really violent thunderstorms! The readings of methane gas we found here is very high and beware for more possible explosions until you get heavy rain! There are no volcanoes in the Bahamas however under the sea floor may have volcanic vents all across the Bermuda Triangle.

"We will be here for a week for more testing on all the Bahama Islands. I'm leaving with the Weather Channel to monitor Emma

Grace for sulfur gas and radiation samples. Just be patient and be prepared. We will keep continue to work with the police and the school for updates. For now, the areas where the sink holes and methane gas explosions will be sprayed with bomb defusing fluid to protect these areas. Thank you very much!" said John Nicolini.

John went back to the helicopter and flew off to the hurricane. The rest of the crew was monitoring reports and Vincent Tino was taking notes. People at the school was wondering what was going on. Police tape kept kids out of the area. The soccer field was taped off. At the helicopter John Nicolini was flying in he was taking samples in the eye of the reforming Hurricane Emma Grace and he found sulfur and radiation and he sent the report to local weather stations.

Meanwhile the military planes and helicopters were taking radioactive samples in Miami, New Orleans and the Caribbean islands, reporting the areas drying up fast from the dangerous chemicals in Emma Grace that made this hurricane so violent and still hanging around!

October 25th Tuesday at 1:12 p.m. sirens were going off in Bermuda as reformed Emma Grace is coming with 99 mph winds! Gusts up to 145! People boarded cruise ships to evacuate to the mainland and people that didn't get out in time were escorted to bunkers located in the mountains then Emma Grace struck Bermuda with no mercy, striking buildings, homes and stores and restaurants! Ripping roofs off, smashing windows destroying camps, villages and a tornado leveled a big church! People and animals were running in the streets to get away from the sudden storm coming out of nowhere!

The tornado hit and leveled a resort and struck a boat marina smashing boats in a million pieces! The tornado continued and leveled the Bermuda airport and planes were tossed like missiles and shredded into a pile of metal; the tornado blew away hangars and more planes were tossed like missiles then the twister got stronger and hit an oil and gas depot and shredded it apart until it blew up like a bomb!

The twister was not done! The tornado struck a city damaging buildings tearing off roofs and breaking windows then it leveled a soccer stadium and hit a hospital before exiting out into the ocean and dissipating into its storm cloud, and then heavy rain. The eye of Emma Grace passed over Bermuda leaving a trail of destruction on the island and now it's heading out to sea then a backdoor cold front broke it up and lowered the wind speed downgraded to a tropical storm with 60 mph winds pushing the storm back into the Bermuda Triangle. Then she picked up speed with 80 mph winds threatened to hit Bermuda again but she passed the island and Virginia Beach was her next target where she stalled and ground away with 80 mph winds now threatening to strike the east coast all the way to New England! From Virginia Beach to Maine there were preparations for evacuations! Thunderstorms hit Virginia Beach spawning a few tornadoes damaging trees and buildings. WNYC out of New York City was broadcasting the news at Times Square in NYC.

"Good evening this is breaking news on WNYC TV channel 5. We have a hurricane warning for New York City. Hurricane Emma Grace is just off the coast brushing Virginia Beach and has moved back out to sea and up the east coast. Please be prepared! This storm could strike anywhere on the east coast as early as tomorrow afternoon. If you need to evacuate you must take buses and use the subway to head uptown. Evacuation centers are available at Yankee Stadium and Madison Square Garden. This is a very powerful storm please get to safe ground away from the Hudson River, this is Vicky Warren reporting on WNYC TV 5."

October 26th, 2022. Wednesday at 2 p.m. was a bright sunny

day in Manhattan and many New Yorkers did not take WNYC news seriously and many people were tying up their boats in the Hudson and some took their boats out of the water. Tugboats and steam ships left the area and military boats and cruise ships left and went up the Hudson River heading toward Canada. A cold front pushed Emma Grace out to sea, and she weakened to a tropical storm with 50 mph winds. 5 p.m. tents were set up at the world trade center memorial and a special dinner was served there for the NYPD and the fire department celebrating Halloween festivities. Food and drinks were served, and marketplace was set up. The New Yorkers are not worried about a weaken Emma Grace out at sea. A big boom was heard, and the water was going out in the Hudson River. A fireman spoke at the diner by the sea.

"Ladies and gentlemen welcome to the NYC evening Halloween ball. My name is Eric Carble NYPD and we do not get together very often since 9/11. The reason why we have to move this Halloween party back a few days is because we have a hurricane coming here by Friday morning, a very dangerous storm but the good news is Emma Grace was downgraded to a tropical storm and we're not going to worry about a little wind like that. This storm had 200 mph winds when she hit Miami and New Orleans and we sent a lot of our people to go and help them, they were hit with waves over 100 feet high and devastated these areas and the Caribbean killing more than 20,000 people! It was the worst storm on record and thank god we have a cold front pushing it away from New York City. Let's all raise our toast and enjoy our feast."

Eric Carble had a long message and the party went well. Bands were playing and people dancing into the night.

The next day Thursday October 27th, 2022 at 6 a.m. the NYPD the fire department arrived to clean up from last night's party, it was a cloudy cold rainy dark morning. The police and firemen noticed something strange down on the Hudson as the water started disappearing rapidly and boats were laying on their sides. It was very foggy, and the water was gone and several boats laid on dry land!

"Jesus Christ! Do you see what I see!?" one fireman said to another.

"It looks like all the water has left the Hudson River! What the hell's going on here!"

"Let's get out of here in a hurry! Something's wrong here! We probably had an earthquake! Let's get out of here!" said the first fireman and they drove away in their vehicles as fast as they could drive uptown. More firemen and police saw the horror and they left the area in a hurry!

7:02 a.m. Emma Grace formed back into a monster sucking all the water out of the Hudson River and building into a mega storm with 130 mph winds right now and she's heading right straight into New York City within the hour. Sirens and lights were seen and blaring throughout Manhattan and people started running in the streets at 7:30 a.m., lightning was spotted and then a loud roar and the ground was shaking triggering an earthquake and then comes a very big wave! Workers at the Freedom Tower watched in shock! Firemen and policemen yelled through loudspeakers while driving uptown toward Harlem.

"Run, run, run, run, run!!!!!!!!!!!"

Worse, people who evacuated started coming back because Emma Grace weakened to a weak tropical storm, ignoring the fact that this hurricane was a very dangerous! The storm strengthened to a category five again during the night with no warning! The giant wave came quickly and struck Manhattan crashing into buildings knocking some of them down and smashing thousands of windows and ripping roofs off; then the winds from Emma Grace arrived to finish the job!

But before the storm winds came, the wave hit first just like seen on the movie, *The Day After Tomorrow*. The wave buried lower Manhattan under 20 feet of water washing yellow cabs, buses, fire trucks police cars and other parked vehicles and drowning people. It pushed the parked vehicles, people and everything in its path through buildings and down Manhattan streets, even boats were washed into city streets before receding back into the Hudson River bowling vehicles and people over to their deaths!

People running uptown saw the giant wave about 200 feet high wash into downtown Manhattan between the buildings and openings crushing everything in its path!!!!!!!!!!! People running as fast as they could running over other people screaming and crying hysterically! People were trampled, others ran into buildings and running up stairways to escape this giant wave, but most didn't survive because the tsunami was too big; not one wave but a series of giant waves buried New York City!!!!!!!!!!! Everything went from a noisy Manhattan to quiet before thunderstorms arrived!

Workers at the Freedom Tower survived as they watched the waves coming in washing everything away! Workers saw the Statue of Liberty get blown over and saw it wash into the Hudson along with ships being tossed around in the waves before the thunderstorms arrived with several waterspouts so workers ran into stairways and tied themselves up with rope and chains to protect them from the wind.

The waves and wind blew the windows out in the lower part of the Freedom Tower and fish, sharks, seals, seagulls and anything from the ocean was uprooted from the water and thrown into buildings just like what happen in Miami and New Orleans; from the waves and wind!

Big waves also struck Long Island, NY and Block Island, RI was hit by a giant wave over 60 feet high washing over the island smashing homes restaurants, hotels and Block Island had serious damage! Block Island and southeastern New England evacuated away from the ocean.

Long Island was devastated but most people evacuated in time; the some did not were killed instantly! Big waves washed over Long Island into the other side and rogue waves hit the Connecticut coastline from Bridgeport all the way to New London CT. Long Island Sound had smashed up boats laying in its wake!!!!!!!!! The hurricane didn't even hit New England yet!

Forty-foot waves washed out the Rhode Island and southeastern Massachusetts coastlines 10 to 20 miles inland causing catastrophic flooding and serious damage to boats and nearby waterfront properties, condos and homes destroyed in Narragansett, RI. And it hit Cape Cod! The waves washed all the way up the eastern seaboard all the way to Maine causing coastal damage!

Now Emma Grace is ready to strike Manhattan dead on! After the tsunami waves here comes Emma Grace up the Hudson River into downtown Manhattan with 175 mph winds!!! The sky was black as the ace of spades at 8:15 a.m. and the lightning was a bright green color. The water from the tsunami waves was rushing in and pulling out taking debris and dead bodies!

A violent updraft pulled roofs off of buildings, picking up heavy objects and throwing them around like missiles! Then a sudden microburst as wind blew straight down with baseball size hail then violent lightning strikes then a tornado touchdown damaging a few buildings before going out into the Hudson River becoming a strong waterspout striking the New Jersey coast. Another tornado hit

Metlife Stadium tearing up part of the stadium seating a NY Giants sign was ripped away from the stadium and tossed into a high-rise building.

The same tornado ripped roofs off of buildings and struck a barn at a nearby farm and a piece of metal struck a running horse and it went right up the horse's asshole! A few minutes later the horse laid dead being blown around in the wind!

At 9:03 a.m. on October 27th, 2022 the eye passed over New York City and the sun came out for about two hours. *The worst is yet to come!!!!!!!*

The sky was clear, and the temperature read 65 degrees on the Times Square bulletin board and then a hurricane warning as the area is flooded. "Please move to higher ground at this time the back end of Emma Grace is on the way," the sign at Times Square read.

10:43 a.m. the sky went from sunshine to a gray color and fast-moving clouds then the clouds formed a pale white then turned yellow, then brown, purple then green then it was the calm before the storm. Thunder was heard and then lightning!

There was a light wind then at 11:02 a.m. the sky exploded! The wind roared at 190 miles per hour into Manhattan smashing windows and ripping objects off of buildings and a wind tunnel with 220 miles per hour ripped through downtown Manhattan and left a trail of destruction all the way into upstate NY.

The second half of the storm didn't last much more than five minutes! Emma Grace blew so much debris into Central Park, every tree was ripped out of the ground and properties and skyscrapers were completely destroyed. Central Park was unrecognizable!

Emma Grace weakened as she raced into upstate New York, New Jersey and Pennsylvania, but she's not done -- not even close!!!!!!! Manhattan got the worst of the wind and waves from Emma Grace.

New England and Block Island Long Island and Cape Cod got the first set of waves, but Philly and New Jersey got the waves from the back end.

At 11:38 a.m. a tsunami struck Philadelphia with 60-foot waves after Emma Grace struck with 90 mph winds in Philly and the waves smashed into buildings breaking windows and tearing roofs off of skyscrapers and condos nearby. Thunderstorms put down tornadoes tearing up neighborhoods! The waves flooded the city of brotherly love under 20 feet of water and there were some dead bodies floating in the flooding. The New Jersey coastline took a good hit from the giant waves from Emma Grace.

A ship was washed into an apartment complex smashing buildings and killing people; gas lines ruptured and there were explosions and tornadoes tore up several neighborhoods well after Emma Grace passed! In Philly people who evacuated were at the football stadium that was flooded; hysterical people watch dead bodies floating by outside the stadium on a beautiful clear day in Philly!

In New York, Yankee Stadium still had people there from the evacuations and flooded under 20 feet of water and it looked like a fishbowl inside Yankee Stadium and fish were seen swimming in the water; sharks too!!!!!!! A man was trying to open a gate in waist deep water to let some of the water out and a shark bit him right in the ass and pulled him under the water and other sharks ate him alive! *What are the chances of being attacked by sharks inside Yankee Stadium!* Stadium officials and the evacuated people were hysterical!

Emma Grace weakened into a tropical low before meeting a cold front over the Great Lakes, where she stalled in Buffalo, NY.

At 3:53 p.m. reality sets in as military helicopters fly over the destruction from Emma Grace. Rescue helicopters rescued people on top of buildings and a whale rested on the observatory platform on the 86th floor of the Empire State Building and a tugboat rested on the other side of the observation deck on fire and a shark was driven through a window and hanging out another on the 99th floor. It had a seal hanging out of its mouth and blood was dripping down the building and the shark was still alive waggling its tail and chewing on the seal.

An NYPD helicopter flew by and the pilot said to another officer onboard, "Officer Richi, can you believe this, a fuckin' shark on the 99th floor of the Empire State Building hanging from one window and out another and it's alive eating a seal!!!!!!!"

Officer Richi said, "I think King Kong put it there!"

Then the chopper fired away at the 99 shark until it blasted into pieces splattering blood everywhere! The dead shark fell to the ground; parts of the 99 shark landed on the observation deck on the 86th floor next to the burning tugboat. Seagulls grabbed the falling seal in midair before it hit the ground!

On Monday, October 31st, 2022, Halloween day was a cold and rainy day in New York City and the flooding receded back into the Hudson River with debris busted up boats and dead bodies flowing back out into the ocean to feed the sharks! Giant earth movers and military tractors pushed debris from city streets from Harlem to the Hudson River and dumped it all in the Hudson. More debris was pushed and lifted and dumped into Central Park; Central Park is now Manhattan's dump site! The debris was set on fire and the area around Central Park dump was evacuated! The debris pushed into the Hudson River was pushed out to sea by hundreds of tugboats.

Giant street sweepers arrived to clean the streets after damaged buildings were knocked down. Buildings that survived this terrible hurricane were swept and cleaned and thousands of dead fish, sea life and birds—not to mentioned dead bodies too!!!!!!!—were removed and swept away by earth movers.

Evacuated people were still stuck at Yankee Stadium until help arrived; the Bronx is still flooded. Dead birds even fish hung in the lights above Yankee Stadium, blood dripping down the light poles, from the giant waves and wind that smacked them there! The dead birds and fish guts are splattered on the lights and on the roof and inside the flooded stadium and surviving sharks eating the dead. Finally, news reporters, the military, National Guard and weather teams were able to enter Manhattan flying over in helicopters to rescue stranded people and animals and get them out of the danger zone. People at Mohegan Sun casino in Connecticut watched the news at a restaurant and bar.

"Good evening, happy Halloween from NBC TV news. New York City was devastated from Hurricane Emma Grace a few days ago leaving a trail of destruction and the death toll at this time is unknown! The storm was so strong pulling all the water out of the Hudson River and away from beaches from Long Island to Ocean City, Maryland and hit lower Manhattan with 200-foot waves and burying New York City under 30 feet of water! There were a series of tsunamis that buried New York City in the ocean. It will take years to get Manhattan back to normal because several buildings were demolished from 200 mile per hour winds from Emma Grace.

"This storm devastated Miami and washed away New Orleans and leveled several Caribbean islands and drowned Atlanta under 50 feet of water! The death toll so far is 55,000 and more than three million people are still missing! This was the worst disaster ever on earth and it has something to do with global warming. The storm raced through upstate New York and it's trapped right now over White Plains dumping heavy rain and the remnants of Emma Grace are still out there!

"Connecticut was spared with heavy flooding and storms. Southern New England was hit with severe flooding and Block Island was blown off the face of the earth from Emma Grace, Narragansett, RI was hit by the tsunami, Newport and Cape Cod were devastated! 70 mile per hour winds and tornadoes damaged the New England coastline from eastern Connecticut, Rhode Island and up the east coast all the way to Maine!

"A man was killed by a shark inside the flooded Yankee Stadium believe it or not! And tons of sea life were tossed into buildings and animals were killed! This is David Festraphano reporting on NBC News. We will keep you posted on further reports from this devastating killer storm."

Everybody on earth was in a state of shock and Mohegan Sun held several evacuations.

PART 3

REMNANTS OF EMMA GRACE CONTINUE TO BE KILLERS FROM TROPICAL TO WINTER AND SHE GETS CAUGHT UP WITH A COLD FRONT AND EXPLODES!

12   *THE BEAT GOES ON!*

The storm stalled over the White Plains and backs into upstate New York spawning tornadoes then hits New Jersey, Maryland parts of Washington D.C. then warm and cold fronts push Emma Grace into the Mississippi River. She becomes a hurricane again and goes up the Mississippi River through the great lakes all the way to Canada before meeting a strong cold front in Canada that pushes Emma Grace on a return trip down the Mississippi all the way to the Gulf of Mexico. She starts up again and crosses central Florida and she makes a return trip up the east coast as a monster again!

White Plains, New York. Heavy rain and baseball size hail is pounding a village in the mountains. The White Plains military-utility camp was a place high in the mountains where evacuations from New York City went were staying in tents and Quonset huts. The huts were heated with wood stoves and also used for cooking and the tents had to use gas and generator heaters and everyone slept in sleeping bags. Igloo sleepers were flown in by helicopters from Alaska to keep everyone warm. A mess hall was a building for people to eat and shower.

November 1st, 2022, was a bad day for weather as the remnants of Emma Grace dumped heavy rain, baseball size hail, strong wind and thunder and lightning and it was cold and the baseball size hail was damaging the tents and people were getting hurt then it snowed during the night and all the next day. Then the storm went through New Jersey dumping heavy rain and flooding cities and heavy snow in the mountains. The cold front pushed the remnants of Emma Grace still packing 70 mph winds through Pennsylvania with heavy rain hail thunderstorms and tornadoes doing some pretty good damage to condos, football and baseball stadiums, and tearing roofs off of buildings, and schools getting hit by tornadoes, and then a snowstorm to finish the job. The damage from this fuckin' storm shows no signs of quitting!!!!!!!

Wednesday November 2nd, 2022. A woman was reading a book at the University of Maryland library and a thunderstorm was going on and the windows were open in the library and a lightning bolt went in one window knocking the book out of the woman's hand slapping the book up against a wall and out the other window then a fire started from the lightning strike! The women screamed hysterically, and she ran out of the library; the book was on fire and papers caught fire and librarians grabbed fire extinguishers to put the flames out! The lightning was so bright, and the thunder was so loud the librarians were afraid to close the windows and ran out of the library. A few minutes later a big oak tree was struck by lightning; the lightning sliced the tree in three!

A basketball game was going on in the evening and a tornado ripped the roof of the Terp Center. Maryland was winning 78 to 75 with 1:23 remaining and Penn State was bringing the ball up the court and they shot a three pointer to tie the game but missed. When Maryland grabbed the rebound the tornado tore the roof off the building and two Penn State players were sucked up into the funnel out of the building. One of them lost all his clothes and the other was thrown into a tree! The first player was sucked up in the funnel and he landed in a ditch on the side of a road naked! The tornado and the storms left the area leaving a trail of destruction on the University of Maryland campus.

The two Penn State basketball players were reunited six hours later. The first player was carried 13 miles away and landed in a ditch; he got knocked unconscious! The second one was trapped in a tree high up with a head injury; at least he still had his cell phone on him when he gained consciousness. The naked Penn State player was found by police and what a story he had to tell! A rescue came to take him to the hospital. The two players and the rest of the Penn State basketball team just didn't have answers for what happened it happened so fast!

Late night and the early morning on November 3rd, the storm hit Washington D.C. A tornado struck Dulles International Airport tossing small planes around like toys and President Tom Brady was ready to board Airforce One and the strong winds blew the aircraft into a terminal breaking glass and damaging the terminal. The president stopped boarding. Lightning struck a fuel truck fueling a plane and the truck and plane burst into flames and exploded like a bomb and the airport was closed for the day!

Then the storm moved toward the White House and the wind blew windows out and the area was flooded under a foot of water! Several funnel clouds past through Washington D.C. causing a panic with people running in the streets and being overtaken by floods.

A soccer game was going on in Camden Yards baseball park at night when suddenly the lights in the stadium flickered then a bright flash of lightning followed by a loud bang then a tornado tore the roof off sending soccer players running for cover then the stadium went dark! The tornado hit an apartment complex in downtown Baltimore and the city was buried under two feet of water and hail. The tornado continued and leveled a few boats in the harbor and lightning struck trees were set on fire and left the city in ruins!

The storm moved back toward Pittsburgh spawning tornadoes heavy rain hail and lightning strikes setting fires and burning wood buildings. A country ranch was struck by lightning and burned to the ground; some people died.

Sunday November 6th, 2022. Part of the remnants of Emma Grace moved into the Ohio River and half stayed in Pittsburgh and the Steelers were playing a football game in the rain at Heinz Stadium against the Cleveland Browns in the pouring rain and thunder was heard when suddenly a microburst came in the stadium with 150 mph winds and players and fans were being blown around everywhere! People ran for the exits like bats out of hell!!!!!!! Some were blown back into the stadium. Several people were hurt and the football players ran to get inside when the wind came straight down from a black ugly supercell then the lightning and then hail filled the stadium a foot deep with hail then the storm moved away and the sun came out. Snowplows plowed the hail off the field and rescuers arrived to move the injured; several spectators were hurt and taken out of the stadium then the game resumed, and the Pittsburgh Steelers won 51 to 27.

The giant supercell went right up the fuckin' Ohio River looking to get stronger and went into the great lakes and formed back into a hurricane! All the storms connected back together after striking upstate NY, New Jersey, Pennsylvania, Maryland then hitting downtown Baltimore and hitting Pittsburgh and now all the severe storms joined together and Emma Grace is being born again as a warm front pushed Emma Grace into the Great Lakes and it turned into a monster once again.

Grinnell, Illinois was its first target and Emma Grace was classified as a strong wave of severe storms with tornado warnings and warning reports from cell phones and radio and TV news. There was not any reason to evacuate before a 60-mph windstorm other than getting into storm shelters. It was a sunny cold day and 6 inches of snow on the ground and Grinnell was not ready for what's to come!

Monday November 7th, 2022. A group of workers were unloading wood from trucks to be cut up to be used for firewood and for heating. Bulldozers lifted giant logs from big trees being cut down with chainsaws and power saws, when suddenly the workers got messages on their cell phones.

"Extreme alert! Please take cover immediately!"

Beep, beep, beep, beep, beep!!!!!!!!!!! The warning kept going over and over! One of the workers called one another to stop production. The big boss came out of a trailer to call his workers to stop working.

He said, "Hey fellas we all need to get to a storm shelter there's a big storm coming with a pack of tornadoes!"

One man said, "It's winter now we're not getting more tornadoes!"

"Manny pay attention to your phone, twisters are coming!" said the big boss.

A bus arrived to take the workers off the work site and took them to a storm shelter bunker located in a mountain and other workers followed in their flatbed trucks. The workers were aware of what Emma Grace had done. They all hunkered down in the storm shelter for an early lunch and they watched news reports on TV.

"Good morning, we have breaking news on the Weather Channel, this is Gary Gray reporting. Emma Grace has started up again and she's in the great lakes threatening to hit the windy city of Chicago, but right now the lumberjack city of Grinnell better take cover right away because you will be first to be hit! This storm has killed more than 55,000 people and more than 3,000,000 are missing and 85 mile per hour winds are just hours away from striking Grinnell!

"Emma Grace leveled several islands in the Caribbean, the Dominican Republic was destroyed and the Punta Cana resort was completely destroyed killing more than 3,000 people and more than 10,000 died in the Dominican Republic. Cuba was destroyed and Miami was devastated and south Florida about 4,000 lost their lives and New Orleans was blown off the face of the earth. We don't have reports of deaths in New Orleans, but more than a million animals were found dead! Atlanta was drowned and 2500 people were reported dead. Bermuda had devastation and New York City was unrecognizable from damage from killer waves more than 100 feet high that emptied the Hudson River and buried Manhattan in the ocean throwing fish and even sharks into high rise buildings! The big waves leveled the east coast!

"We have a report that a man was killed by sharks swimming in the flooded Yankee Stadium! Tornadoes, thunderstorms hail flooding caused catastrophic damage in upstate NY, New Jersey, Pennsylvania and Maryland. Two Penn State basketball players were sucked out after a roof was blown off during a basketball game at the University of Maryland. They both survived with injuries. A microburst hit the Heinz Stadium in Pittsburgh during a football game and 450 people were hurt!

"Then this storm went over the Ohio River spawning tornadoes on one side of the river and a snow storm on the other now these storms joined together with the remnants of the very powerful Emma Grace and this unusual storm is coming right up the great lakes and Grinnell you better be ready soon and Chicago you will be her next target, take cover now! This is Gary Gray reporting, the Weather Channel."

The big boss with his name tag Rocky Cookie across his green and blue flannel shirt, and Manny stopped outside of the storm shelter to look outside and a huge shelf cloud appeared with giant thunderheads moving at a pretty good rate of speed and they heard thunder!

Manny said, "There it is! It's coming!"

Rocky said, "Let's get inside this storm is going to be a bad one!"

A woman was working in a barn brushing down horses and feeding them when she heard a big boom while she was talking on her cell phone then she heard thunder and she went outside and she saw the big black clouds coming fast rotating into a funnel then she locked the barn door and she ran to a storm shelter in the ground near the barn. When she got there the wind picked up and she got in the shelter safely. Then tornado!

The twister hit the barn and the horses were whinnying and crying like crazy! The barn was blown to pieces and the horses were tossed around like missiles! The girl in the shelter heard the wind coming hard and bang! She heard *crash boom bang!* The barn was hit, and the frightened horses were screaming! A few seconds later, everything went quiet! The girl cried staying in the shelter, she knows what happened! Then she heard thunder and a hard rain.

Then it stopped and she got out of the shelter and she saw what happened, she was hysterical! The barn and everything in it, was gone! The barn had seven horses, hay, hundreds of pounds of it, and saddles and any equipment used for horses all disappeared! The barn was wiped slate clean to its slabs and her house was untouched by the tornado.

She went looking for her horses and there were only three nearby the other four were long gone! The first horse was thrown into a big oak tree stuck in the tree with a broken neck and branches punched the horse's body and blood dripped down from the tree and the head was hanging off the body. She cried so hysterically she threw up! Then she saw a second horse driven into the ground with its ass upright and a metal fence post driven right up the horse's asshole and out its side in a pool of blood and a raccoon was eating the dead horse! The girl covered her mouth in shock, later she threw up again! Then she saw a third horse wrapped around a telephone pole with no head and she saw the head laying in a brook! She was so hysterical she passed out!

When she woke a short time later, she staggered to her house. She got on her cell phone and there was no service. On the way to her house, she saw fish flapping around on the ground and raccoons were eating them. Then she saw a dead deer with no head and two missing feet and two dead pigs up against a snowbank and she saw blood in the snow! All the trees were blown away and she saw dead birds laying in the snow with black field rats, raccoons and ravens eating them! It was a nightmare in hell this poor girl experienced! She got in her house and she locked the door and she checked her house for damage, and everything was OK. She laid on her bed and she cried herself to sleep.

A few hours later her cell phone was working and there was a warning: "This is a warning from the National Weather Service. An F5 tornado has hit your area and you must evacuate and get help, *beep, beep, beep, beep, beep!* I repeat: this is a warning from the National Weather Service. An F5 tornado has hit your area and you must evacuate and get help. *Beep, beep, beep, beep, beep!*" The girl called 911 crying.

"Hi this is Cindy Atkins and I live at 333 Cornhole, Street Grinnell, IL. A tornado hit all around my house; it hit the barn killing all my horses and animals please help me!!!!"

"Stay where you are! Are you in your home?" asked the 911 dispatcher.

"Yes."

"Stay there a helicopter is coming to get you," said the 911 dispatcher.

The helicopter landed in the girl's driveway to bring her to safety. Emma Grace spawned several tornadoes and wind damage destroyed the town of Grinnell. Farms, schools, malls condos camps and everything was unrecognizable! Trees were blown away and dead animals laid everywhere leaving a trail of destruction; the tornadoes had winds greater than 300 miles per hour! Emma Grace is now a giant killer once again coming up the great lakes making a direct aim at Chicago! It was 11:11 p.m. the night of November 7th, 2022 when the windy city of Chicago gets warning.

Before this fuckin' bitch got into the great lakes the Weather Channel was trying to figure out what this storm is doing because it's even overtaking winter weather and building huge thunderheads and overriding snowstorms and crossing unusual areas and leaving a trail of destruction wherever it goes! Weathermen got together to sort out what is going on and a meeting took place in a conference room at the Weather Channel with men and women who work there.

"Welcome to the Jim Cantore conference room here at the Weather Channel my name is Tim August the head of oceanography and atmosphere cycles. We have a storm that we're not familiar with and we need to find a way to stop what is happening before it kills everybody worldwide! We had hurricanes, typhoons, cyclones across the globe with high winds and tsunami waves many times before but nothing like this!!!!!!!!!!!

"How many people have seen the movie, *The Day After Tomorrow?* The warm and cold weather superstorms with killer tornadoes and basketball size hail and then freezing everything solid and destroying the world! We had many meetings and talks about this movie about could this really happen, and the answers was no! Not quite like that, unless an asteroid about a pretty good size hit the earth blowing a hole in the ozone layer but our magnetic field will keep that from happening! If that was true it would have happened a long time ago and not during our lifetimes! We get hit by meteorites all the time and most of them blow up in the upper atmosphere."

Tim August continued after sneezing and blowing his nose, "Excuse me it's allergy season! The events that happened on that movie may have happened 65 million years ago, but the Weather Channel didn't exist during the dinosaur days!" Everyone in the room laughed hysterically! Then Tim August continued after sneezing and blowing his nose again!

"Excuse me again! Well ladies and gentlemen I hate to disappoint you, but this event has happened just like on the movie in our own atmosphere!!!!!!!!! Hurricane Emma Grace was born on August 20th and she's still going! Before this storm left the African coast Emma Grace killed a thousand people dropping hail from violent thunderstorms bigger than duck pin bowling balls and hit a resort and an erupting volcano with nuclear warheads stored there and blew the volcano and the island out of the water setting the upper atmosphere on fire and causing a mega blast sinking ships and killing thousands triggering tsunami waves!

"The blast dried up Emma Grace pushing the storm so high in the sky the flames burned their way out during the fallout. When cooling occurred in the stratosphere the fires finally burned out and when the dust fell back down to the water the hurricane started up again and went on its attack! This storm has radiation, sulfur deposits and volcanic materials and the energy is so severe there is no stopping it! We do not have a plane that can fly that high to put the flames out the only hope we have is when this storm moves up the great lakes and dies out when she reaches Canada or very cold air

"Right now, Emma Grace is a strong hurricane ready to hit Chicago and we have planes flying in her right now. This storm has 120 mile per hour winds, that's very unusual that far north! Emma Grace has been coming and going and hanging around for almost three months!! It is very scary! This storm killed about 60,000 people and the death toll may never be known and there are more than three million still missing!

"The Caribbean, Dominican Republic, Cuba and other islands were buried. Miami was destroyed, New Orleans was blown off the face of the earth and Atlanta was buried under 50 feet of water and the Bahama islands were evacuated from sink holes and Bermuda was devastated before New York City took the brunt of Emma Grace extracting all the water out of the Hudson River and dumped it on Manhattan burying New York under 50 feet of water. The storm emptied the ocean tossing fish, sea life and birds into buildings! A man was killed by a shark attack inside Yankee Stadium, what's the chance of that happening!!!!!!!? Then the storm hit New Jersey, Maryland, Pennsylvania before crossing the Ohio River and up the great lakes! The University of Maryland was hit by tornadoes and the city of Baltimore suffered severe damage. Two Penn State basketball players were sucked out of an arena when the roof was blown off during the game. Then the city of Grinnell was destroyed by violent weather and now Chicago is about to be hit!

"If you believe the events from the movie, *The Day After Tomorrow* were bad, Emma Grace is much worse! Who would ever believe a hurricane would do this kind of damage! This storm blew up mountains, that's unheard of! We have no defense against Emma Grace! The thunderstorms are more than 20 miles high to pull down so much cold air to fuel this hurricane to keep going anywhere it wants! The scary thing about this storm his how it's pushing cold fronts backwards to find more water to accelerate! We have a report from our planes the storm has hit Chicago."

"Aircraft 3253, what do we have, Tim August over!?"

"We have circulation and the front part of the storm has hit buildings and broke windows and some roofs were torn off and some boats were destroyed from 85 mile per hour sustained winds and we have thunder and lightning and we are flying in the eye right now and the rest of the storm was downgraded to 100 mph winds and we will be exiting the storm soon because it's beginning to get dark. Ron Justin, air 130 flight 3253, over."

"10/4, Tim August, over."

13   THE NORTHBOUND STORMS

On November 7th at 4:37 p.m. the storm hits Chicago like a bomb and many people were caught by surprise! It was a beautiful sunny day and it was 62 degrees and fishing vessels and tour boats were out in the water until storm warnings brought them back in. Everything was shut down in the city and signs were warning people to take cover, Emma Grace is coming! And a deep freeze will follow everyone must get inside.

People on the late shift in office buildings looked out the window and saw rain pounding on the windows and bright fast flashes of lightning and heard a howling wind.

A custodian was cleaning a conference room in one of the skyscrapers with a big picture window about 60 floors high and he was watching the storm outside and the rain was hitting the window so hard it was ready to break the window was vibrating in and out then a bright flash of lightning lit the sky up like daylight and suddenly a strong gust of wind came and blew the window in!

The custodian tried to grab on to a table, but he was sucked out to his death just like that! Emma Grace grazed a few buildings breaking windows and ripped a few roofs off! A couple tornadoes touched down to help with the destruction! Lightning struck boats in Lake Michigan. The workers took the elevator down to the ground floor in the building where they lost one of their workers, the custodian. They were in the mechanical room to have their dinner and turned on the TV to watch the news.

"Warning, this is NBC News, Hurricane Emma Grace is hitting Chicago with 100 mile per hour winds damaging buildings, boats and beach fronts. This is an unusual hurricane in the great lakes and the worst storm ever on earth and this storm is heading straight up Lake Michigan threatening to strike Michigan and Wisconsin and she may merge with Winter Storms Benjamin and Clitina," said NBC news before the lights went out.

The workers used Black and Decker bright flashlights for lighting and to get around.

The custodian has not come down yet and it's time to go home and the workers kept calling his name: "Kevin, Kevin, Kevin!!!!!!!!!" No answer!

One worker said to another, "He must have gone home already. I am not walking up 60 flights of stairs, fuck that!!!!!!!"

The workers went up the stairs to the ground floor to leave the building and water got inside the building and the city of Chicago looked like a flowing river! Trees were blown through city streets and cars, trucks and buses were floating by them crashing into one another and leaving a pile like bowling pins laying in a pit!

One worker said, "Oh my fuckin' god!!"

Another worker said, "I guess we're not going anywhere!"

Then the eye of Emma Grace passed over and a bright full moon shining over the damage and flooding in Chicago.

A helicopter flew over and a voice came from a loudspeaker from the helicopter, calling, "Please get to higher ground, a tsunami is coming. I repeat, please get to higher ground a tsunami is coming!"

The workers stranded in the building heard the warning and went up a few floors calling Kevin and there was no answer. The workers took cover on the eighth floor in a room with no windows to protect them for what's to come!

Emma Grace moved up the great lakes and merged with a snowstorm. The snowstorm was big enough to strike Chicago dumping six inches and then the snowstorm left Chicago to meet the very powerful Emma Grace racing up the Great Lakes! A polar vortex dropped temperatures to six degrees freezing. When Emma Grace met the snowstorm, the energy sucked up water from the Great Lakes just like it did in the Hudson River and Chicago was hit by 30-foot waves!

The city was flooded under five feet of water, some areas were under 15 feet of water! Before daybreak the tsunami flooding froze solid as temperatures dipped to 6 below zero! Then Emma Grace met the big snowstorm and raced up Lake Michigan all the way to Canada and a huge winter storm and bitter cold temperatures were coming from Lake Superior. All merged crossing Lake Heron and hit Lake Ontario and struck Toronto dead on; Toronto gets the worst of it!

Later the Emma Grace-winter storm remnants hit upstate NY. Crossing into Vermont, New Hampshire and southern Maine where Willy Bird lives and another whiplash cold front pushes the storm right over Boston. The cold front polar vortex pushes the storm all the way out into the Atlantic Ocean until it reaches the Bermuda Triangle. All the way to Fort Lauderdale Florida where it redevelops into a hurricane where Emma Grace gets her name back. Then she's coming right straight up the fuckin' east coast all the way to Maine before she finally dies in the Canadian Maritimes!

Let's get back to the snowstorm in Lake Michigan, let's not ruin this story!!!!!!!!!

At 5 a.m. on Tuesday November 8th, 2022 the Emma Grace snow-storm ruptured shipping lanes in Lake Michigan and dumped blizzard snows and strong winds causing catastrophic flooding on both coast-lines sinking boats and flooding freezing solid from the bitter cold. Icebreakers were frozen in place. Warnings came across all TV stations in Wisconsin and Michigan from this dangerous winter storm.

"Good morning, we have breaking news at 6 a.m. on Tuesday November 8th. Hurricane Emma Grace struck Chicago with serious wind damage and 30-foot waves caused catastrophic flooding and Winter Storm Benjamin dumped 6 inches of snow in a short time followed by a rare November deep freeze and cars, trucks and buses will be frozen in place in its wake. The city's east side will be shut down until a thaw comes. Boats and beach fronts were totally destroyed! Emma Grace has merged with Winter Storm Benjamin after hitting Chicago and she will get her new name. Benjamin is now striking the Wisconsin coastline with 100 mile per hour winds and dumping six inches of lake effect snow per hour. The town of Degnan better be ready because you're next! Benjamin is expected to merge with Winter Storm Clitina coming off Lake Superior by noon today and become a super snow maker and hit Ontario Canada and Toronto by tonight.

"At 6:08 a.m. this morning the following areas must take cover right away! Dayton WI, Degnan WI, Green Bay WI, Great Gorge WI, Focker WI, Worcester WI, Finger Lake WI, The University of W,I Thunder Bay WI…. Please take shelter at the university barracks if you can get there because these areas may receive more than 10 feet of lake effect snow from Benjamin and Clitina; remnants of Emma Grace by tonight! If you get stuck in these storms later today, you will die! Expect 6 to 10 feet of snow with 100 mile per hour winds, snow drifts 50 feet high and 30 to 60-foot seas! Not to mention, thunder and lightning and snow twisters!!!!! You must get to shelter now before it's too late! Emma Grace has killed nearly a million people and it's the same system! Please take warning. This storm is very dangerous! This is Eric Lynch reporting from the Weather Channel."

At Degnan, Wisconsin 9:30 a.m. on November 8th, people were boarding buses to evacuate. It started thundering then lightning then sleet started falling that quickly turned to snow and two inches fell in less than a half hour! Sand trucks and tractors were plowing the streets right away so people can get to safety. The airport was closed, and the National Guard arrived to help clear the streets. By 11 a.m. there was seven inches of snow on the ground, blowing and drifting and less than a half hour later everything was a standstill, vehicles and snowplows were getting stuck in place! Military helicopters had to rescue their own help and people were still out driving around, fuck them!!!!!!!!

The Green Bay Packers were still practicing in 15 inches of snow at the stadium until the wind picked up drifting snow in minutes and dangerous lightning! The football team went inside to take cover and a bolt of lightning struck a light pole knocking out the electricity! The power was out everywhere and 25 inches of snow had fallen then around 1 p.m. the storm passed and the sun came out but the wind kept howling and blowing snow; the Wisconsin coastline did not get the 10 feet of snow predicted by the Weather Channel as the storm moved out quickly but they did get 10 foot drifts! But they're not out of the woods yet!

The back end of the storm moved up the middle of Lake Michigan, but big waves and bitter cold were on the way. A 40-foot wave struck Degnan burying the town under water, then followed by a 30-foot wave, then a 20 footer then a 10 footer leaving total devastation and when it got dark a deep freeze kicked in freezing everything solid!

Several people came out to help shovel snow when the sun came out and the wind stopped, they saw the big waves coming one after another and people tried running to higher ground, but nobody made it and they were all killed! The snow and drifts were too deep to overcome. Subways were flooded and people were killed, by drowning, and electrocution! More people died from the flooding than the snowstorm. While Wisconsin was getting buried alive around 2p.m.

Military helicopters flew over Chicago to view the damage; it was a sunny afternoon and temperatures warmed to the 30s. The coastline of Chicago was covered in ice with some dead people lying in frozen blocks and cars, trucks, buses and trains frozen in place. The subway was flooded and froze over with dead people in it and trains on their sides.

Gas lines ruptured and there were several fires burning. The west end of Chicago had survivors who evacuated and were also flooded from the giant waves! Several police and fire trucks closed off the city not letting people in. The former Sears tower was damaged with several broken windows. Glass panes from broken windows made a picture show stuck in frozen icebergs! People in the tower high up can look down and see the destruction in lower Chicago and the lake side but the west end was not too bad; some parts just got the snow.

Evening came and the deep freeze froze the Wisconsin coastline solid. Around midnight Benjamin-Emma Grace remnants merged with Winter Storm Clitina and got a new name coming out of Lake Superior, heading to the city of Justine Ontario Canada where it's really gonna get bad and the storm is expected to strike Justine around 4 a.m.

Before dark military helicopters and weather planes flew up on both sides of Lake Michigan to view the damage. There was wave damage and busted boats and damaged buildings in Wisconsin and

Michigan. The damage left a trail of destruction in a pile of snow and ice all the way up Lake Michigan on both sides! The Wisconsin coast got water from the waves; the Michigan coast was hit by ice tsunamis that bowled neighborhoods over like bowling pins with incredible damage and then froze over during the deep freeze! Several people that did not take this storm serious like instructed by news reports were killed!

In Justine, Ontario was a mild day about 45 degrees, and it was nice and sunny but a big mega storm was coming. The city experienced a mild earthquake that triggered gas line ruptures during the day and the gas company turned off the gas to fix the problem and it was successful. They kept the gas off because of the storm that's coming; the city also lost power from the mild earthquake. Then around 8 p.m. on the 8th of November Justine police drove around calling on loud-speakers for everyone to evacuate.

The city had no lights and was in the dark. People lit candles, flash-lights and hurricane lamps for lighting to get around. Bears mountain lions and wolves were crossing neighborhoods where people were, and the police had to shoot them while evacuating people! People heard *pop, pop, pop, bang* while police shot at the animals in wooded areas and told people to get out on loudspeakers.

"May I have your attention please this is the Justine metro police: you must leave your homes and get to higher ground there is a mega lake effect snowstorm coming with 100 mile per hour winds, the storm will reach our area by 4am. Please go to the following areas; Camp Jayglenn ski resort located on Mount Michigan 2200 feet in height, St. Catharine's church located 630 feet level on Mount Michigan and Canadian mounted barracks at the foot of Mount Michigan, you can board shuttles to take you up the mountain to these cites! I repeat, may I have your attention please this is the Justine metro police: you need to leave your homes and get to higher ground there is a mega lake effect snowstorm coming with 100 mile per hour winds, the storm will our area by 4am. Please go to the following areas: Camp Jayglenn ski resort located on Mount Michigan 2200 feet in height, St. Catharine's church located 630 feet on Mount Michigan and Canadian mounted barracks at the foot of Mount Michigan you can board shuttles to take you up the mountain to these cites."

The Justine police drove around all night on loudspeakers with the same message to make sure people get to safety. Shuttle buses followed the police and people boarded them passing in the streets to take them to the mountain Michigan evacuation zones. The police shot animals, such as bears, wolves and mountain lions that got in the way; the animals were trying to get to safety because they also knew that a big storm is coming.

People in Chicago were escorted to the United Center before the evacuation to get food and keep warm. Football and baseball stadiums were open for people to get help and food. In Michigan the National Guard closed off areas damaged by ice tsunamis from Emma Grace-Benjamin. The evacuees were taken by buses to the big house where the University of Michigan plays football. During games they were thrown out! In Wisconsin it was the same there. People were being rescued from flood waters and bused to higher ground. Several people were killed in the floods and frozen to death from the cold.

Midnight, Wednesday November 9th, 2022. Winter Storm Benjamin who took over from Hurricane Emma Grace merged with Winter Storm Clitina coming out of Lake Superior. Now Justine Ontario Canada is next. Airplanes flew in the eye of this storm to warn shipping lanes that something bad is coming.

Clitina is now a super storm carrying 60-foot waves and dumping 10 inches of snow per hour dragging across the Great Lakes; more indescribable damage from tsunami waves hitting the coast of northern Michigan and 140 mph winds with incredible lightning. This fuckin' bitch is taking its sweet fuckin' time building into a super fuckin' monster sucking up so much water from upper Lake Michigan. Panicking coastlines were waiting for this bitch for hours!!!!!!!!!!!!!!!!!

Emma Grace-Benjamin is showing this giant how it's done! Suck up as much water as possible and drown everybody in its wake burying cities under her terror, just like Emma Grace did!!!!!!!!!! On November 9th at 4:07 a.m., police were driving around the evacuation zone in Justine and it was clear with a light wind and 42 degrees. A half hour later there was no change in the weather.

One cop said to another, "Where the hell is this snowstorm?"

At 4:44 a.m., a policeman was looking at his watch when suddenly a chill and fast-moving clouds were coming covering the moon and now it's overcast. By 5 a.m., policemen were parked at Tim Horton's coffee shop and were drinking coffee and eating breakfast. A few minutes later it was pouring! The TV was on at Tim Horton's and the policemen were watching the news.

"Good morning this is the Canadian United National Trust TV News report. We have breaking news; a killer winter storm is on the way. The city of Justine must take cover immediately! This storm is going to hit Justine dead on! Expect heavy snow, 5 to 10 inches per hour, 100 mile per hour winds, thunder and lightning, and 50-foot waves. Then a deep freeze to follow! Winter Storm Clitina is the same system from Hurricane Emma Grace and Winter Storm Benjamin. Emma Grace has caused worldwide destruction killing an estimated 3,000,000 people! Please get to higher ground at this time; Justine is now under a tsunami warning and a severe thunderstorm warning. Please take cover right now! This is Victoria Tiverton reporting."

Right after the news report, the rain was really coming down and then lightning and then it got brighter then thunder and more lightning then sleet was coming down and then it was getting windy and the thunder was getting louder and the lightning was very bright!

One of the policemen said, "We better get out of here and get up to Jayglenn's before we get trapped here this storm is getting bad!"

The policemen paid their tab and left. The employees of Tim Horton's hurried to get everyone out and close the coffee shop to get to higher ground.

At 5:35 a.m. the wind started howling and 30-foot waves struck the coastline smashing boats marinas and neighborhoods in low lying areas. A policeman was sleeping in his police car when he heard a roar and it was snowing. He heard water gurgling and he started his police car and he sped off in time putting his police flashers on and racing uphill before the tsunami caught him; he saw the big waves in the rearview mirror! At 6:08 that morning, the storm arrived in Justine and so did the waves almost catching a policeman sleeping! Policemen are not supposed to be sleeping in their cars anyway!

Before the storm and waves came the military's mounted marines were preparing the evacuated residents of Justine at a hotel motor lodge at Jayglenn Ski Resort sitting near a big fireplace.

"Good morning, my name is General Kevin Gold from the Canadian mounted marines. We have a good fire going and continental breakfast will be served buffet style after a brief message.

"We have a bad lake effect snowstorm coming from a storm system that's been around for three months. It began as a hurricane that came off the African coast and it hit an erupting volcano with nuclear warheads stored there and causing a mega explosion blowing a hole in the ozone layer and became a mega storm going out of control. Hurricane Emma Grace killed as many as 3,000,000 people and caused mega destruction along the east coast and the storm was strong enough to come inland until finding water again and strengthening back into a hurricane until meeting Winter Storm Benjamin before merging with newly formed Winter Storm Clitina and now we have a mega hurricane-snowstorm!

"We need to take this storm very seriously. If you go outside right now, you may not come back! This storm demolished cities, look what it did to New York. It has blown up mountains and blew islands out of the water! We're in the direct path of this storm this is why we're here. When it's over the city of Justine may not be there! This storm system is the worst ever on earth. Hurricane Emma Grace had wind gusts over 300 miles per hour. Now we have a snowstorm that is more than 1500 miles wide bigger than Lake Superior coming right at us.

"The storm is here and it's snowing, and we have thunder and lightning. Stay away from windows because we're expecting 100 mile per hour winds and blizzard- whiteout conditions. We have 1500 people here and we may be stuck here until spring. We have no electricity and no gas, but we do have plenty of wood to burn for cooking. The hotel is heated with pellet stoves and lighting and hot water from generators. We have bunkers, the hotel basement will hold a lot of people. We all need to come together as a team and help one another until this disaster passes. We're expecting 10 inches of snow per hour and 100 feet on the ground when it's over is not out of the question! Be prepared because something really bad is coming. Get in line to get your food. Thank you," said General Kevin Gold.

People waited in line for the breakfast buffet and General Gold kept giving instructions throughout the day and people sat in front of fireplaces to keep warm. By 7:30 a.m. there were 15 inches of snow and wind blowing snow drifts up against the windows. Lightning was flashing in all kinds of colors, pink, yellow, green, blue and purple with very loud pounding thunder. By 9 a.m. there was three feet of snow on the ground and one hour later the storm was at full force now there's five feet of snow on the ground and the drifts covered the hotel windows all the way up to the fourth floor. The wind was blowing 100 miles per hour blowing and drifting snow at record heights. Wooden structured buildings and homes were blown away from the wind. There were snow tornadoes helping with the destruction! Huge waves buried low line areas, drowning everything standing. A man was sleeping in a sleeping bag and he was buried in the snow. Roaming animals were stuck and buried alive in snow drifts. Three feet of additional snow fell by 1 p.m. before the storm passed and the sky cleared. Justine got 8 to 10 feet of snow on the ground and drifts 50 feet high. Then a deep freeze and a lot of damage!

14   THE CANADIAN EXPRESS

The storm moved toward Lake Ontario and Toronto is Clitina's next target; the same storm is now called the Canadian Express keeping her name. The winds from Clitina calmed down a lot but the snow and thunderstorms are still dangerous! C.U.N.T. news in Toronto had warnings from the coming storm; the TV station is located at the top of the Canadian National Tower.

The next morning was Thursday November 10th, 2022. It was a sunny mild day about 50 degrees and people were out walking around going to coffee shops and people were going to work. At 9 a.m. cruise ships were pulling into port coming in from China to get ready for a Chinese festival in downtown Toronto, the city is expecting a big crowd this weekend because the United States will be celebrating Veteran's Day tomorrow. Tents were set up and tied down getting ready for the festival and workers were working on the outdoor ice rink and making ice sculptures. Wood structures were being set up and painted. Concert stages were being set up outside and in the Rodgers Center where the Toronto Bluejays baseball team plays. A newscast came over the billboard inside the Rodgers Center.

"Good morning, this is the Canadian United National Trust TV News. A deadly snowstorm is heading for Toronto the same storm system from Hurricane Emma Grace that destroyed the U.S. eastern coastline that leveled New York City! The city of Justine received at least 8 feet of snow in less than 24 hours with winds over 100 miles per hour and 50-foot drifts from Winter Storm Clitina. This storm is now called the Canadian Express and the winds from this superstorm have been downgraded to 40 to 50 miles per hour but still dumping heavy snow and strong thunderstorms. This storm is still very dangerous. There is no need to evacuate but you must take this storm serious because of its history. We are expecting strong winds, heavy snow and violent thunderstorms; snow drifts and serious flooding. Please be advised, C.U.N.T. news reporting!"

Cruise ship Ding Dong Tours from the island of Q'klitores came to visit Toronto and the tour got off and their first visit was the Canadian tower.

"Good afternoon welcome to the city of Toronto Ontario Canada. The Canadian United National Trust TV news station is located on the top floor of this tower and the tower is named the Canadian united national tower and the number one bank is the Canadian United National Trust Bank! C.U.N.T. It is not under a nice name, but it is what it is!

"Let's take the elevator to the restaurant where breakfast will be served." said Chi Chung. Translators spoke in Chinese.

The elevators took the tour up to the restaurant to eat pancakes, French toast muffins, orange juice and coffee. The sky was a clear day turn to a yellow color, then gray, then green and then a brown color, the wind picked up and then it stopped, and the sky cleared up again and it was a blue sky!

Everything was OK on Thursday afternoon on the 10th of

November. The two went on a tour with trolley trains that took tourists through downtown Toronto. A few hours later it was dinner time at the tower and the men and other visitors were arriving before dinner before 5 p.m. People were sitting down, and bottles of red and white wine came out first, then salad, then chicken soup, pasta, French fries, then chicken roast beef and oven baked potatoes or rice was served, and the restaurant was packed with people! Everyone was enjoying a nice family style chicken dinner in the tower restaurant when suddenly the storm was coming.

It started out with rain. Then around 7 p.m. lightning was seen and then thunder. The lightning was getting brighter and it was getting windy. Crowds line up ready to board the elevator to go up to the tower restaurant waiting in heavy rain and thunderstorms overcrowding the elevators. Suddenly a loud bang of thunder and the elevators jolted, and people were screaming; it felt like the elevators were going to break off! Then when the elevators got to the restaurant and the doors opened everyone clapped.

One woman said, "Oh, god, we made it!!"

Another lady said to the elevator director, "Take me back down, I lost my appetite!"

Every table was filled and dinner is ready to be served. The storm is here and looking out the windows you can see fast moving clouds below and flashes of lightning! The restaurant started rotating around and classical music was playing while people were eating. The lights were dimmed lower and restaurant waiters and waitresses were lighting candles. Then the wind outside was howling and the restaurant was shaking and rocking, and people started screaming!

"Ladies and gentlemen don't worry about the rocking and shaking it's always like this when there's a storm everyone you'll be OK!" said the restaurant manager. Then the crowd quieted down.

Then a wild display of colorful lightning flashes. People looked down at the fast-moving cloud deck and looking up you can see the moon and stars as the tower restaurant disc kept rotating around and backwards.

A woman had too much to drink and she got up from her table and she walked over to the edge and she looked out the window and a gust of wind shook the restaurant and she lost her balance and she fell up against the window. A waitress helped her get up and she staggered back to her seat and she threw up all over the place. Finally, she was removed by the staff! A few people were disgusted with her behavior. The area was cleared and cleaned up and the restaurant smelled like puke!

Outside it started to sleet and then it was snowing. People were waiting for elevators to go up to the tower restaurant and some were getting off. The restaurant was still packed with people and suddenly the lights blinked off and on and people are screaming! Then a lightning bolt shot out of the top of the clouds hitting the windows shaking the restaurant tower violently! People were screaming hysterically and getting away from the windows! Then this bright flash of lightning followed by a loud bang!

The lights went out for good because lightning struck the main generator of the tower and the elevators packed with people stopped and stuck midway up high above the Rodgers Center and the tower was swinging back and forth jerking against the tower elevator cables. The wind was blowing so hard the cables were ready to break the elevator windows. They were in the clouds stuck up there and the lightning was so bright you could not look at it. People were screaming and crying stuck on the elevators! People were hysterical in the restaurant and candles and lightning flashes was the only light.

The restaurant crew was talking among themselves. "This is not a normal storm nothing like this has ever happened, we may be in trouble!" The manager came out with a loudspeaker to try to calm the crowd down.

"Ladies and gentlemen, we lost power just stay calm. We're having an unusual storm this evening, just stay in your seats and we will get you out of here when we get the lights back on. The generators take time to come back on, as soon as the storm passes, we will get you out of here safely!"

People were getting sick and throwing up and the tower restaurant smells like puke again! Then a vicious massive lightning bolt struck and smashed a window and people were getting sucked out like a vacuum! Others tried to hold on for their lives and the entire restaurant was in ruins; more windows gave way and part of the tower roof started to give way and more people were getting sucked out to their deaths along with tables and glass breaking everywhere! The manager tied himself to a pole to avoid being sucked out as he watched the horror in shock crying!

Then another positively massive lightning bolt coming out of the top of the clouds struck the freight elevator packed with people snapping the cables sending 50 people to their deaths! The elevator landed on top of the Rodgers Center smashing into pieces and going through the roof and landing inside! People laid dead, splattered guts on the Rodgers Center floor and the falling freight elevator left a big hole in the roof.

The lightning strike also set fire to the restaurant forcing people to jump to their deaths! Fire wrapped around the restaurant finally triggering sprinklers and some people were still in the restaurant holding onto things to avoid being sucked out! A little while later the storm moved away heading for Niagara Falls and Buffalo, New York.

The news warned about a dangerous storm coming with

thunderstorms and 50 to 60 mile per hour winds; there was no need to evacuate but the storm was still dangerous, however when it came back over water it picked up speed rapidly with 100 mile per hour winds with gusts as high as 160 and dumping over two feet of snow in Toronto and drifts 10 to 15 feet making it hard for fire and police and emergency vehicles to get through getting stuck in snow drifts leaving Toronto in a disaster zone!

Firemen went up skyscrapers to try to put the flames from the tower restaurant, but it was way out of reach! There was no way to get to the tower fire until the storm goes away. The fire has to burn its way out until the storm is over.

Two hours after the storm fire helicopters flew up to help put out the flames and the fires were finally out but smoke was still smoldering. Rescue helicopters arrived to rescue people left in the restaurant after fire helicopters hosed down the smoldering ash! It was a scary scene getting people out in rescue baskets and fire helicopters continued to hose down hot spots. It took hours for rescues to reach the dead because the snow was so bad and too deep! Finally, military earth mobiles with giant plows arrived to push the snow and clear streets in downtown Toronto and city snowplows followed. Police on loudspeakers warned there is a curfew for 24 hours. Some dead bodies were found in the snow laying in blood and broken up dead bodies and splattered guts were found!

"Oh my god! These dead bodies leaped from the tower on fire!" a fireman said to a police officer.

"I know, it's 9/11 all over again! We got a lot of cleaning up to do!" said the cop.

People in the Rodgers Center restaurant and hotel had to be evacuated when the freight elevator fell through the roof killing all those people! The Rodgers Center is used for an evacuation shelter if something happens in Toronto. Sirens were sounding all over the city when the tower restaurant was struck by lightning setting it afire! People on the ground were in shock from what they were seeing!

The first thing people did in the rain, sleet and slushy snow was head to the Rodgers Center but were chased away by the Canadian Mounted Police for safety reasons and were told to get into a warm building somewhere. Later people were still coming to get in the Rodgers Center and the doors were locked. A few minutes later was when the freight elevator struck by lightning blew off the tower restaurant and falling through the roof, setting off alarms and sirens all night long and would be ignored until the storm is over and the streets are cleared.

The next day was November 11th, Friday, 2022. About 10 a.m. the police fire trucks and rescuers made it to the Rodgers Center ready for the disaster that followed! Police and rescue rushed in to see the indescribable nightmare!!!!!!! The band Coldplay from England was playing tonight; not now!!! The freight elevator landed on their equipment smashing it into pieces with dead body parts blood and guts hanging everywhere! And bodies splattered in a pool of blood on the floor and hanging from the rafters; believe it or not one person was still alive, and he was rescued.

The Rodgers Center stunk like rotten flesh and workers were getting sick and puking all over the place adding to the horrible smell!!!!!!!!!! The rescue police and firemen opened all the doors to ease the stench and had to wear masks and special equipment to remove the dead. Birds flew in and animals from outside helping the cleanup!

Ravens, raccoons and foxes all came in for dinner eating up loose body parts and the guts! Later dogs came in to join the feast and bobcats as rescue workers and coroners were removing the body parts and then the animals were doing a good job eating the leftovers, but they were fighting with one another and multiplying! You wonder where all these animals come from with two or three feet of snow on the ground and going into buildings. The workers were trying to get the animals out until they started getting aggressive!

Then the firemen came in with fire cannons spraying fire at them and all the animals ran out of the Rodgers Center in a hurry! Then they closed the doors to keep all the creatures out! Other firemen were using fire extinguishers to put out fires the fire cannons made.

The band's equipment was demolished! The speakers were smashed, and the drums and guitars were smashed into pieces. The band Coldplay was very upset over what happened. Body parts and blood and guts laid in the ruins! The damaged equipment was moved, and the Rodgers Center floor was hosed down and cleaned up. All the events are canceled for the remainder of the weekend. The restaurant, stores, mall and the hotel in the Rodgers Center was roped off and closed.

Residents and visitors had to board buses with skis on them and were taken to the Raptors arena where the Toronto Raptors and Maple Leaves play to evacuate the city. Later in the day about 1:30 p.m. the sun came out and the temperature rose to 50 degrees and the snow was melting. All the events this weekend are canceled! All the Chinese dragons and tents were damaged or blown away!

Nobody thought this storm would be this bad! Everywhere it goes it kills thousands of fuckin' people!!!!!!! But they were aware that danger was coming! Windows in downtown Toronto were blown out in some building and roofs were ripped off! Winter Storm Clitina-Canadian Express came through with 160 mile per hour wind gusts and whiplash thunderstorms leaving a trail of unimaginable destruction; the same storm system from hurricane Emma Grace!

Now Niagara Falls is next. Niagara on the lake is a beautiful nice and clean city with 6 inches of snow on the ground and a peaceful evening and it was a Friday night and danger was lurking not far away. People were at a pub bar eatery watching a hockey game on TV. The Buffalo Sabres were playing the Toronto Maple Leaves and it was a 2-2 game with less than two minutes to play when all of a sudden, the game was interrupted by breaking news.

Someone at the bar yelled, "Did you hear what happen in Toronto last night?!"

"Good evening, we have breaking news on the Canadian United National Trust news network! Winter Storm Clitina, the Canadian Express, a very dangerous storm, struck Toronto leaving a trail of destruction and killed hundreds of people last night. Lightning struck the Canadian United National Tower—"

While people were watching the news, the lights went out and Niagara on the lake went pitch dark! Then it got very quiet. People slowly got out of the bar with only candles lit. The snow shadows helped people get to their cars to leave then a bright flash of lightning then thunder and then it started raining turning to freezing rain before turning to snow.

People started driving uphill and a police car arrived, and the police said on a loudspeaker, "Everybody drive uphill away from the water, a bad storm is coming!"

The cop made the announcement over and over until the streets were clear. The owners of the bar eatery living above the bar finished cleaning up under candlelight ignoring the police warnings. Blew out the candles when they finished cleaning and went upstairs to bed. It was a couple that owned the pub. It was thundering and lightning and sleet pounding outside, then it stopped, and it got quiet. *The storm is reloading by sucking the water out of Lake Ontario.*

A loud roar was heard, and the ground was shaking and vibrating just when the couple got to bed. They got up and got dressed and ran down to their car when suddenly a wall of ice-cold water washed them away! The couple was killed instantly, before they left the pub and it was all gone in seconds!!!!!!!

A 30-foot wave washed Niagara on the lake away in minutes and a series of big waves after that! Homes and businesses were washed away before their eyes leaving devastation and death in low line areas then the storm was over but not before 50 mph winds and a deep freeze froze the city solid! Temperatures dropped below zero and the city was frozen under 5 feet of ice and the trees were frozen solid and power lines froze and broke off. The back end of the storm stayed over water dumping feet of snow and 100 mph winds heading for its next target, Niagara Falls.

Back to Niagara on the lake, police fire and rescue went to the damaged area and it was flooded! Fires broke out because of broken power lines from the ice. The Canadian Express hit Niagara Falls with heavy snow powerful wind and dangerous thunderstorms. About 3 a.m. on the 12th of November a foot of snow fell on the city of Niagara Falls Canada; by 6 a.m. 4 feet of snow was falling in Buffalo, NY. And it was coming down at 6 inches per hour! The storm stalled over Lake Erie and unloaded over Buffalo, NY. Lightning struck buildings in Niagara Falls and snow-covered streets and then the cold and everything was iced over and the city lost power leaving a mess. *At least no one died in the paradise of Canada!*

A different story in Buffalo that's getting buried in tons of snow! Snowplows went to work right away moving snow and getting stuck because the snow was coming down so hard it was a blanket of white and the blowing and drifting and 100 mph winds made things impossible to move. People out in the storm died there! By 9 a.m. there was 7 feet of snow on the ground and it was coming down even harder with thunder and lightning! Lightning struck buildings down as snow was burying them, even homes buried in snow was struck by lightning and snow drifts higher than 50 feet. By 4 p.m. on November 12 there was 13 feet of snow on the ground and drifts over 100 feet blowing off of Lake Erie and Lake Ontario.

At Ralph Wilson Stadium snowplows and heat machines worked all day and night to get ready for the Jets, Bills game on Sunday at 1p.m.; the heat machines melted the snow and ice so the game can be played. By game time it was still snowing but the wind stopped and Buffalo received 22 feet of snow and 150 foot drifts before it was finally over but the game was still on and people made their own seats in the snow because there was so much! Believe it or not the stadium was filled.

The game was tied at 7-7 by halftime and the snow was letting up but thunder was still heard then the sky cleared, and this fuckin' storm was finally over! The sun came out by the second half and the temperature was 9 degrees. It was 17 to 17 at the end of regulation and the game went into overtime and no one scored, four field goals were missed by both teams and the game ended in a tie. All that mad rush to beat the deep snow to see the Buffalo Bills play the New York Jets and nobody wins!

The storm moved north toward Watertown, New York near Lake Ontario but stayed inland striking Watertown with a minimal snowstorm with light winds and thunder. Snow crossed into Vermont meeting another cold front pushed the storm into the White Mountains of New Hampshire, where it stalled and dumped more than 5 feet of snow before moving on.

It was now six p.m. Sunday November 13th, 2022. The football players and fan followers inside Ralph Wilson Stadium watched the news on TV at a restaurant located in an underground bunker in the basement of the stadium.

"Good evening: we have breaking news from Winter Storm Clitina-Canadian Express on NBC. Buffalo received more than 20 feet of lake effect snow which is not a surprise the way the storm came in with some very dangerous wind and lightning damage! We do not know how much damage came from this winter storm or have any reports of deaths. Homes and businesses were struck by lightning even through heavy snow.

"The Bills-Jets game went on as usual despite 150-foot snowdrifts in some areas. Fans came into Ralph Wilson Stadium in snowmobiles. Snowplows were getting stuck and the city is at a standstill. This is the same storm system from hurricane Emma Grace for the last three months and it's leading up the damage in winter storms. Niagara Falls Canada received 14 inches of snow and ice. But no reports of deaths but Niagara on the lake was hit hard with snow and ice and big waves then a solid freeze, there were reports of deaths there, but we do not know how many.

"On Thursday November 10th lightning struck the Canadian Tower restaurant killing hundreds of people and a crowded freight elevator was struck by lightning and landed on the roof of the Rodgers Center going through the roof killing several people in Toronto. Three feet of snow fell there and winds over 100 miles per hour broke windows and ripped roofs off of buildings canceling all events for the rest of the Veterans Day weekend.

"Clitina devastated the city of Justine dumping 8 to 10 feet of snow with 50 to 60-foot drifts and severe flooding from big waves leaving a trail of death and destruction. The city may be buried until spring. The east side of Chicago was devastated by this storm where several people have died and froze to death! This is the worst storm of all time. We will keep you posted for updates. NBC news reporting!"

The people that were at the game were trapped there living in tunnels and the football team stayed in the locker rooms or some-where in the stadium. The NY Jets football team was airlifted from the stadium and flown back to Metlife Stadium where it was raining. People cannot go to their homes for a long time until this fuckin' snow melts, in Buffalo! Some tunnels lead to storm drains that lead to some homes. Everything is snowed in: the city is buried!

People at home had to get out on their roofs to shovel the snow off so their homes many don't collapse! People rode in snow mobiles to help others push the snow off of roofs. Heavy earth mobiles came in to start plowing and removing snow to get to stuck vehicles and some people were found dead in their cars. Military earth power plows had to push and remove snow and dump it in Lake Erie to get through Buffalo. In Buffalo they do a good job removing snow. In Niagara Falls everything was back to normal by the end of the day.

Monday November 14th, 2022. Removal was going well in Buffalo but the city of Niagara on the lake was a disaster zone buried under a lake of ice! Trucks dumped sand and salt to get to the lower end of the city by the lake. Ice breakers came in from Lake Ontario to break up the ice from the tidal waves and trees; homes and villages were destroyed, and the ice was removed so the city can get back to normal. The ice was placed on barges and taken out on Lake Ontario to be dumped! Some dead bodies were found from people who drown when the unexpected waves struck! The upper end of Niagara on the lake survived.

A big clock in a park outside upper Niagara on the lake read 11:11 a.m. on Monday November 14th and the temperature was 42 degrees. It was a nice and sunny day. The weather got better in the hard-hit areas so cleanup can be done. In Toronto most of the city was cleaned up. A lot of snow melted, and debris and broken glass was removed along with all the dead bodies! The Rodgers Center was cleaned up and the doors will be locked for the rest of the winter.

The only thing untouched was the Canadian tower. One elevator was working; the one that goes to the TV station at the top of the tower. Rescue helicopters dropped off rescue workers to find any more dead bodies in the damaged restaurant and a few more were removed in bags and taken away. The Toronto firemen removed fire debris from the fires and window workers were removing broken windowpanes and installing new windows.

The roof on the Rodgers Center was being repaired and a new freight elevator was installed to bring new tables, chairs and restaurant furniture up to the restaurant. A sign at the Rodgers Center read: "the Tower Restaurant will reopen in two weeks" in English and in French. It was a slow process in Justine the city was snowed in and flooded and would probably be that way until spring. Chicago recovered during the thaw.

15   THE CURSE OF EMMA GRACE

It was Tuesday November 15, 2022. Lincoln, New Hampshire. A meeting at a ski lodge with park rangers about the coming storm. The sky turned very dark and it was snowing hard with a light wind but there was lightning and thunder. Skiers were wrapping up for the day and went to the lodge, took their equipment off and went to dinner and the meeting followed. The restaurant in the lodge had a nice big warm fireplace going and everyone gathered in front when the meeting took place; there were only 10 people there.

"Good evening ladies and gentlemen welcome to the Lincoln Lodge. It's a slow day and evening here, but the 7 inches of snow today makes skiers delight. My name is Mike Hunt the head ranger here at Lincoln ski lodge. We have a big snowstorm coming this evening and we need to take this storm very seriously! This storm is the remnants of Hurricane Emma Grace, Winter Storm Clitina and the great Canadian Express! This storm is coming here; that's right we're next! This storm system has been tearing up the east coast and the Midwest for the last three months! It is not as bad as it has been but it's a very tricky storm. We're expecting 3 to 5 feet of snow here in the White Mountains tonight also expecting white out conditions strong winds and thunderstorms.

"Vermont got 4 feet of snow earlier today and lightning strikes did some damage setting fires. A barn was struck in Bourne, Vermont by lightning and killing more than a dozen horses! This storm was worse than any storm anywhere on earth! Hurricane Emma Grace killed an estimated 3,000,000 people; it leveled the Caribbean, Miami, New Orleans, Bermuda, the Bahamas and New York City to a point where there is nothing left! Emma Grace had 300 mph winds and 150-foot waves and spawned more than 50,000 tornadoes! On August 22nd, 2022, Emma Grace blew a volcano and island in the Caribbean out of the ocean and setting the sky on fire for two weeks!

"The storm was strong enough to reach the Ohio River and came up the Great Lakes merging with Winter Storm Clitina and it blew away the east side of Chicago, buried parts of Canada alive in more than 10 feet of snow and tearing up parts of Toronto killing thousands of people. The storm had radioactive positive lightning strikes coming out the top of the clouds and blew the windows out of the Canadian Tower restaurant sucking people out like a vacuum! Also, a freight elevator was struck by lightning and landing through the roof of the Rodgers Center killing everyone aboard! The restaurant was also struck by lightning setting the place on fire killing the remaining people there! The horror was so bad people had to leap to their deaths!

"Then the storm hit Niagara Falls burying them in a foot of ice then Buffalo was buried alive under more the 20 feet of lake affect snow and 100 mph winds. The Jets and Bills game was played believe it or not, that's a surprise! The game ended in a 17-17 overtime tie. Lightning hit buildings and people were found dead there too! The storm weakened on November 13th, but Vermont got whacked with heavy snow and violent thunderstorms burning buildings and killing animals!

"Tonight, it's our turn. The storm is here right now, it's snowing and there are thunderstorms coming. We may escape most of the wind but take this storm seriously! It has killed millions of people! I want to warn you when you go skiing tomorrow watch out for avalanches because the weather warmed up and now there's 3 to 5 feet of snow coming during the night and then it's going to get really cold. Wet snow and powder snow move fast when it's heavy and deep. Tonight, the ski lifts are closed and all day tomorrow because of this storm! If you want to go skiing tomorrow, you go at your own risk! Thank you, this meeting is adjourned. Enjoy the nice warm fire and the bar is open until 1am," said Ranger Mike Hunt.

The next day the skiers ignored Mike Hunt's warning and they went skiing anyway! After breakfast they were off. About 4 feet of snow fell during the night and it was still snowing, and it was coming down pretty good with a few cracks of thunder! At 10 o'clock in the morning the skiers enjoyed a great time skiing in the deep fluffy snow downhill and cross-country skiing.

About a mile away in their adventure there was lightning, and a bolt fried a tree and one skier almost went through it! He was screaming after the strike; the skiers made it back to the lodge in fright because of more lightning and very loud thunder roaring through the mountains and lightning strikes everywhere! The skiers were a mile and a half from the lodge when the thunderstorms came and they had to ski very fast, like they were racing, fearing they would get struck by lightning in the open field. The skiers made it safely back to the lodge.

Mike Hunt said to them, "Are you people crazy going out in this weather?!"

Later in the day it was still snowing, and the skiers waited until the storm passed, they ate lunch and sat in front of a warm fire in the fireplace. Then around 4 p.m. the storm passed, and the sun came out and half of the skiers fell asleep in front of the fireplace the others watched TV or played video games and playing cards; those who woke up joined in with the games. Mike Hunt was putting more wood in the fireplace to get a good fire going! Later a steak dinner was served with drinks, martinis, Manhattans, vodka drinks, beer and wine.

Then around 8 p.m. the skiers went out again using bright Black and Decker flashlights hooked up to their helmets and they skied until midnight enjoying five feet of fresh snow. It was 10 degrees when they got to the lodge just after midnight and they went to the bar and party in front of the fireplace for the rest of the night eating snacks and playing games. The next day the ski resort reopened and buses with more skiers arrived and it got crowded. The ski lifts were open, and the Lincoln resort was in full swing again.

Thursday November 17th, 2022. A cold front crossing over Maine met with a nor'easter coming up the coast and the remnants from Emma Grace got caught in the middle of the coastal storm and the coming deep freeze. The coastal storm was rain and the remnants from Emma Grace-Clitina and the Canadian Express has light snow. It meets the deep freeze cold front and turns the snow into ice then it meets the warm nor'easter off the coast of southern Maine and the storm turns into a triple whammy superstorm off the coast of Maine. *This is the cold front that will push the remnants of Emma Grace out to sea all the way to the Bermuda Triangle and it re-intensifies and she gets her name back and starts over until she finally dies right where she met this cold front.*

The University of Southern Maine really gets it!!!!!!! Then Boston Massachusetts will be next before the storm gets pulled out to sea after striking Boston. The weatherman does not know what these storms are going to do. The Canadian Express was a dying storm by itself and a rainstorm was coming up away from the Maine coast and the cold front was on its way. At 2 p.m. on the 17th, it was a clear day with a few passing clouds and a mild day in the 40s, the forecast is calling for a clear and very cold night.

At 6:22 p.m. on the campus of Southern Maine University, students were walking through campus and it was snowing quickly turning to freezing ice and students started slipping and falling. It was so slippery they couldn't get their footing and students were getting hurt falling in these ice pellets. One girl fell hard, and she broke her hip! Rescue workers struggled to get to the girl because the ice was so slippery, they had to crawl to get her and sliding on the pavement to get to the rescue. The girl was lifted carefully into the rescue and it had to drive very slowly on the ice.

Later it was raining ice and it was freezing on contact. Trees and telephone wires were covered in ice and the wind picked up and branches started breaking off trees and falling on electrical wires and knocking out power through the campus. Then it was thundering and lightning and the wind picked up and here we go again! The rain came down so hard it started freezing over icy surfaces and then a thick sleet was pouring down and this unexpected storm comes out of nowhere! A security guard came out of a building and he lost his footing and he landed on his back hitting his head and later he ended up in the hospital. Someone saw him go down and he was picked up in a snow mobile and taken to the university infirmary, the hospital on campus. A newscast came on TV.

"Good evening this is the WWME channel 3 news in Portland Maine a freak storm has developed over southern and eastern Maine with heavy rain, ice, strong winds and thunderstorms may be the remnants of Winter Storm Clitina-Canadian Express re-developing. It has caused major structural damage on the campus of the University of Southern Maine where there were injuries. The forecast was calling for a clear and cold night but just before 6:30 p.m. it was snowing then turned to ice and heavy rain freezing on contact then pouring sleet and thunderstorms and trees and telephone wires fell from a sheet of coating ice knocking out all the electricity on the campus of southern Maine. The University was on lockdown in the dark in less than an hour. We have some brutal ice storms here in Maine but nothing like this. The campus is now reporting wind gusts over 100 miles per hour and broken windows and roofs ripped off! Trees down and telephone poles snapped in half!

"We are getting a report from the Weather Channel that the remnants from the Canadian Express merging with an ocean storm and a polar vortex cold front and it now all coming together and may become a bomb winter storm/superstorm! The Weather Channel will fly into this storm to identify what's happening by tomorrow morning. Please stay tuned for updates; we have a possible superstorm developing, WWME TV 3 news reporting"

Maine residents were watching the news updates on this freak storm raising the heat in their homes keeping wood stoves and fireplaces lit and getting heavy blankets and quilts out getting ready for what's to come!

Back at Southern Maine, there were no lights students walked around with flashlights in their dorms, the campus was in the dark with flashes of lightning and strong winds and raining ice leaving the campus buried in a sheet of ice. One of the students went to the window in her dorm room and she looked out suddenly a strong gust of wind blew the window out and she was sucked outside and dragged across campus and she was thrown into a tree where she was stuck there and she froze to death! Her roommate came to the room and saw the window blown through and she screamed hysterical.

She kept crying, "Where's Amy, where's Amy!"

A couple of her male friends went out looking for her and she was nowhere to be found. The boys struggled walking through the ice and the bad weather and one of them stepped on a downed livewire and he got fried like a marshmallow! The other boy ran for his life slipping in the ice and screaming for help!

Around midnight the storm passed, and a helicopter flew over the campus a military helicopter with a loudspeaker warning everyone on campus to stay put.

"Ladies and gentlemen please remain indoors because it's too dangerous to be outside we already have deaths on campus from the storm!"

The temperature dropped to eight degrees and everything was frozen solid during the night. Electric crew worked all night in the bitter cold to restore electricity to the campus. The trucks had chains wrapped around the tires to get around in the ice and snow; sand and salt trucks were dumping heavy loads of sand and salt to get around all this ice. The storm did not dump much snow until it got out over water at three o'clock in the morning. The polar vortex high pressure pushed the storm off the coast of southeast Maine and headed for Boston Massachusetts but not before stalling for a couple of days spinning like a top. The storm caused big waves threatening shipping lanes and islands off of eastern Maine. Fishing boats had already been damaged and a massive evacuation was on the way.

By 5 a.m. back on the University of Southern Maine campus, trucks arrived to dump sand and workers shoveled the sand on sidewalks and stairs so students could walk; the university was closed for classes for the remainder of today. Reality sets in when the sun rose the campus looked like another planet! The entire campus was covered in ice and icicles hung off of buildings.

The Weather Channel and military planes flew into this newly formed nor'easter in the eye of the storm and one weatherman said to another, "Hey bro, it looks like the curse of Emma Grace is ready to start up again; it's not a tropical system but it's the same storm system of Emma Grace, Winter Storm Clitina and the Canadian Express where she gets her name right now! This storm has been brewing for the last three months killing millions of people and this polar vortex is finally pushing the storm out to sea."

The Weather Channel posted warnings about this very powerful storm noontime on the 18th of November. Back at southern Maine at least two people have died, and several students were hurt. The girl in the tree was found frozen to death hidden in branches and a boy was electrocuted! A security guard was in the hospital with a head injury; people heard on the news. Fishermen at a bar listen to the warnings from the Weather Channel.

"Good afternoon, we have breaking news a major ice storm struck the University of Southern Maine leaving two people dead and several injuries. The storm left the campus in a mirage of ice and it darkness during the night with no heat! The storm came unexpectedly. The weather was calling for a clear and cold night but the Canadian Express that crippled Canada leaving a trail of destruction and death!

"The weak storm caught up with a polar vortex cold front pulling the nor'easter coming up the Maine coast and turning the storm into a bomb superstorm! This storm system is the same system from hurricane Emma Grace that has been going on for three months and the curse of Emma Grace is not going away!

"The storm right now is stalled off the Maine coast and going out to sea; watch out Boston you might get clipped by this storm in one or two days! The storm is located stalled over Eagle Island with 70 mile per hour winds with gusts over 100!

"The following areas must evacuate at this time from Portland Maine down the Maine coastline all the way to Boston Massachusetts and Cape Cod and the islands. Prepare for some very big waves! Shipping lanes for all boats to be taken out of the water. Everyone must evacuate the coast and move inland because this storm is very dangerous, Luke Grenchal, the Weather Channel."

People on East Island saw lightning and the wind picked up and it was raining with sleet and snow coming down. About 9 a.m. residents of East Island boarded boats to evacuate to the mainland and boats anchored in a river far inland the Maine coast. East Island was a ghost town except for two men who decided to break into the bar called the Fishnet Pub and have fun drinking all the booze until they passed out!

Hours later the storm blew all the windows out of the bar and the power was out now there's no heat and three feet of snow on the ground now these two drunks are stuck there being hit by debris from outside tossed into the bar! One guy was hit in the head and he was knocked out and he froze to death! The other man went looking for blankets to keep warm while he was drinking a bottle of bourbon. Then he gathered wood from outside to light a fire in the fireplace and he fell asleep; he doesn't know what happen to his friend and he passed out in front of the warm fire. A few minutes later the wind blew a piece of burning wood across the floor in the bar and the bar caught fire and burned to the ground!

The man woke up feeling the heat and saw the bar burning down; he said, "Holy shit! Matt, we gotta get out of here!"

He called for his friend. There was no answer, so he left the bar trapped in three feet of snow and rain and ice blowing in his face and lightning and thunder and snow drifts and he made it home. The fuckin' bar burned to the ground and his friend Matt is dead! The man made it home drunk. He has no heat and no lights, so he grabbed a hurricane lamp and a bunch of blankets to keep warm.

He said to himself, "I'm not lighting my fireplace and burn my house down!"

The city of Justine was still snowed in with no electricity and the dead is still unknown, from the Canadian express. In Toronto they were still carrying out the dead in body bags but at least the snow was melting so coroners can find the rest of the dead. Half of the Ding Dong tour was feared dead most of them being blown out of the Tower restaurant from the killer storm a week ago. Boats went searching for bodies all week long in Lake Ontario and a few were found. The city of Toronto was closed off for a week to clean up and search for the dead.

In Niagara on the lake there were a few deaths, but the city is up and running a week later. Niagara Falls recovered after the vicious storm last week dumping more than a foot of snow and buried in ice. Buffalo is still snowed in and the dead may not be found until spring-time! In Vermont and New Hampshire several animals were killed and if any were dead it would not be known until the next thaw. Southern Maine got buried in ice two fatalities so far and several injuries and the storm is stalled off the coast of Maine working down toward Boston and Cape Cod.

People were coming out of the TD Bank garden after a hockey game in Boston and the Bruins who beat the Montreal Canadians 4 to 1. The crowd went to an Irish bar called McMahon's Irish Pub. Everyone wearing Bruins clothes in the bar drinking and eating having a Bruins victory party and they were watching the news on TV.

"Good evening we have breaking news on News Watch 10 in Boston. A deadly storm is on the way from a backdoor cold front. Remnants from Emma Grace, believe it or not! After what happen in

New York and many places we need to get prepared! The storm has moved off the coast of Maine being pushed by a polar vortex directly toward Boston, the storm is moving very slowly and may strike Boston late Saturday night or early Sunday morning. The storm right now is out at sea and building into a mega nor'easter with very strong winds heavy snow and ice and thunderstorms and we have to get ready, this storm has killed millions of people! We will keep you posted on reports news 10 will let you know when to evacuate. News 10 Boston reporting."

People at the bar cheered, "Let's have a hurricane party!" The night went on OK.

At 3 a.m. on November 19th it was snowing, and part of this killer storm was here but it was moving away from Boston and threatening Cape Cod. Boston got three quick inches of snow and thunder and lightning and some strong wind then the huge storm moved away, and it got cold. It was 14 degrees in downtown Boston and the plows were out moving the snow and clearing the streets. By 3 p.m. on the 19th it was light snow and a dark gray sky. The storm was making a comeback and an evacuation was ordered.

At the Encore casino they were boarding up all the windows and the hotel was evacuated. Trains and buses picked up people to take them to safety. Hotels in downtown were evacuated and planes were leaving Logan Airport to get away from the storm. All the boats from the harbor had to be taken out of the water and the coastline was evacuated. By 6 p.m. the sky cleared. After all that work Boston was spared. The city shut down and boarded up.

The storm moved toward Cape Cod and they were not so lucky. Sunday November 20th, 2022. At 5 a.m. police posted an evacuation driving around with a loudspeaker.

"May I have your attention; we have a bad storm coming you

must evacuate and get off the island immediately!"

The police were calling all day long to get everybody out. A bus in Provincetown was loading people when suddenly a big wave washed them away into the sea. People started screaming when the wave came, and it was over in 30 seconds! Nobody had a chance when the early 7 a.m. dawn wave hit; about 60 people were killed! The wave was about 50 feet high! Buildings were washed away, and Provincetown was devastated!

The storm quickly came ashore dumping about 5 inches of snow per hour with 100 mile per hour winds and thunderstorms and blew the town of Touro off the map; everything was washed into the sea by 50 to 60-foot waves. A 100-foot wave struck Norsic Lighthouse Beach and it washed great white sharks into town and they died being blown in the wind and buried in snow drifts and the storm moved out to sea but the waves kept coming!

People evacuating were racing to get out of Cape Cod as quickly as possible and there were accidents everywhere! The waves were so high buses and cars were being washed away. A giant wave moving 100 miles per hour went down the Cape Cod canal washing ships up on land like toys and the Mass Maritime Academy was completely destroyed! Most off the Cape evacuated days ago and those who did not were killed! All of Cape Cod suffered catastrophic damage from the giant waves and 25 inches of snow and severe flooding and the cold to follow froze everything solid.

By 3 p.m. on the 20th of November the temperature dropped to 7 degrees and Cape Cod was covered in ice. A great white shark was washed up against the Norsic lighthouse tower and froze solid. The sun came out and the sky cleared, and the storm was gone but the big waves kept coming to finish the job.

Martha's Vineyard and Nantucket were evacuated before the

storm hit and big waves caused a lot of damage on the islands too! The storm and the big waves were pushed out to sea by evening. The storm didn't last more than 5 minutes when it struck Martha's Vineyard and Nantucket. The storm was pushed all the way past the Bermuda Triangle. Homes, businesses, churches, restaurants were blown off the face of the earth by huge waves and high winds on Martha's Vineyard and Nantucket!

The polar vortex pushed the remnants of Emma Grace all the way to her grave where she started; back into the Caribbean before she rises again just like Jesus Christ! But that's later! The polar vortex pushed cold weather from Canada all the way to the Carolinas before going out to sea for good and the result will give Emma Grace her name back! Wednesday November 23rd, 2022 Emma Grace is re-developing slowly in the Caribbean behind the Bermuda Triangle; she's not organized just yet.

Back in Canada, the city of Justine the weather was getting warmer and some of the snow is melting from the Canadian Express. Part of the city was being plowed and getting cleaned up and snow being moved.

But there's another problem in Justine, polar bears are invading the area. A man wakes up early in the morning to find a bear on his roof. He called 911 on his cell phone to report the bear and a bear remover arrives and he gets out of his van. He's got a ladder, a baseball bat, and a shotgun, and a mean junkyard dog!

"What are you going to do," the homeowner asked.

"I'm going to put the ladder up against the roof, then I'm going up there with the baseball bat and knock the bear off of the roof. When the bear falls off, the dog is trained to grab the bear by its legs or his balls if it's a male, and not let go. The bear will be subdued enough for me to put him or her in the cage in the back of the van." He hands the shotgun to the homeowner.

"What's the gun for?" said the homeowner.

"If the bear knocks me off the roof, shoot the fuckin' dog!"

The bear remover went up on the roof to chase the bear off with the baseball bat and he got the bear off the roof and the homeowner shot it right in the head shattering the bear's brains with the shotgun! It was a big polar male bear and the junkyard dog grabbed the bear by his balls and dragged it to the van and workers and the homeowner helped put the bear in the van and the bear removers left. The homeowner had a mess to clean up in his yard, shoveling snow and the bear's brain guts and blood. Several polar bears were being shot by bear keepers in Justine. Over 30 polar bears invaded Justine and were put down and the city was in fear.

16   THE RETURN OF EMMA GRACE

November 23rd, 2022 at 2 p.m., the same system from Emma Grace was re-organizing in the open Caribbean Sea and heading right between Florida and the Carolinas. The mass of the storm was huge with a well-developed eye, but the storm was weak right now and the weather planes went in to see if it's tropical and the winds were 45 mph and the storm got her name back: the return of Emma Grace!

News from the Weather Channel warned the public in Florida that Emma Grace is back! Orlando Florida 6 p.m. on the 23rd of November, Wednesday, a political party was going on at the Orlando Convention Center and President Tom Brady was there. Breaking news came out on TV screens with the Weather Channel interrupting the party; everyone stopped to watch.

"Good evening we have breaking news; tropical storm Emma Grace is back: the storm has been just renamed after it was pushed out to sea by a cold front and she's located in the Caribbean Sea working her way through the Bermuda Triangle and may strike anywhere from Jacksonville, Florida to Kill Devil, North Carolina within two or three days and come right up the east coast and strike Cape Cod again as a strong nor'easter or hurricane. Emma Grace, a weak tropical storm has sustained winds of 45 miles per hour with gusts up to 65 miles per hour. This storm is strengthening, and she's scheduled to become a hurricane again! Emma Grace has been a dangerous storm for more than three months, changing names in winter storms and killing millions of people!

"On Sunday November 20th Winter Storm Clitina-Canadian Express wiped out almost all of Cape Cod killing hundreds of people and burying Cape Cod under two feet of snow and 100-foot waves caused catastrophic flooding and cold freezing everything solid. The death toll may never be known. The Caribbean, Miami, New Orleans, New York City, parts of Chicago, and Canada, and Toronto, and Buffalo, NY were completely destroyed. Emma Grace the worst global storm ever on earth had winds as high as 300 miles per hour spawning more than 50,000 tornadoes moving inland. Then it went into the Lake Superior leveling east Chicago under 50-foot waves before meeting Winter Storm Clitina and covered the city of Justine, Ottawa under 10 feet of snow and buried Buffalo under more than 20 feet of snow.

"This hurricane met with the Canadian Express in Lake Michigan coming from Lake Superior and powerful whiplash thunderstorms followed by a hard freeze killed thousands in Toronto from positive lightning strikes. 150 mile per hour winds blew the windows out of the Canadian Tower restaurant killing everyone! An elevator with an estimated 50 to 100 people was struck by lightning and fell from the restaurant crashing through the Rodgers Center leaving Toronto in total devastation!

"The storm wiped out Niagara on the lake, the death toll there is unknown. The storm dumped 5 to 8 feet of snow in Vermont and New Hampshire killing thousands of animals. The storm hit southern

Maine dumping three feet of snow followed by a hard freeze. The death toll there is unknown! Boston was spared with little damage from snow and ice until finally destroying Cape Cod and the islands, the death toll is unknown in Cape Cod Martha's Vineyard and Nantucket. Most of the Cape and the islands evacuated before this killer storm came. The city of Boston boarded up and evacuated.

"The killer cold front pushed Clitina-Canadian Express way out to sea until it became a strong rainstorm in the middle Atlantic and now it's tropical and has her name back. We will keep you posted, Emma Grace is back but the hurricane season is almost over and hopefully she moves north and weakens then she will be done, but don't let your guard down this storm is unpredictable and very dangerous! Vickey Victoria, the Weather Channel." The convention party went on as schedule after the brief bad news report.

The next day was Thursday, November 24th, 2022. Jacksonville boarded up windows and evacuated before being told to be on the safe side. South Carolina and North Carolina followed suit; board up remove the boats and get the fuck out!!!!!!! Weather planes flew into Emma Grace and she picked up a little now with 53 mph winds and not a big threat toward land yet.

Airforce One with Tom Brady flew over the frozen Cape Cod, Martha's Vineyard and Nantucket and it looked like a frozen wasteland with several buildings destroyed covered in ice and snow, but no bodies were found. Airforce One flew up the eastern seaboard all the way to Portland, Maine and everything appeared normal; still cold up here but ocean waves were calm, and the storm is gone. The chopper flew low over the frozen campus of the University of Southern Maine and it looked like it was back to normal. In Canada it will take until springtime for things to get back to normal. Then Airforce One flew to Chicago, Wisconsin, and Michigan and things there were getting better but were still snowed in and iced over! The president flew over Buffalo, Vermont and New Hampshire and everything was snowed over. Then Air Force One flew back to Washington D.C. *All the flyovers from the president but nothing can be done until spring; everywhere is buried under snow and ice; there are probably thousands of dead bodies lying under winter's wrath!*

Cruise ships arrived were evacuating people away from Puerto Rico, the Bahamas and Bermuda and taking them to military camps where tents were set up in the barren land of the speakeasy! Eleven p.m. on the 24th of November this fuckin' cunt is making a direct aim on Puerto Rico! The weather planes were making their last advisory flight in the eye of Emma Grace and she's still a tropical storm with 50 mph winds heading for Puerto Rico. Cruise ships were loading for evacuation two hours before the last advisory. The ships left Puerto Rico heading for the Gulf of Mexico.

The weather planes shot rockets of dry ice into the storm hoping to dry it up some before leaving. The plan did not work; it made the storm worse and it doubled in speed two hours later! Emma Grace is getting angry and her winds are now up to 100 mph with gusts as high as 150. The storm went from a weak tropical storm to a mile-wide stovepipe vortex monster!!!!!!!

It was 1:17 a.m. Friday November 25th, 2022. San Juan, Puerto Rico. A group of college kids on vacation was having a hurricane party on a beach and it was a partly cloudy windy night and the water was calm with a shiny half-moon. The kids were having drinks on the beach and swimming in the water, minutes later lightning was spotted.

One of the kids said, "Get out of the water, it's lightning!"

One boy said, "Emma Grace is on her way, but she's only a tropical storm, we can handle 50 mile per hour winds!"

People in San Juan ignored evacuating after being told too; the storm is on the other side of the island! The sky was clear, and the eye passed over Puerto Rico sparing most of the island but the back end hit San Juan real good! People who did not evacuate, a chosen few in the city and on the beach enjoying a nice evening walking around got a big surprise! A few flashes of lightning appeared and no thunder, suddenly the sky cleared! Then it got very quiet and the wind stopped.

The kids on the beach cheered, "It's over, the storm is gone!"

"Too bad! Come back Emma Grace!" one boy said, and she came!

The sky clouded up and it was getting foggy and then the wind picked up and the water was getting choppy, then lightning and thunder, then the rain was coming down hard!

One boy said to the other, "Be careful about what you wish for! Emma Grace is here bro."

The kids just kept partying as the storm was getting worse and lightning flashes turned to cloud to ground strikes and hail rained down the size of baseballs and the wind was a hell of a lot stronger than 50 miles per hour! The party goers went from celebrating to fear in a matter of seconds; they had a mile to go to get to safety. It was a long beach and about 20 party goers were getting blown around and into each other and tossed up in the air and thrown into the water!

The kids were screaming and crying running for their lives and lightning was striking the ground making fear even worse! The kids bled when hail stones were hitting them in the head; one girl was killed by the hail and the wind swept her out in the ocean! Two more boys were blown out to sea and had to swim to a buoy with lightning strikes around them!

About 16 of the 20 made it back to the hotel surviving 85 mph winds blowing at their backs and being belted with baseball size hail and were full of blood when they got to the hotel lobby. Three of the kids passed out on the floor! The hotel clerk called 911 on cell phones speaking in Spanish and help never arrived then the lights went out as hotel workers were covering the injured with blankets; they had to deal with lightning flashes to see what they were doing. The wind was blowing so hard the windows in the lobby were ready to blow in. The hotel workers moved the injured to a room away from the windows.

The windows were buckling from the strong wind suddenly they blew in! The whole wall was blown in and a man was picked up and thrown up on a foyer and he was able to get up and run away. The whole front of the great Omni Hotel in San Juan was blown away!

People who were out walking around got inside and went to their rooms when the storm was coming. People sleeping in rooms facing the beach had to be evacuated and get other rooms in the basement on the other side of the hotel; it was a good thing because the windows and the whole side of the hotel were blown away! Some people had to hang on to things all night until it let up.

Emma Grace stalled right directly over San Juan all night long! A waterspout hit a row of Tiki bars along the beach in front of the damaged hotel about 20 of them and blew them all away! All you can hear was a roaring wind and glass breaking all fuckin' night long! The storm finally went away at 6:06am!

The two boys had tied themselves to a buoy and hang on for the night battling 4-foot waves. When daylight came the destruction was unimaginable. Later the two boys untied themselves and swam to shore to the hotel to find their friends. Injured people kept calling for help in English and Spanish and finally help arrived.

A Coast Guard boat arrived from the U.S. to help the injured. Then a Coast Guard hospital helicopter landed on the beach loading up the injured and then boats came to evacuate the rest of the island. Eighteen of them made it but two girls died, and they were never found.

Emma Grace is now in the Bermuda Triangle right between the Bahamas and Bermuda taking aim for North Carolina. People in the Bahamas saw an ugly rotating mass out in the ocean spinning stationary and moving slowly. Weather planes flew back into the eye of the return of Emma Grace once again getting reports back from the Weather Channel.

"C130/23 this is Vickey Victoria. Do not fire anymore dry ice rockets into the storm, we may have made it worse from last night because dry ice and radioactive materials do not mix. The storm doubled in speed and 100 mile per hour winds struck the Omni Hotel in San Juan Puerto Rico last night and there was a lot of damage. We do not know if there were any deaths!"

"Vickey, I read you over, we have a well-developed eye and sustained winds of 130 mph with gusts past 150. And Emma Grace is slowly moving toward the Carolinas. This is Greg, the co-pilot, c130/23, over."

"Ten-four, Greg, c130/23, please keep the Weather Channel posted," said Vickey.

The Carolinas were evacuating boarding up buildings and getting boats out of the water and the highways were jammed but moving along. People delaying getting out stopped at grocery stores and the shelves were empty and stopped at gas stations and there was no more gas! Some cars got stuck on the highway after running out of gas making a travel nightmare for the people leaving at the last minute! A newscast came out on their car radios while driving north following the traffic.

"Good afternoon, we have an extreme weather alert! Hurricane Emma Grace is heading for the outer banks of North Carolina by 4 p.m. this evening! You must leave all coastal areas immediately! The storm has winds over 140 miles per hour and moving between the

Bahamas and Bermuda at 18 miles per hour and prepare for the worst! This is a very dangerous storm! Expect tidal waves strong straight-line winds, deadly lightning heavy destruction even waterspouts and tornadoes!

"This storm struck San Juan Puerto Rico killing at least three people and injuring several and causing serious destruction last night! This storm has been going on since August 20th killing more than 3,000,000 people and devastating all the east coast and in Canada and now, she's back. You must take this storm seriously if you do not want to be the next victim! Karen Colt World Network News radio!"

At 3:13 p.m. the waves arrived before the storm hitting the outer banks with 50-foot waves, smashing up a few boats and washing oil tankers up on sand banks and homes and beach front properties were destroyed before the storm came! A meeting took place at the Weather Channel about the storm. A group of weathermen and women and a speaker trying to make sense of this very powerful storm.

"Hi ladies and gentlemen we have a superstorm that we cannot do anything about. It has blown up mountains, blew islands out of the water demolished cities and radioactive lightning even dominating winter storms and pouring through warm and cold areas like nothing. It is a global catastrophic disaster! We did everything we could do to keep people safe but it's at a point that this storm may never end! It appears something else that we do not know of is causing this once in a lifetime superstorm! The only hope we have is if this storm finally runs out of gas in the Arctic Ocean at the end of the hurricane season in a week. Thank you, my name is John Matthew, superstorms specialist."

At 4 p.m. on Friday November 25th the storm hit part of the outer banks of North Carolina destroying coastal areas. The storm moved up the east coast staying offshore, and the Virginias are next, being hit by big waves. There was a massive evacuation on the east coast from the Carolinas all the way to Canada before news reports came in. People know what's coming: the return of Emma Grace, she's a killer once again!

TV stations warned people living within 50 miles from the coast to get out! If ships and boats are still out there, leave them behind and get out! This storm is carrying 50 to 100-foot tsunami waves! A warm front coming up the east coast is helping to fuel this killer storm.

When Emma Grace left the Bermuda Triangle it hit the outer banks of North Carolina really hard with winds over 100 mph and now is a Category 2 hurricane with winds as high as 100 mph. The storm has a mile-wide vortex with a well-formed tight eye showing signs of strengthening!

New York City is in great fear already have been destroyed and people still there were taken by cruise ships going up the Hudson River to upstate NY because Emma Grace may hit NYC again. In Cape Cod and the islands there's nowhere to go; if there's still people there, they're going to stay there, still snowed and iced in! In Long Island, the subway is dead, flooded and out of service all the way through New York City.

Ferry service is evacuating people and moving them to Connecticut and boarding buses from CT to mountain areas in CT and Massachusetts. People had to stay in hotels or military camps away from the water. Rhode Island, Cape Cod and the islands may get the worst of this storm! Evacuations from all of Rhode Island were taken in buses to the Mohegan Sun casino staying in the hotel and bedding was set up in conference rooms in the casino. Most of the evacuating people were taken to Twin River Casino, Hotel and Event Center. The Tiverton Casino was closed. Hundreds of people went to Tiverton Casino and were told to go to Twin River in Lincoln, RI or drive to evacuating centers in Boston. The city of Boston was spared from the winter storm but ready and waiting for the return of Emma Grace! Hotels and hospitals were taking evacuations from Rhode Island and Massachusetts.

The Maine coast evacuated moving inland. There were no immediate evacuations in Vermont, New Hampshire or western Maine. Everyone living by the coast was ordered to move inland 50 miles away to avoid being washed away!

The storm stayed off the coast passing the Virginias, Washington D.C. and Maryland, but coastal areas were struck by 60-foot waves washing homes and businesses off the map. Boats were taken out in time, but some oil tankers were left behind and were washed up on shore making a mess of the east coast all the way to Long Island NY. An aircraft carrier was found in a river in New Jersey resting up against a row of buildings. There was an oil slick in New Jersey as the waves are striking before Emma Grace arrives. Fifty-foot waves washed the boardwalk away in Atlantic City. By 6 p.m. on the 25th the storm is destroying the New Jersey coastline and moving very quickly!

A rainstorm over New York City will join Emma Grace when she comes; the rainstorm spared NYC pushing Emma Grace away and she hit Long Island dead on with 120 mph winds! Sixty-foot waves washed Long Island off the map and the winds got stronger, 130 with gusts as high as 180 mph! Everything standing on Long Island was blown into the ocean and the inner bay along the Connecticut coastline was flooded. Every building on Long Island was severely damaged or blown off the face of the earth!

By 8 p.m. Emma Grace hit Rhode Island with 200 mph winds and gusts past 250! Block Island was destroyed for the second time and the entire state of Rhode Island was destroyed. Westerly, RI was wiped slate clean and the Rhode Island beach front properties were blown off the face of the earth! Narragansett, RI was a sand pit in seconds there was nothing standing! 100-foot waves finished the job!

The eye of Emma Grace went over Cape Cod and the islands, finally this nut is starting to break up! The area was hit by big waves causing severe flooding, but she is busy in Rhode Island that got hit the worst! East Greenwich, Warwick, Cranston were wiped out. In Providence, Emma Grace was starting to exit and weaken but not before she finishes off the Ocean State.

The city was flooded under 20 feet of water as Emma Grace washed Narragansett Bay into downtown Providence, Pawtucket and the Attleboros causing catastrophic flooding not to mention 25 inches of rain that fell across Rhode Island during the storm! Roofs were blown off of buildings, all the windows in all buildings were blown out and homes and wood structures were blown off the face of the earth! A pair of violent tornadoes destroyed the Brown University campus and several buildings on the east side of Providence were leveled! A tornado hit Pawtucket before Emma Grace exited into Massachusetts.

A cold front pushed Emma Grace right over Boston! The city of Boston evacuated from the winter storm and people were staying in high rises to avoid being swept away from tidal waves. The electricity was shut off from North Carolina all the way to Maine along coastal areas because of the giant waves; people were told to evacuate a long time ago and people listened this time knowing how bad this storm is: this fuckin' thing just doesn't want to go away! The storm devastated Attleboro, Seekonk, Rehoboth and riding the coast and hit Boston and all the suburbs around the city.

A tornado demolished Dorchester, every building was shattered like splinters and debris was flying around like missiles! Another tornado went right down Rt. 93 destroying businesses. Another tornado leveled Quincy, another tornado demolished Braintree and subways were flooded by heavy rains! A tornado damaged building at Harvard University and the football field was damaged. A violent tornado went through Logan Airport damaging several planes and hangars were blown away and a terminal was destroyed, and a fire started.

Boston was spared from Clitina but the return of Emma Grace is coming to finish the job! The waves came first 40 to 50 feet washing into downtown before the worst of the storm arrived in a few minutes. A tornado hit the Encore Casino blowing out windows and tearing off roofs and boats in the harbor were destroyed. People were in the casino when the tornado hit running and screaming running to safety! Another tornado went right down Route One smashing businesses and malls leaving a trail of destruction! Everett, Lynn, Chelsea and Peabody were leveled by deadly tornadoes! This fuckin' storm is not here yet spawning all these tornadoes! Slot machines and gambling tables laid in the harbor outside with busted up boats and Tiki bars laying in the water destroyed by the wind.

Big waves arrived to do more damage! The waves flooded downtown Boston then by 11 p.m., Emma Grace arrived with tsunami waves and 150 mph winds! The wind came first tearing roofs off of buildings and then windows were blown out in several buildings and 100-foot waves washed bridges away! The Tobin Bridge, gone! The tunnels and subways were flooded. The roof of the TD Bank garden was blown off and walls collapsed, and the TD Bank Garden was destroyed. The Boston Celtics basketball floor was in view buried under water! Fenway Park was flooded, and the Green Monster was cracked! Buildings in Kenmore square were struck and damaged by tornadoes! The subways were flooded and buried under 15 feet of water from the waves and flooding. The storm dumped 35 inches of rain in downtown Boston and the winds damaged several buildings; some buildings collapsed from the wind, flooding and being struck by tornadoes!

Emma Grace moved out of Boston and struck Salem, Massachusetts with wind damage and flooding. A cold front pushed this fuckin' cunt out to sea after devastating downtown Boston! The storm hit part of Hampton Beach and went up the Maine coast quickly all the way to Nova Scotia by 1 a.m. on November 26th. In 24 hours, Emma Grace hit San Juan, Puerto Rico and raced up the east coast all the way to Canada, leaving a trail of destruction! Hampton Beach and all of the Maine coastline was damaged by waves and high winds. The wind was still blowing 100 miles per hour with gust as high as 150 when she hit Nova Scotia at 1:18 am. Nova Scotia did not evacuate; the province was told they would not get winds over 50 miles per hour.

Are they in for a big surprise overnight! 100-foot waves; a series of huge waves struck an oil platform rig and buried it into the sea and then the giant waves hit the coastline. Residents at a hotel could feel a cold damp breeze and it was low tide, but the waves are coming! First the wind and thunder and lightning and heavy rain it was coming down so hard and the wind was getting stronger until windows started breaking and the hotel walls were buckling ready to blow through.

A hotel clerk said to a bunch of crowded people, "Everybody get to the north side of the building and stay low, a bad storm is coming!"

A few minutes later, the first wave struck washing over an island where the hotel stood in Nova Scotia, the next thing everyone was tumbling in the high waves and pulled out to sea and everyone died, about 100 people who were staying at Hotel Darby in Nova Scotia all vanished in less than two minutes! A second wave, a 200-footer washed boats and wiped out islands and seaport villages and fishing ports into the ocean and smashed ships and oil rigs up against rocks splintering everything to pieces! Emma Grace wanted one more blow job before she dies in Canada! Hundreds if not thousands of people were killed, and Nova Scotia was totally destroyed in less than 20 minutes buried under the sea! More series of giant waves arrived to drown Nova Scotia completely!

The storm heading up into the Arctic Ocean met a strong bitter cold front that slowed Emma Grace down as she was downgraded to a strong ocean storm passing Prince Edward Island where she brought some big waves about 25 feet high causing coastal damage. Then Emma Grace met the frozen icebergs of Greenland that finally swallowed this fuckin' cunt! The storm moving into a mega cold front in the arctic ice to put this storm to sleep for good! The sky cleared and the waves calmed down.

17   THE GRAVEYARD OF
EMMA GRACE

t was Sunday, November 27, 2022. It was 45 below zero much too cold for a hurricane to survive. It was a sunny bitter cold day and ice fog was coming off the icebergs in Greenland where the remnants of Emma Grace froze to death!!!!!!!!! Forget about Thanksgiving this year because Emma Grace had it for a meal, but thank god, she's dead now!!!!!!!

Before the return of Emma Grace, some rebuilding was being done after her ruins! In New Orleans is now a huge military camp with three new schools being built, Speakeasy Elementary School then Emma Grace County Prep Regional Vocational Technical Junior Senior High School Community College. The third school is Speak Easy Volcano University.

The city of Atlanta is back to normal, other than some buildings had to be knocked down from hurricane and tornado damage and some condemned from flooding. New homes and businesses were being built in Atlanta. Miami will take years to rebuild and the same for New York City, New England and Nova Scotia, Canada. In Miami and New York City boat marinas were gone, only military boats remaining. The city of Justine, Toronto and Buffalo has no chance for recovery for at least 6 months to a year. Justine in Canada and Buffalo, NY will be snowed in until spring! The naked lady in the water island- Q'klitores was blown off the face of the earth from Emma Grace! Tollgate Island was swept away, and the return residents are living in tents. The Lesser Antilles Islands, people are coming back, and the recovery will be slow. Antigua was destroyed and will take years to recover.

Some people came back only to see their property gone! All Caribbean evacuations were forced to go back to the cruise ships and taken back to their islands from Oldtown, Texas so new evacuations can come in when Emma Grace hit New York City. The Dominican Republic will take a while to recover with residents living in tents or homeless, Hispaniola was completely destroyed. In Cuba recovery will take a while; prison guards are still shooting escapees there! In Puerto Rico a hotel was leveled and three people have died then it took two days for Emma Grace to finish the job; as she moved quickly from the outer banks of North Carolina all the way to Canada leaving a trail of destruction before the ice cold weather swallowed her whole!

It was almost a week before electricity was restored for the east coast. The news came on TV stations a few days later after power was installed in many places.

"Good evening this is the 6 p.m. evening news on Newswatch 10 in Boston. Hurricane Emma Grace struck Boston on Sunday afternoon causing serious damage and spawning several tornadoes! Hotels were damaged and the Encore Casino took a hit with broken windows and roofs ripped off and the Encore Harbor was damaged with slot machines and tables joining damaged boats and broken debris splintered in a million pieces! The TD Bank Garden was destroyed along with Fenway Park, and Kenmore Square was devastated by tornadoes and subways were flooded. Buildings in downtown Boston suffered broken windows and roofs ripped off! The death toll in Boston or in Rhode Island may never be known.

"We have breaking news: Nova Scotia was completely destroyed, and hundreds and thousands of people are feared dead! Two hundred-foot waves struck Nova Scotia on Sunday night washing the island off the map and damaging oil rigs, ships, and reshaping the land. The storm hit Prince Edward Island with 25-foot waves, but we do not have a report of deaths there. The remnants of Emma Grace were downgraded to a powerful rainstorm weakened by a bitter cold front that killed her tropical storm character! It was a long three-month killer path for the return of Emma Grace and the winter storms and the Canadian Express that made her so powerful! This storm has killed an estimate of 3.5 million people and 8 million are reported missing. Cleanup may take months or years, Lisa Klit News 10 Boston news."

Nova Scotia was leveled! On the 29th of November when the tides went out dead bodies and dead fish laid on shore; lobsters and giant squid washed up on shore dead! Boats were busted up like an accordion and wood and damaged structures laid in splinters! Several people who did not evacuate in Nova Scotia were killed in minutes! The giant waves washed everything away! In Boston everyone evacuated early; anyone who didn't was killed!

In Rhode Island everyone evacuated! The Twin River Casino was destroyed but everyone got out in time; the casino and hotel were blown off the earth by 150 mph winds and serious flooding! The only building standing in Rhode Island was a bowling alley: Lang's

Bowlarama. A dead great white shark laid in the Lang's parking lot with seagulls, ravens and pigeons pecking on its remains! The rest of Rhode Island was destroyed.

The Newport Harbor looked like a pile of splinters with people removing wood debris putting it in their cars to use for firewood! The Ryan Center on the URI campus looked like a pile of metal and buildings destroyed like in a junkyard! The beaches in Rhode Island were unrecognizable with debris and dead fish laying around and sea birds eating the dead! Seals and dogfish were washed into downtown Providence, with several dead fish! A whale washed up in the Providence River and it ended up dying where they have the Waterfire! Birds were eating the flesh on the dead whale and big water rats were running around in Waterplace Park in downtown Providence looking for food to eat and scaring the public! A great white was lying on the roof of the Dunk Center and it was being removed by a crane truck and placed into a dump truck and taken to the Narragansett Bay to be eaten by other fish and birds! Bulldozers came to break down damaged buildings so rebuilding can be done. Most of the state of Rhode Island was destroyed and damaged buildings can be used for firewood!

Gina Raimondo was in Kennedy Square in downtown Providence drinking a cup of coffee looking at all the debris and it looked like the end of the world! She puked her brains out!

In Westerly all the way to the Connecticut state line everything was shredded to matchsticks! The Foxwoods Casino in Connecticut had broken windows and roofs ripped off! A dancer at a strip joint at Foxwoods was dancing when the roof ripped off and she was sucked out into the storm and she lost her titty bra! She came back in the strip joint covering her weapons! Some of the slot machines were damaged from the flooding but people were still playing in the poker room. The Foxwoods Casino took a good hit from the flooding, with damage to buildings-hotels from the wind. And the bay between Connecticut and Long Island was filled with debris from Emma Grace! The Mohegan Sun casino was filled with evacuated people but there was some serious flooding and no electricity, and a lot of slot machines shorted out and they were turned off. The generators were on for lights, but people played the table games. The rest of Connecticut suffered severe flooding.

New York City was closed-off because it may take years to recover because there was so much damage! Buffalo is snowed in until spring and Atlantic City is leveled! The boardwalk is gone, and dead fish, jellyfish and shellfish were washed to shore from Emma Grace and the seagulls and seabirds had an open buffet for months because so much dead sea life washed up on shore!

The New Jersey coastline was littered with smashed boats and ships washed up on shore; an ocean liner was washed up on to rocks and leaking oil on public beaches! The oil caused an oil slick killing sea life and birds plus a stench that the return of Emma Grace left behind! The coastal destruction went all over the east coast from Maine to the outer banks of North Carolina. Boats piers and beach fronts were leveled from waves, wind and struck by lightning.

On Wednesday, November 30th, 2022, Airforce One flew over the destruction all the way up the east coast and beach front damage for hundreds of miles; it looked like the end of the world.

"It will take years to fix this!" said President Tom Brady, flying over in Airforce One.

The destruction from the tsunami waves was so severe the helicopter couldn't land. "This is unbelievable at least 10 miles inland has been destroyed!" said the pilot flying Airforce One!

Gas lines ruptured and caught on spilled oil from overturned oil tankers and caused a massive inferno in New Jersey and Pennsylvania. Hundreds of boats and ships washed up on beaches on Long Island. The Long Island sound was loaded with debris. Several structures were damaged across Connecticut, and in Rhode Island looked like a pile of rubble and Cape Cod and the islands were blown off the map! Buzzards Bay was loaded with debris all the way up the east coast past Boston all the way to Maine. The southern Maine campus evacuated off campus before the return of Emma Grace arrived and the campus buildings were no longer there being all washed away by the 100-foot tsunami waves!

The waves got worse when Nova Scotia was struck by Emma Grace; what a mess she did leaving a world ending massacre! With catastrophic destruction and death! Oil rigs ships washed up on shore smashed to matchsticks and dead bodies and fish littered the land. The destruction was so bad like the end of the world! People tried to make their way back in damaged places still flooded and unrecognizable! Military and Coast Guard helicopters landed in Nova Scotia during low tide to scoop up the dead. Boats worked into flooded areas to look for dead bodies because no one will survive in 100-foot waves; just watch the movie, *The Perfect Storm.*

North Carolina boats moved through dead fish and debris to look for possible survivors and found some! In Baltimore Harbor there was no change, all busted up like everywhere else with debris and dead bodies. Many dead bodies were being removed from New Jersey; hundreds of dead bodies found in destroyed hotels in Atlantic City. More dead bodies were removed from the Hudson River and the New Jersey coastline. More dead bodies were found in Cape Cod and more along the Maine coast and thousands in Nova Scotia in Canada. For three weeks daily the Coast Guard and rescue flyovers looked for survivors and remove the dead. Fish were pushed away with tugboats to ease the stench of the dead and great white sharks arrived by the thousands for an open buffet! The damage from Emma Grace raised a worldwide panic as people are wondering what is going to happen next.

It was now Saturday, December 24th, 2022. Christmas Eve midnight mass with Pope Theodore Francis Green with his name tag on his gown saying mass at the Vatican and his sermon was about the end times!

"Good evening my dear brothers and sisters, merry Christmas to everyone! This past year was the worst ever on earth! I hope 2023 will be a better year. Right now, we are in the rapture from the Lord, we have been at this very end the last ten years! In August we had the worst storm ever that killed as many as 5,000,000, people and 10,000,000 are still missing. Hurricane Emma Grace blew mountains and islands out of the water and demolished the Caribbean islands, Dominican Republic, Cuba the Bahamas, Bermuda parts of Puerto Rico and destroyed the east coast of the United States all the way into Canada, killing millions of people! Miami, New York City and New Orleans were blown off the face of the earth with 300 mile per hour winds and 150-foot waves drowning ships and oil rigs and recondition the land and turning the earth upside down! Cruise ships sank in the Bermuda Triangle killing thousands from Emma Grace.

"Have you seen the 2004 movie, *The Day After Tomorrow,* that was a movie about violent hurricanes that turned into winter storms wiping out the east coast of the United States all the way into Canada and worldwide violent storms with thunderstorms, killer tornadoes 10 pound hail stones and violent winds. New York froze over after a tidal wave flooded New York City and then a snowstorm and freezing temperatures killed people, with only a few who survived. Scientists and weathermen said that something this from that movie will not happen in our lifetime, but scientists said that it could happen! The only way something like this would happen if a large asteroid blew a hole in the ozone layer destroying the earth's magnetic field! A violent volcano can do something like this.

"My dear friends, one did and *The Day After Tomorrow* movie came true, but Emma Grace was much worse! This hurricane struck an island with nuclear bombs stored in an active volcano while it was erupting and caused a mega explosion that blew the island and the volcano out of the ocean. It set the sky on fire pulling down radiation that fueled Emma Grace into a superstorm!

"This hurricane was the devil tempting god for the final judgment. We may fall from the devil, but god will raise his people! We're in the rapture! If you read the Bible it says that one day you will hear a loud noise in the sky, that's the lord calling, and everyone will start disappearing right in front of your eyes! We're at the beginning to enter the gates to heaven to be with Jesus Christ! Hurricane Emma Grace has already taken millions into its final days.

"In October 2021, a third of California burned to the ground killing about a million people! In Australia, Indonesia, Philippines, Brazil and India fires killed more than 20,000,000 people in 2021. In the year 2020 the president of the United States Donald Trump was ruled the antichrist of the world just like Hitler during World War Two, in 2018-19 Syria was demolished. In December of 2019, a massive earthquake in Afghanistan and Pakistan killed about 2,000,000 people. And finally, the threat of world war three draft in July of 2020.

"The violence all over the world is getting out of control helping the devil lead the way! My dear brothers and sisters we need to be ready the end times are here. The earth is burning up and challenging the devil: it's cooling off from the rapture of god. Name of the father and the son and the holy spirit. Amen," said Pope Theodore Francis Green.

The Christmas mass went on and when it was over people gathered outside the Vatican wishing everyone a merry Christmas exchanging gifts in the pouring rain. A little while later a bright light came from the dark sky of the blessed Virgin Mary. Hundreds of people coming out of the basilica and the Christmas mass were amazed and everyone was praying well into the night singing Christmas songs until the vision went away a few minutes later.

Sunday was Christmas Day, December 25, 2022. Coast Guard boats in Nova Scotia finally got on land when the flooding went down and went into damaged buildings to search for more bodies. During a snowstorm, it was a very cold dark gray day in the snow was really coming down. Suddenly a loud noise was heard followed by a bright flash of lightning and the Coast Guard working crew leaving one building and going into another saw a brightening in the sky in the 15 degree cold and a vision of the blessed Virgin Mary appeared in the sky and stayed there for 10 minutes. One Coast Guard worker called for his friends.

"Jay, Glenn, Tommy and Ricky, look up in the sky it looks like the lord is calling! It looks like the Virgin Mary!"

"Manny, let's get the fuck out of here before we become Nova Scotia's next victims, let's go! We gotta get out of here!" said Glenn.

The crew left in a hurry fearing the vision. Once they got back in the boats before the tide went out the vision disappeared! *The vision was coming from the heavens telling everyone below that all the bodies were raised for people still there to understand that all the dead from Hurricane Emma Grace went to heaven from Nova Scotia.*

No bodies were found on Christmas day. The day after Christmas crews went in again to find bodies in the ruin Nova Scotia and again no bodies were found. It will be springtime before cleanup will be done in Nova Scotia.

In Boston, evacuations were coming back in some areas. During the massacre the Boston Celtics and the Bruins were on a long west coast road trip. The New England Patriots beat the Philadelphia Eagles 31 to 13 in Foxboro on Christmas Day. Gillette Stadium survived Emma Grace with some light damage, but they had almost three feet of snow from this storm. Hotels started running again finally after a month in downtown Boston and people staying in the hotels watched the news on channel 10 in Boston.

"Good evening this is breaking news on Tuesday December 27th, 2022. Lisa Klit reporting on the 6 p.m. news. The three-month storm from the return of Hurricane Emma Grace a month ago has many more numbers with destruction and death! It has been a horror show! The combination of storms has killed 7.5 million people and 12 million are feared missing. There's more than a trillion dollars in damages, the official toll may never be known, and many areas may never recover! More than 690,000 dead have been recovered in Nova Scotia and more than a million in Canada alone! 33 violent tornadoes touched down in local Boston neighborhoods leaving a trail of destruction.

"The Encore Casino will reopen on New Year's Eve. A series of tsunami waves has leveled Cape Cod, the islands and several Boston bridges were washed away. The TD Bank Garden will take some time to be rebuild, the Boston Celtics will have to play the remaining home games at Boston College as well as the Bruins because the campus was not hit too bad from Emma Grace.

"Rhode Island has been blown away and it will take years for them to recover. Brown University and the east side of Providence was flattened by violent tornadoes. The Twin River Casino and hotel was blown off the map from 200 plus mile per hour winds and the town of Lincoln, RI wiped slate clean like a sandy desert!

"Western Connecticut, Vermont, and New Hampshire survived most of the destruction but there was damage they too getting a lot of snow. A lot of deaths and property loss reported in Maine and there still looking for bodies. Overturned ships and damaged boats and marinas will stay that way for years to come. New York City and New Jersey all the way to North Carolina have so much damage that may never be recovery there for years. New Orleans was blown off the map leaving a field of scraps and people living in tents; some new schools are being built there and the Superdome still stands. Miami will be shut down for months to come to rebuild. This is Lisa Klit, news watch 10 Boston."

People coming back were escorted to some areas but most of downtown Boston was seriously damaged.

The next day was Wednesday, December 28th, 2022. The Weather Channel and military and the NASA volcano crew had meetings to try and understand how such a storm like Emma Grace was so strong! Military ships helicopters and planes landed on Tollgate Island where military workers were rebuilding. New buildings were being built and a hotel is being built being run by David L. Sanberg. He wants Tollgate Island to be a resort like Q'klitores. The meeting will be held on Thursday the 29th of December.

A hurricane wall was built around Tollgate Island to protect the island from being struck by these big storms. The wall is 30 feet high because there are 20-foot waves here on high tide during big storms. Before this meeting takes place on Tollgate Island a military ship traveled to where Q'klitores once stood and everyone aboard saw the ghost of Olivia stationary above the water where the hotel and volcano once stood.

Everyone aboard the ship cheered, "Hi Olivia!!!!!!!!!!!"

The apparition appeared for a few minutes and then it went dark. It was a hot night and it was 94 degrees at 10 p.m. on the 28th of December in the southeastern Atlantic Ocean. Divers jumped off the ship to look for evidence of any pieces of the hotel, bunkers or clues of the island; it's the third time the military and weather teams were here and found nothing! With undersea search lights and mini submarines looking for clues and there was nothing but rocks and sand; they saw two bull sharks fucking but that's about it! The search was over, and the ship remains dock there for the night. Olivia's ghost appeared once again about 3 o'clock in the morning.

In Toronto, Canada another dangerous winter storm was coming raising fear another Emma Grace might be brewing. Winter Storm Fungoo raced over Toronto with 90 mph winds with thunderstorms and dumping 8 inches of snow per hour; the storm came with no warning; the thunder was very loud and the lightning was very bright! People started running trying to get aboard trains to get out, but everything was shut down. The storm lasted a little over five hours dumping 40 inches of snow and a few windows blew out in buildings and roofs were ripped off and a giant snow tornado went up Lake Ontario and the storm was gone in the middle of the night.

No deaths were reported in this storm, but downtown Toronto was buried in snow and the city was at a standstill once again. The military earth movers arrived to move the heavy snow late in the evening when the storm was over. The next day military helicopters were flying over the east coast of the United States trying to make progress from the destruction. The National Guard took over seaports from Miami all the way up the east coast all the way to Maine. Canada was being guarded by their army.

It was 6 a.m. on Thursday December 29th, 2022. Back where the island of Q'klitores once stood several divers jumped off a ship to find the evidence of Q'klitores and once again nothing was found. Two more military ships with divers came to help out and they found nothing. The ships went back to Tollgate Island for the 3 p.m. meeting in a military closed in tent.

"Good afternoon ladies and gentlemen. My name is Sergeant Adam Santini the general manager of Tollgate Island formerly from the naked lady in the water before Hurricane Emma Grace blew it up! Some of you people we may have met before and today we welcome several people back hoping to reunite here on Tollgate Island.

"First, let's welcome the NASA volcano crew, volcanologist leader Vincent Tino and his crew, Amy Amitriptyline, John Nicolini, Jay Domers, Paul Arts, Linda Lincoln and newest member Robert Elsworth. We also have Doctor Raymound W. Hallowmostraphoni-agalleriabarringtoncommonwealth, just call him Dr. It! We also have Texas Ranger Clayborn Roots with us today and Vincent Tino will be our speaker. Vinny please."

"Thank you, Sgt. Santini. Ladies and gentlemen, we just experienced the worst storm ever on earth and it's finally over. But why did this happen? Well I have answers. When Emma Grace struck the Mount Flow volcano, we had so many explosive materials including a bomb called the mission hl1200 more than 200 times greater than Fatboy used in Hiroshima and Nagasaki. This is a nuclear weapon we were not supposed to use unless world war three broke out and got out of hand. Nobody knows we have this bomb. We're lucky we didn't blow the whole world up.

"When Hurricane Emma Grace struck the erupting volcano, the blast sucked all the insides of this volcano high into the atmosphere out into space in seconds and the shockwave triggered a tsunami over 200 feet high drying up the storm setting the stratosphere on fire. When the dust settled, Emma Grace started up again two or three weeks later and she became a super monster from space with radiation, volcanic materials and the energy from this super nuclear warhead. We are lucky the bomb blew straight up instead of blowing out or the whole world would have been gone!

"We have another bomb called the EMP, electric magnetic pulse. If we drop one of those there would be no electricity, no power no nothing. Your car would not run, nor computers or phones everything will not work. The reason why hurricane Emma Grace was so strong and so damaging was caused from this hl1200 mission; we had two of them stored in this volcano. No information must be leaked out from this meeting or we will be behind bars forever!

"One more thing before we end this meeting: when Hurricane Emma Grace went up into Canada it raced up to Greenland and into the Arctic Ocean meeting a bitter cold front with temperatures more than 40 below enough to kill the storm's energy. Divers will be here for the next three months with the NASA volcano crew to find any more evidence on what happened. From now on and forever, no more nuclear warheads will be stored inside volcanoes. This meeting is adjourned, thank you very much," said Vincent Tino!

The military and NASA dive teams spent months looking for fragments of the island-volcano and found nothing!

New Year's Eve, Saturday, December 31st. 2022 was a massive celebration all over the world with fireworks going off everywhere welcoming a new year after the disaster of hurricane Emma Grace! Memorial services were held during New Year's Day.

Five years later there was not much change. New Orleans was still a desert with small buildings being rebuilt. Miami, New York City, and the east coast were still in ruins; most of the buildings in Miami and NYC had to be knocked down leaving most of the east coast cities in a pile of bricks! The disaster on the east coast was still unsafe and flying over in planes and helicopters there was still a big mess! Miami and NYC were closed off to the public and taken over by the military. Long Island, Cape Cod, the islands and New England states started rebuilding, but it's still a mess and it will take years to finish rebuilding. Tall buildings and bridges were never rebuilt. The sea shore littered with damage ships and ocean debris stayed there! Only the dead were removed; the death toll in the millions will never be known for years to come from Hurricane Emma Grace and the east coast is still a ghost town!

THE END

AUTHOR'S NOTE

If this book becomes a movie, they should have the Christian song: "The Revelation Song" play while helicopters are flying over all the damage on the East Coast and the ruins of New York City, Miami, New Orleans, Dominican Republic, and the sink holes in the Bahamas, the damaged islands in the Caribbean, and the explosion of Mount Flow on Q'klitores ending with the nuclear mega blast in the ocean and the upper atmosphere on fire.

CHARACTERS

David L. Sanberg: owner of the hotel and resort on the island of
    Q'klitores.

Olivia: the island's ghost.

Dick Hurts: is a lawyer and now he's living in Holden, Massachusetts

Patty McGroin: his girlfriend. Originally from Bangor, Maine.

Willy Bird: the rapist escapee from the island now he's the head dean
    of students at the University of Vagina in Saskatchewan, Canada.

Admiral Quonset Point: cruise ship Irene.

Ding Dong Tours: Chi Chung.

Donald Paderka: tour guide.

Richard Dennis: helicopter tour pilot.

Sergeant Adam Santini: National Guard leader.

Raymound W. Hallmostraphoniagalleriabarringtoncommonwealth: the islands doctor and counselor; known to be called, Dr. It.

Dick Dickey: casino pit boss and hotel host.

Helen Lladova: show designer, fashionista and a judge.

Officer Clayborn Roots: Texas Ranger.

Mount Flow: the volcano.

The NASA volcano crew of six:

Vincent Tino: the leader. John Nicolini: news reporter.

Jay Domers and Paul arts: work crew in the volcano.

Amy Amitriptiline and Linda Lincoln: monitor and computer readers.

Lories: the casino.

Emma Grace: is the hurricane.

Peter Peckershaw: picture designer.

www.ingramcontent.com/pod-product-compliance
Lightning Source LLC
Chambersburg PA
CBHW051148030726
47504CB00004B/1094